I0613100

Frances Dana Barker Gage

Elsie Magoon: Or, the Old Still-House in the Hollow

A tale of the past

Frances Dana Barker Gage

Elsie Magoon: Or, the Old Still-House in the Hollow
A tale of the past

ISBN/EAN: 9783337027193

Printed in Europe, USA, Canada, Australia, Japan

Cover: Foto ©Andreas Hilbeck / pixelio.de

More available books at **www.hansebooks.com**

ELSIE MAGOON.

ELSIE MAGOON

OR

THE OLD STILL-HOUSE IN THE HOLLOW.

A Tale of the Past.

BY

MRS. FRANCES DANA GAGE.

PHILADELPHIA:
J. B. LIPPINCOTT & CO.
1867.

...Act of Congress, in the year 1867, by

MRS. F. D. GAGE,

...District Court of the United States for the

...District of New Jersey.

(ii)

DEDICATION.

TO THE

Friends of Temperance.

I COMMEND MY HUMBLE VOLUME, WITH AN EARNEST
HOPE AND PRAYER, THAT HE WHO HEARS THE
RAVEN'S CRY AND MARKS THE SPARROW'S
FALL, MAY MAKE IT, IN THEIR
HANDS, A MEANS
OF GOOD.

THE AUTHOR.

(v)

PREFACE.

THE story of Elsie Magoon was written some years ago, at the request of a friend who was struggling to aid the cause of Temperance on the borders of the Mississippi. Believing then, as now, that no fiction can be wrought by the imagination equal in intensity of romance to the every-day realities of common life, I collected a few incidents which were stored in my memory, and wove them together with a thread of narrative; adding little to the facts, but changing names and localities, lest the actors, or their descendants, should be recognized by their neighbors, even at this late day.

In the character of Elsie Magoon, I have endeavored to portray a true woman, filling her place as wife, mother, and member of society. Such wives and mothers are the great need of the age.

(vii)

ELSIE MAGOON;

OR,

THE OLD STILL-HOUSE.

CHAPTER I.

"MAYBE I ain't tired!" said Richard Magoon, as he threw himself down upon the threshold of his log-cabin, one of the first warm days of April, fanning himself vigorously with his straw hat and wiping the perspiration from his brow.

"What have you been doing?" asked his wife, who sat near, nursing a beautiful babe of a year old.

"Cutting timber in the Narrows."

"I thought you had cleared all the land you wished to plant this year."

"So I have; but I wanted some building-timber."

"Building-timber! Now the barn and wood-shed, the poultry-houses, and sheep-fold are built, you ought to rest one season."

"I know; but I am in debt. When I borrowed that five hundred dollars of your step-father, I expected that I should have paid it off before this time; but I find that a debt is like a snow-ball, gathers as it goes,"—and Richard cast his eye at the huge piles of snow that lay down in the yard, slowly melting beneath a spring sun.

"Yes, like a snow-ball it gathers," replied the wife, "and like a snow-ball our means will melt away, and leave us nothing, I'm afraid, by-and-by, to show for all our years of privation and care."

"That's a fact, Elsie,"—and Richard sprang nervously from his reclining posture, and fanned himself more vigorously,—"that's a fact, and if I don't go at something better than I've been doing these years past, I may as well quit, for I don't make the two ends of the year meet, nohow."

"Oh! you must not get discouraged, Richard. You know we have got a great many things done that won't be to do over again—clearing and fencing, and putting out the orchard, and building. The orchard is beginning to bear; you have some nice stock coming on; a fine flock of sheep; and four colts that will soon be fit for market, besides the old horses; and such nice fat hogs! I am sure, Richard, you can begin to pay something this fall, if you don't go to building any more, to take——"

"That's just what I want to build for, to help myself out of this fix! I've a thousand bushels of corn on hand. Every neighbor has more than he can sell, and it's all going to waste for want of a market. Old Deacon Hill was along last week, and has been advising me to build a 'Still-house,' and go to making whiskey. We can't take the corn down the river, and there's no sale here; but we can sell all the whiskey we can make, at a good profit; besides, the slop will fat my hogs; and so I can turn my farm and labor into cash quicker, than in any other way. I just made up my mind *I'd do it,* and we've got the logs nearly all ready."

"Oh, Richard! I would n't. A 'Still-house' is always a dreadful thing in a neighborhood. Don't you remember——"

"It's no use talking, Elsie! I *must* do that, or worse. That debt has *got to be paid,* and I never can do it by raising corn at ten cents a bushel, or feeding pork for a cent-and-a-half a pound; and that's the best I can do. Besides, I don't see what objection you can have to a 'Still-house.' I shall see to it myself, and keep it straight."

"Well, I don't know, Richard; you think so now, —but somehow,—well, I don't know. But it seems to me I would n't try it." She paused, as if she dared not put into words the fear that fell upon her.

Poor Elsie Magoon! how her pale cheek grew paler, there in the moonlight, as she looked down upon the noble form of her husband. Shadows wild and fearful flitted before her — shadows that made her blood chill, and prompted her to press her babe closer to her heart,—shadows that made her tongue stammer, and the thoughts to come and go, struggling for utterance, and yet not to be spoken.

"Well, it's no use arguing the matter. I see no other chance to get out of a bad scrape. I have made my bargain with Wright to do the coopering work, and with Thompson to build the chimneys, and with Samson to come and set it in operation, and do the

millwright work for a horse-mill; and it is to be completed by the fourth of July. I bought Crane's mill-
works, over on the creek. He was n't able to rebuild
his dam, after the fall rains washed it out. So I've
nothing to do but put up the building and move over
the machinery and set it a-going; and I want you to
get ready for a raising a week from to-morrow; it
will be a heavy job."

"Oh, Richard! why did you not tell me about it
before you went so far?"

"Because I was *determined* to do it; for, live this
way, pinched to death for means to get along, and
never having the satisfaction of saying, 'I owe no
man anything,' I won't; so there's 'the word with
the bark on';" and Richard rose with a bound, went
down to the gate, and with a loud voice called in his
sheep to the fold.

There were few finer-looking men in the land than
Richard Magoon. He was not what the novelist
would call a "handsome man," but his was a noble
splendor that attracted one more than beauty. Six
feet two inches he stood among men; finely propor-
tioned, and full of athletic vigor. His face was florid,
yet free from freckles; his eye of the kindliest gray,
his hair a dark brown, soft, curly, and brilliant as a
woman's; his voice full and rich, yet sweet and soothing; and a truer or kinder heart than Richard Magoon's, never throbbed beneath a blue hunting-shirt
of a good-wife's spinning. While he leads his flock of
forty fat sheep to the ample log-fold, we will tell you
of Elsie, his wife, the heroine of our tale of the past.

We have called her beautiful,—and beautiful she was, with her brilliant complexion, her deep blue eyes, and flowing, auburn locks,—and the radiance of a loving soul, flooding every feature.

But it was not the beauty of Elsie Magoon,—it was her native good sense, her high morality, her untiring patience and courage,—which made her the "bright, particular star" of the neighborhood; the one sought after in all emergencies, for advice and counsel, for aid and comfort, by the wives and mothers whose fate had been cast, like hers, amid the trials and privations of frontier life.

Both the farmer and his wife were natives of Massachusetts, and had brought with them to their new home the sterling virtues and indomitable force of will and character, native to the air of their beloved State. They were called "educated" people in those times—that is, they possessed a good knowledge of the common English branches taught in the rude school-houses which then dotted the hillsides and hollows of New England; and in which the stimulus of *birch* generously supplied any deficiency in the mental appetite;—they used their mother-tongue without the vulgarisms of phrase and pronunciation which so often render the Yankee dialect in the mouth of the untaught native, ludicrous to "ears polite."

The cabin of the Magoons, made of rough logs, stood upon the banks of a beautiful stream in the interior of Ohio, called by the aborigines "Wahoo." It wound through a wide valley hemmed in on either side by hills, having a rich soil, and a not

2

inhospitable climate. After the first settlement was made, emigration began to pour rapidly in upon the new colony, and the sound of the axe and the mill grew every day more frightful to the timid denizens of the forest, who had hitherto held undisputed sway of its fastnesses and solitudes, except as the Indian hunter now and then intruded upon them with the twang of his bow, or the crack of his rifle.

Richard Magoon was twenty-eight years of age — his wife but twenty-four. They had taken the advice of Dr. Franklin, and married early—he at twenty-one; she, in the girlish days of seventeen. Seven years they had been toiling together on their farm. The "old man," of whom the money was loaned, was Elsie's step-father; and the money thus loaned to the husband of his dead wife's child, was money that had belonged to the mother,—the gift of her kind old grandfather,—but which had become the step-father's by marriage; and thus the money which the mother would have given to her only daughter, and which could have been spared from the rich man's purse and not have been missed,—was only lent, at heavy interest, to her husband, through the mother's earnest intercession. Now that the mother was gone, the selfish man added interest to interest, making the burden of his wife's children heavy and oppressive.

Elsie watched the receding form of her noble husband till it was lost to her in the obscurity of the night. Then, slowly rising from her chair, with a deep sigh, she laid her sleeping babe in the rude cradle, and, stooping over it, left a kiss upon its fair

brow, as she breathed forth a mother's anxious solicitude in the words, "God help thee, my poor child!"
Why she spoke thus she could not tell; or wherefore
the deep foreboding that had so suddenly shrouded
her spirit in gloom.

"Oh! it *is* hard," said Elsie, as she turned away
from the cradle to light a candle from a glowing coal
upon the hearth; "hard to think that my mother
should toil as she did, thirty years in that house, that
was all hers, when *he* came there; that the money
grandfather meant for her children should become *his*.
Hard, that money, home, labor, all are now his, and
we must be so oppressed; when, if she had *owned* anything, or been anything but a slave, she would freely
have given *me*, her only child, this little portion.
Now, it will all go—home, and all—to his haughty
relatives. Well! it can't be helped. But it seems to
me it's very wrong."

Elsie picked up a coal with the tongs, blew it into
a blaze, and lighted her candle. Just then Richard
came in. Seeing her troubled look, and the tears
struggling in her lustrous eyes, he stepped up to her,
looking tenderly in her face, and said, "Don't be troubled, Elsie; all shall go right for your sake."

And the two sat down by their home-table, to chat
away the evening hour. For they obeyed the injunction of St. Paul;—he loved his wife even as himself;
and she "reverenced" her husband. Their days were
given to necessary toil, but their evenings to each
other.

CHAPTER II

THE soft, clear April-weather, that had set the bluebirds twittering, and brought out the violets and anemones by the brook-side, and the sweat-drops upon the brow of Richard Magoon, at the commencement of our story,—had passed away, ere the day came for the raising of the "Still-house;" and in its place were cold, scowling skies, and bitter frost, covering the earth with frozen sleet and snow.

"Had you not better put it off, Richard, for a few days?" asked Elsie, as she looked out at the cheerless prospect.

"No; I could not send round word now; and half of them would be here, in spite of my efforts, if I were to try. Besides, Stillman raises his barn next Saturday, and the farmers are too busy to lose more than one day in a week. It's a bad day, and no mistake; but I must put up with it;—there's no help for it now."

"Where is Joe going with the horses?"

"Down to the Ford," said Richard, looking every way but at his wife, and working at his teeth earnestly with a splinter.

"What for?" asked Elsie, in a troubled voice.

Richard did not answer. At that moment Joe emerged from the shed, with a keg that might have held five gallons, and placed it in the wagon.

(16)

"Richard," said Elsie, with a firm voice, laying her hand impressively upon his shoulder, "don't do *that*. It's a cold day, and if you get whiskey among those men, there will be trouble. You know what Truman, and Smith, and Sheldon are. Why will you yield to what you know is wrong, and run the risk of having your own work spoiled, and perhaps somebody killed or maimed for life. Oh! it is terrible to give whiskey to these men at raisings,—it always ——"

"Well, Elsie, it's no use talking *now*. You've opposed me from the first, every step I've taken. I've trouble enough without so much opposition from you. You know the men won't work without whiskey, and it would be a great idea for me to ask them here to help build a 'Still-house,' and then go to preaching about their letting whiskey alone!"

When one step toward wrong is taken, we must either retrace it, or take the next. To stand still is seldom possible. Richard had determined on doing what his own conscience condemned, and he could not bear that Elsie should prick his sensitiveness to the quick, with truths against which he had no argument. Elsie turned away with a sad heart. He had never spoken so unkindly to her before. "She had opposed him from the first." So she had. How could she do otherwise, when she felt that only evil could come of his plan? And yet she must *seem* to acquiesce; or, at least learn to keep silence, and let the wrong go on, lest she should arouse within her own household a spirit of antagonism that would turn all the sweet waters of life into bitterness. So with her customary

2*

light step, but a heavy heart, she turned to her work.
According to the usual customs on such occasions,
Elsie had asked the assistance of the wives of several
of her nearest neighbors in preparing the dinner and
supper, for the husbands who were to take part in
"the raising." And, as Richard turned to leave the
house, Mrs. Smith and Mrs. Sheldon appeared, and
received a neighborly welcome.

"Good morning, Mrs. Sheldon — Good morning,
Mrs. Smith. This is a disagreeable morning for you
to turn out. I hardly expected either of you. I'm
sure I ought to be obliged to you for coming over."

"Well, you need n't be much obleeged to me, no-
how," said Mrs. Smith, a little, dapper woman, in a
home-made, butternut-colored linsey dress, and clean
blue-and-white checked apron of her own spinning.
"You may just thank my old man, for I'd never
come anigh to help raise a 'Still-house,' if *he* had n't
a-said I *should*. But he promised he'd take me down
to the Ford next week, and let me sell my dried‘
apples, and git some things for myself. You know
Judge Bryant let me dry all the windfalls me and the
children could tote, last fall; and I've kep' them all
winter, just 'cause I could n't git to go down. He
says Miller is giving three-quarters of a dollar a
bushel now for real good ones; and I know there
ain't none better than mine."

"Why did n't you let Tom Gifford take 'em in the
fall?" asked Mrs. Sheldon.

"Well, just 'cause I could n't git 'em down."

"But Mr. Smith went down so often," said Elsie.

"Yes, he went down nigh onto every day, and could have taken 'em just as well as not; but if he had, not a red copper would I ever 'a' got; and I worked too hard for them there apples, to let him drink 'em all up in whiskey, I tell you."

A cold chill swept over Elsie.

"Well, now we're here, set us to work; we didn't come over to set round," said Mrs. Sheldon. A pile of squirrels and quails, which Richard's unerring rifle had brought down the day before, were to be prepared for a pie; a huge turkey lay by the door, to be made ready for the workmen. Pies were to be made, and bread prepared for the brick oven that was being heated in the yard; and soon the active hands of the women were at work.

"When did you hear from Mrs. Truman?" said Mrs. Sheldon, as the two sat by the fire, paring apples for pies.

"I was down there last night, and she's mighty bad, I tell you. Oh! but it's dreadful to live with that man. Her face is all black, and her back is that lame she can't turn herself in her bed, where he beat her."

"He beat her! Why, I heard she fell down the steps."

"Yes, that's what she told; but Sally told me that Truman come home high, and went to whipping little John; and she took his part, and then he fell on her and beat her pretty nigh to death, and would 'a' killed her, if Sally hadn't thrown a blanket over his head, till Mrs. Truman ran into the smoke-house and locked herself in, and he did n't know where she 'd gone; so he just swore hisself to sleep, and then she come in and got into bed; and she 's not been out since, poor thing!"

"Oh! what a dreadful thing this 'Still-house' will be," said Mrs. Sheldon, leaning over and whispering to her neighbor, with a shake of the head.

"It will be just that; and if I was Elsie Magoon, I 'd put a stop to it."

"She can't do it, Mrs. Smith. That Richard Magoon has an awful will of his own; and it 's my 'pinion that, if she was to say much, he 'd be setter in his way than he is now. She 's mightily troubled— I can see that in her looks; but we mus'n't let on — it will make her more so; and, dear knows, she 's feeling bad enough!"

Thus the women chatted on in an undertone. The forenoon passed; a capital dinner graced the humble board. The wind had softened, the sun came out; and the ice and snow fell from the logs, leaving them in a slippery and dangerous condition.

Thirty men had gathered for the work. They were men, for the most part, of strong hands and willing hearts, and the work went on with straightforward regularity. Log after log was rolled up, notwithstanding their bad condition, by the main strength of bones and muscles. No machinery helped their weary labors; and when Elsie sounded the horn for dinner, the building was up to the second story, and all counted it a good job done.

As they gathered to dinner, it was easy to be seen

that a part of the company were merrier than the
natural flow of spirits would induce. Smith, Sheldon, and Truman, especially, were in a high state of
exhilaration. They were among the stoutest men in
the township—big, brawny, sensual, and proud of
their physical proportions; and in the rude sports of
the backwoods always first. At the raisings too, they
did the work of giants, and their prowess and strength
were rewarded by a double portion of what, in those
days, was esteemed the greatest "treat" that could be
bestowed'—the favorite whiskey-punch, or egg-nog.

Smith and Sheldon were not habitual drunkards,
although they were occasionally found "the worse for
liquor." But Truman, the giant of the trio, had of
late become a daily victim to the fearful habit, and
the sun seldom went down upon him a sober man.
At dinner, he was uproarious in his fun, and laughed,
talked, sung, shouted, and kept the table in a roar of
mirth.

"That Truman is as drunk as a fool," said Mrs.
Smith to Elsie, as they were cutting up the pies at a
side-table; "and, between you and I, Smith is as
high as a cat's back. Oh! there'll be awful times
afore night, for when Truman is so, he always wants
to fight."

Elsie's lip quivered, but she choked down her
emotion, and went on with her work.

"Hurrah, boys!" shouted Truman. "Don't eat
all day. Three cheers for Mrs. Magoon's pies, and
then come along."

The cheers, loud and long, were given, and fell

upon Elsie's ear like an insult. To think that *she* should be cheered þy a set of noisy topers !

The afternoon wore on. With every tier of logs their work became harder, their nerves and muscles more weary; and large draughts were made by many of the party from *the keg*, in the hope of gaining the needed vigor

About four o'clock a dispute arose, as to the comparative strength of Truman and a new-comer in the neighborhood, named Scott. A wrestling match was proposed. In vain Richard begged them not to spend their force in fun, and insisted that both were strong, and had done well; but sides were taken for both parties, and all hands stood still to see the contest.

Scott was a broad-shouldered, active fellow, sober, and many years the junior of Truman, who was already staggering with liquor. The trial of strength did not last an instant; with quick energy and action, Scott lifted his antagonist off his feet and laid him prostrate, while a loud shout of triumph went up from one side, and a hiss of derision from the other. In a moment Truman was on his feet, and, with clenched fist, glaring eyes, and the maddened fury of a maniac, pitched upon Scott, who stood with his back to him, and with one blow felled him to the ground. A melee ensued, and, for a few moments, the fight seemed to become general. But, luckily, there were sober ones enough to quell the tumult and command peace.

Truman and Scott went back to their work reluctantly, Truman muttering, that "he'd fix him before night."

The building was nearly finished — the last heavy log was being rolled up; all hands were striving to do their utmost. The loud "heave ho" cheered them. "Stick to it, boys! up with her! there she goes! heave ho! once more, my hearties!" One effort more would have laid the ponderous log in its place. One effort more, and the walls of the 'Still-house' would have been completed. At that critical moment, when every nerve was strained, and every hand doing its best, the heavy lever of Truman slipped from its place and fell with its whole weight upon the hands of his next neighbor, who let go his hold with a cry of pain. The log began to slide. There was not force enough to sustain it. Eyes were turned aside to see what was the matter; the equilibrium was lost, and in an instant down it came, crushing all in its way.

"Out of the way, boys!" shouted the foreman, and, springing to the right and left, all escaped but one. Scott, the young giant, the bold, athletic farmer, who, seeing the danger, strove to avert it to the last, found it impossible to get away, and was crushed beneath the ponderous weight. It was but the work of a moment to extricate him, but it was too-late. One shriek of pain, one gasp of fearful agony, and the eyes rolled back, the lips quivered, the tongue spoke the words, "Mary — wife," and all was still.

"Good God!" exclaimed Richard, "he is dead."

"Yes, by G—d!" said Truman, "and it's just what

I meant to do. The impudent devil has got his pay! I knew he'd hold on to the last, and I let go my hold on purpose to ——"

"To kill us all, you villain!" cried Richard, seizing him by the throat and hurling him out of the way,—while he rushed to the aid of those who were lifting the crushed body from beneath the logs. The excitement was terrible,—and while the calmer among them were making a rude bed of boughs on which to lay the body yet quivering with death-throes, the more impulsive were for lynching Truman upon the spot. Curses, groans, and prayers were mingled in sad confusion. A messenger had run to the house of Magoon for camphor and bandages, and, bursting in among the women, cried out, "Scott is killed; a log fell and crushed him; he did n't live a minute; Smith's hands are broken to pieces; give me rags and camphor, quick!"

· Scott lived upon the adjoining farm, which he was just clearing, and his young wife had come over to help Elsie in getting supper. With a wild shriek she flew to the scene of disaster, threw herself upon the mangled body, and pressed her bloodless cheek upon his.

"He is not dead—no! no!—he shall not die. Harry! Oh, my husband! Good God! *Do something* for him! Oh, can't he be helped! Who did it? What did it? Oh, Harry, Harry, speak to me once —oh! just once!"

She could not believe him dead; and her terror, her despair, filled every eye with tears, and every heart with anguish. Elsie came and stood beside her, pale as marble, but with tearless eyes. One look she gave to Richard, as she took the hand of poor Mary in hers; she spoke no words; but, "your own work spoiled and somebody killed or maimed for life," sounded in his ears like words of doom. Smith's hands were fearfully crushed; the bones in his right hand were laid bare of flesh, and broken in three or four places, and the cords and sinews severed at the wrist. "Maimed for life," and he the father of a large family! Scott was dead, and Truman—what would become of him? All this passed, in an instant, in review before him, and he groaned aloud.

Mary clung to her husband until, from the violence of her grief, she fell in convulsions beside him, and was carried away in the arms of the men, and laid upon the bed in Richard's cabin.

Elsie sat all night by the moaning young wife, who talked and prayed, and prayed and sung, until, worn and exhausted, she slept,—only to awake to a more fearful consciousness of her bereavement.

"Elsie," said Richard, as the crimson glow began to show in the east, "let me sit and watch by Mary, and you go to bed. You will be sick with your hard day's work, watching, and excitement."

"Oh! Richard, promise me—promise me that you will go no further with that 'Still-house.' Give it up, and we may get over all this; go on, and this will be but the beginning of an end which we cannot see." And she threw herself sobbing upon his bosom, and rested her weary head upon his shoulder,—

3

her stern self-control all gone at the sound of his kind words.

"It has been a terrible day, Elsie; but then I don't see as it was my fault, particularly. Everybody uses whiskey, and you can't keep such men as Truman from drinking; and when they drink, they're not to be trusted. We might have a thousand raisings, and not have such another accident."

"Harry! Harry! Harry!" shrieked Mary, waking from her sleep. "They said he was killed—crushed under the log!" And she attempted to leap from the bed. They flew to the side of the poor maniac, and were making unsuccessful efforts to quiet her, when old "Granny Hall," the Indian "doctor-woman," as she was called,—who, without the learning, had more native skill in disease than many a diplomaed M.D. of our times,—came in, sent by a neighbor who had a superstitious faith in her power over all the "ills that flesh is heir to."

If force of muscle could give one such power, she might, without fear of contradiction, lay claim to it; for she was a woman of proportions so huge as to afflict with fear all timid folk. Although called the Indian Doctor-woman, it was not because the blood of that race was in her veins, but because having been carried off in her youth from a frontier settlement, she had learned during her seven years captivity among them, all the secrets of the medical art in their rude hands; and there was no root or tree of the forest whose medicinal virtues were unknown to her. The hardy life of these children of Nature had brought to its fullest development the frame of the robust maiden. Day and night, storm and sunshine, were alike to her; nothing appalled, everything seemed to nourish and strengthen her; and now, going her rounds before the day had fairly dawned, she had found herself in the neighborhood of this fearful disaster, news of which had travelled on the wings of the winds, from neighbor to neigbhor.

In reply to her knock upon the outer door, they had bid her "come in,"—and her large figure now loomed up in the early morning twilight, until she looked powerful enough to be some Genius of the Forest, coming to lift the fearful burden of suffering from their shoulders.

"Lord bless me! Elsie Magoon, what's the matter here?"

"Oh, Granny! we're glad to see you. Pray give this poor thing something to put her to sleep,—she raves so!"

"That I will, honey, in no time;" and without further ceremony the old woman drew a tin cup from a capacious leathern pocket which hung at her side, raked over the dying coals upon the hearth, and forthwith set a handful of leaves steeping. Then she joined Elsie at the bedside, and laying her great, cool palm upon the fevered brow, seemed as if by magic, to still its torture.

The decoction was soon administered, and when Mary had sunk into quiet slumber, the old woman insisted on being left in care of her, while Elsie should rest. "Now, honey," said the rough but kindly voice, "you just go lie down, or you'll be where *she is* 'fore you knows it; go right 'long, Granny knows."

Too feeble to resist, and too miserable to care to oppose the well-meant command, Elsie threw herself upon a couch. But not to sleep. Scene after scene of that fearful drama, with many others supplied from the dreaded future by her kindled imagination, passed in vivid detail before her. Nothing seemed too horrible to follow with logical certainty upon this opening scene of horror. Next to her own Richard, young Scott had been the pride of the settlement. And now he lay dead; and that fatal "Still-house" had been consecrated to its evil work at the outset by the best blood of the neighborhood.

Reader, did you ever live in a frontier settlement? Did you ever hear the howl of the wolf upon the hills, or the shrill scream of the panther in the forest, and sally out, rifle in hand, with your dog at your heels, to hunt out the wild intruders upon your grounds, or to guard your precious sheepfold from the foe? Have you ever started with affright, and felt your blood chilling in your veins, as the warning of the rattle-snake by your path, reminded you that your legs were unbooted, and the enemy near by in ambush? Did you ever hear the fearful cry of "Child lost!" in the wood; or any of those things which startle the heart, and call out the sympathies of neighbor for neighbor, friend for friend, in a new country —a forest home?

If you have, you will know, better than any one

can describe to you, the deep interest in each other's welfare which is felt in a neighborhood of new settlers. Mutual danger makes mutual ties of interest. Neighbors widely scattered, exposed to common and various perils, cannot afford to be indifferent to each other's fate; and thus become by force of circumstances, the best and most steadfast friends.

It has been said that "we never thoroughly hate one whom we thoroughly know;—and thus it is that in new neighborhoods and countries, assistance is rendered with an unselfish, impulsive cheerfulness, which you seldom find in the changed circumstances of after-years.

3 *

WE left Truman in the hands of the crowd, which for a while seemed determined to satisfy its anger by dealing with him in the most summary manner. Many cried, "Hang him!" others, more humane, insisted upon tying him, and whipping him "within an inch of his life." But Richard, who felt that evil enough had been done already, and that Truman's assertion that he had let the log slip purposely, had been only a drunkard's boast,—persuaded them to release him.

This allayed the madman's fury, and as he staggered homeward, he blubbered and wept like a child over the horrible accidents of the day. His wife was never the sweetest-tempered, and the tale, that Truman had purposely let the log fall, had reached her ears before he made his appearance, and created in her turbulent bosom a terrible tempest. Naturally nervous and excitable, full of energy and fire, taught by precept and example to scold and storm when things went awry, she was in no mood now to lead her besotted husband into a calmer and better state of mind. Her married life and its manifold trials—such as they must ever be to woman in the home of a drunkard—had done nothing to soften or sweeten her temper; and the pert, exacting girl had become the uncompromising termagant, at forty.

(30)

Poor Truman had been in a state of repentance, for the last mile, on the road home. Mad he was, when the log slipped — mad with whiskey — ready to rejoice over the fearful work; but the sight of that poor wife, and her wild, frantic woe, had pierced his soul, and wakened its remorse.

The long road home, the coming twilight, and returning reason, left him subject to the good angels for a little time, and he wept and prayed, as he strode along through the darkening forest.

But as he reached the stile, and half climbed, half rolled himself over, Nancy caught sight of him, and began her attack in such a way as threw him on the defensive at once, and scattered his good resolves as the tree throws off its leaves at the touch of an October frost.

"Now," began she, "now you've gone and done it, have ye?"

"Gone and done what, you old wild-cat?"

"Yes, I should think you'd ask what! Tom Wilger's been along an hour ago, and told me all about it. It's no use trying to make me believe you did n't do it. You're a wicked old wretch, and you'll get yourself on the gallows, or in the pen'tentiary, and bring disgrace and misery on us all, 'fore you're done. It'ud been better if your own old head had a-been under, instead of Scott's — that it would!"

Away went tears and repentance; away went good resolves, and up rolled the whirlwind of wrath.

"Now, look you here, Nancy, I'm not agoing to take sich as that from you, nor no other woman; and

if you don't shut up and get me some supper, I'll
turn you and every tarnal young one out of the
house, and help myself. This house is mine, and, by
the Lord Harry, I'll be master of it,"—and away
went the club which he carried as a cane, into the
group of children, who stood, like a flock of frightened quails, in the corner. Truman was thoroughly
aroused, and Nancy, who was really a loving mother,
and feared the effects of his malice upon the children,
calmed down a little.

"Well, just sit down now, and quit your behaving,
and I'll get you the best I can,—God knows, it's
poor enough."

And while he poured out oaths and imprecations,
she hurriedly set his food before him, knowing that
he would soon throw himself upon the bed, and go
to sleep for the night; and then slipped out to milk
her cow, and give vent to her burdened heart in sobs
and tears.

Oh! earth, earth, how beautiful thou art; and yet
how full of sorrow, of bitter anguish, and despair,
are the hearts of thy children! Truly has it been
written, "that the sins of the parents shall be visited
upon the children to the third and fourth generations." Truman and his wife were the legitimate
offspring, in mind and body, of those who had given
them birth;—and who may not foretell the future
of the poor stricken ones who gathered around the
sobbing, scolding mother—glad to take shelter even
in her bitterness, from a drunken father's violence
and wrath? If the children of such parents come up

in sin and depravity, shall the boasting moralist, who has entered upon his manhood without the taint of an inherited passion in his veins, — who has been fostered by a gentle mother's Christ-like love, and a father's calm discipline and resolute morality, — who has been trained to truth and right, and taught daily lessons of temperance at the home hearth, not only by spoken words, but by the habitual practice of self-control and self-denial, — fold his hands, and say to the wretched wanderer from the path of right, "Stand by — I am holier than thou!" Rather let him return thanks for the many blessings he has received, crying, "Father, forgive them; they know not what they do;" solemnly asking his own heart, if, with their training and temptations, he should have done as well as they.

It was a glorious morning. All traces of the late storm had passed away; the sun rose in gorgeous splendor and brightness, and shone down upon the beautiful holly, lighting it up as if for a holiday festival, rather than for a funeral.

The Wahoo, as we still prefer to call the river, was a coquettish little stream that went meandering through the broad rich valley at will, tying itself almost into bows and knots, and then gliding away, like a line of silver, through a quiet meadow, or beside the sloping hills. It was now raised above its common level by the rain and snow, and, just released from its bondage of ice, went singing and dancing along, making a cheerful accompaniment to the twittering birds, and sending up fresh incense to heaven, with that of the opening buds and bursting leaves.

Oh! it was a beautiful day, when young Scott, in the prime of early manhood, was to be returned, — "Dust to dust, and ashes to ashes." Far and wide had spread the news of the terrible catastrophe, and there was a gathering of the people for miles around. In the city, your next-door neighbor may die and be buried. You see the signal of crape at the door-knob; you turn coldly to the paragraph in the morning paper to learn of what disease, and at what age, he or she has died; and then go to your business, to remember them no more. But in a new country, a death calls the neighbor from his plough, the housewife from her cares; and the tear of sympathy falls free and full, while the heart grows softer and kinder for its sorrowing.

This too was the Sabbath; and as the sun rose to the meridian, and the first hour of his declining was marked upon the cabin-floor, the people gathered from East and West, from North and South, until the cabin of Scott, where the body lay, could not hold a tenth of those who came. Elder Peters, the venerable pastor, who had been summoned from the next village, proposed that they should repair with the coffin to the maple grove near the grave-yard. When they arrived there, seats were made of logs and rails for the men, chairs and stools from their farm wagons accommodated the elder part of the matrons, and the younger stood, or took turns with the older men. Many a meeting had been held in this lovely spot, beside the little log meeting-house and the rural grave-yard; but never one so solemn, so full of deep warning as this.

When all was arranged, the old, gray-haired preacher arose and offered a fervent prayer in behalf of the people. Then came the hymn —

"Hark! from the tombs a doleful sound —
  Mine ears attend the cry;
Ye living men, come view the ground,
  Where you must shortly lie."

And the deep bass of the voices of a hundred men, and many more of the softer treble of women, filled the forest with the full notes of stirring pathos. Wild, deep, and fervid was the solemn dirge that echoed through the valley from the lips and hearts of the assembled crowd, a heartfelt requiem for their lamented dead.

When the opening exercises were closed, the old man arose and took his text from Christ's Sermon on the Mount, all of which he first read with impassioned emphasis. "Blessed are they that mourn, for they shall be comforted," he repeated; and for half an hour he sought to bring hope and consolation to the stricken kindred, most of all to the old father and mother, who had come, laden with years and sorrow, to lay in the grave their last-born, who, like Benjamin, had been their darling. There were brothers and sisters too, who sat in the space for mourners around the coffin; and as the aged pastor's words fell soft and low, they wept long and freely. At last he addressed himself more directly to the audience:

"My friends," said he, "I am an old man, and, you know, the Psalmist says, 'our days are three-score years and ten; and if, by reason of strength, they be fourscore, yet is their strength labor and sorrow.' I have passed the common age of man, and am travelling on to the fourscore; yet I cannot say as yet, that my labor is sorrow; for God has blessed my weakness, and made me joyful in his own strength. But I may never be spared to come to you again, or you be allowed to meet here in such numbers; and I have much to say to you this day. Go bury your dead and return here for an hour."

Plain and simple was the old man's speech, and the people, who knew and loved him, obeyed without question or hesitation.

Meanwhile the widow, in her weakness and partial unconsciousness, had been left in the care of kind, old Granny Hill, who had "strength enough left in her old bones," she said, "for many a good turn yet." While the poor young thing slept, she sat by the window, and with her spectacles before her eyes, and her Bible spread on the little stand, commenced reading. Her hands lay listlessly over the arms of the old high-backed chair, while her body sought repose from the cushion behind. The words grew more and more dim, and at last she nodded in very weariness. Then she roused herself, drew out her snuff-box, took a pinch, rubbed her eyes, and read again. Again she nodded and dozed, and, dropping her head against the chair, fell fast asleep.

Soon after her nurse fell asleep, Mary opened her

eyes. Where was she? She could not tell. All things about her were new and strange. She closed her eyes again, and visions of terror floated about her; gradually they assumed form and shape, and,—like a sudden waking from a sound sleep,—the dream, the confusion passed away, and the dread reality stood before her. She raised herself in the bed, and discovered the sleeping woman. She looked about— *her all was gone.* She cast her eye out of the window down across the meadow to the sugar-grove, and there was the assembled multitude.

She sprang lightly from the bed, and slipped down the path by the fence, just as they were lowering the remains of her husband into the dark vault below. As the minister lifted his hat from his aged brow, to return thanks to the bearers, who had borne the bier hither upon their shoulders, and to ask the blessing of God upon them all, a wild cry was heard, and the wife broke through the solid circle around the grave. Ere they could stay her course, she let herself into the grave, and lay moaning upon the coffin. Shriek after shriek pierced the air:—

"Oh! he is not dead, he is not dead! You shall not bury him! He was well yesterday morning; so strong and good! He went to build a 'Still-house'— who killed him? Oh! God, have mercy—help— help—he is *not* dead, he is *not* dead!"

With maniac fury, she tried to tear the lid from the coffin with her feeble hands. Intense excitement stirred the people.

4

"Sing," said the aged minister,—"sing in full, soft chorus:"

> "Oh! God, our help in ages past,
>   Our strength in years to come,
> Our shelter from the stormy blast,
>   And our eternal home!
> A thousand ages in Thy sight,
>   Are as an evening gone—
> Short as the watch that ends the night,
>   Before the rising sun."

The men were trembling, and the women weeping in the tenderest sympathy; but the pastor's words quieted them, and their voices rose, in a low, plaintive, soothing air, gradually swelling into a louder note of triumph and faith. The wife became more and more calm; at last her sad cries ceased, and she lay sobbing and helpless, and made no resistance, as strong men lifted her in their arms from the grave, and gave her into the hands of her friends.

"Come away," said Elder Peters, "and lead her from the grave;" and still singing, they walked back to the grove; while the friends placing the widow in one of their wagons, drove with her to her father's house.

The preacher called his flock around him, and, in words not eloquent, but weighty and true, preached the first Temperance sermon that ever was heard among the swaying boughs of that old forest—perhaps the first ever preached in Ohio. He spoke unflinchingly, fearless of censure. He held up before them a picture of themselves. He pointed to the new-made grave, recalled the anguish of the crushed wife, and spoke of the orphaned child. "All this," said he, "is but the beginning—an earnest of what is to follow—from that accursed building just now reared in your midst."

"My friends," cried he, with vehemence, "I am an old man, yet have my lips never knowingly tasted ardent spirits. The voice of my angel-mother taught me, with my morning prayer and my evening thanksgiving, to shun this snare, set for the feet of the unwary. Will any man say I am the worse? How can a Christian pray, 'Lead us not into temptation —deliver us from evil,'—and yet put the deadly cup to his lips, and help to *make, buy,* or *sell* that which — will bring upon us scenes like this we have just passed through? What caused the accident of yesterday? Rum! What made that wife a maniac? Rum! What has cast such a gloom over the neighborhood, causing you to assemble here, with grieved hearts, to bury away out of your sight, in the very spring-time of his manhood, a good man, a brother and a friend? Rum! And yet, my people, you are joining hands to build a temple, here in this wood, consecrated to the use of that demon which destroys so much of your peace. Pause, before you go further! If such things are done in the green tree, what shall we expect in the dry?"

The old man talked thus for nearly an hour, in the most earnest manner, regardless of the frowns of the men, or even of the abrupt departure of Deacon Hill, who left the grave, and stood moodily apart. Richard Magoon was too manly to show any displeasure, but his face, despite his efforts, betrayed the feelings that were struggling within.

The old man closed, by offering a pledge somewhat like that of the "American Temperance Society;" but none would sign it—no, not one; and as they went away to their homes, the majority of the men called the old man crazed. But the women thought there was at least "method in his madness," and that his words "were words of truth and soberness." Elsie Magoon did not sign the pledge; but in her soul were treasured up resolves never afterward broken or forgotten.

CHAPTER IV

FIVE years!—what a moment they become, as we look back upon them! No matter how full of fear and sorrow,—no matter how full of pain and anguish in the passing,—they dwindle to a mere span when we look back upon them through the long lanes of life.

Nor does it matter if the moments were filled to the brim with gladness;—if every pulse told of a happiness akin to Paradise;—if joy gave wings to the hours then; they now are as the distant visions of a fevered dream.

Five years have gone by since they buried the victim of the "Still" in the solitary church-yard by the sugar-grove,—since they bore the maniac wife to her kindred,—and since the strong-hearted Elsie Magoon resolved, in the silence of her own spirit, to wage life-long warfare with the demon of destruction.

The April sun had come out bright and beautiful after that solemn funeral, as if the children of men were pure and good. But light and warmth had never come again to the soul of the bereaved wife. From the funeral scene in the sugar-grove, until she ceased to wander by the brookside, and gather spring violets for her hair, she had remained a maniac; always awaiting *his* coming, and forgetful of all things

4 *   (41)

save that trusting love which had been the most real
and blissful experience of her young life.

They laid her to rest one bright May-morning by
his side, and shed tears of quick sympathy above her,
while in low and gentle whispers they said, It is
better so,—she goes to meet him who was so murder-
ously torn from her, and who waits her coming in
the beauty of his youthful vigor, and the purity of
his early love.

Truman still lived by the roadside, his cabin more
fearfully desolate, his wife more turbulent and un-
happy, his children more wild and ungovernable,—
and he, a loathsome sot. He worked still, at times,
but every night found him staggering under the weight
of his daily draught. Whiskey then had one virtue
that it can not now boast. It was free from drugs
and deadly poisons. A virtue!—no, we will recall
that word. It had no virtues: it had only a property
that lengthened into years the tortures which now are
often ended in a few days.

Smith and Sheldon were both given over to the
fell demon which groaned and spouted in the hollow
all the year round; for the steam-engine was but a
clumsy affair, and its labored, unearthly sounds might
easily, by the agonized fancy of the suffering, have
been mistaken for the shrieks of lost souls.

Many new-comers—or, as they were called, "Bush-
whackers"—had moved into the neighborhood, settled down in their cabins upon government land, and
managed to live by working "by the day" for the

farmers about, and every one of them was a daily frequenter of the old " Still-house."

The land was rapidly passing into the hands of owners, being cleared and put under cultivation. The county seat, " Down at the Ford," as it used to be called, which, five years ago, was but a very small collection of very small houses, had swelled into quite a village, and an active trade was kept up between its merchants and the farmers

Money was not a very abundant article in those days. The merchant bought his goods on credit; sold them for the products of the farm, the field, and the wood which he floated down the rivers to New Orleans, in winter; where they were exchanged for cash, or groceries—such as sugar, tea, coffee, fish, and molasses. These were at first brought up the Ohio on the slow-moving keel-boat, but, after the year 1815, by steamers which plied at intervals upon the waters of the Ohio and Mississippi, making the trip, sometimes, in the short space of forty days. But every year added to their speed, and also to the impetus given to improvement in the new country. The town of Smithville—named from its proprietor—had now become, in the phrase of the times, a "wonderful growing place."

Richard Magoon's "Still-house" was a great help to the people;—of course it was. Did he not hire all the squatters to work on his great farm? Did he not buy all the corn and rye in the country round? Were not all the apples ground into cider at his mill, all the peaches mashed into pummice, and the surplus of cider and peaches worked into brandy there?

His mill, too, supplied the flour and corn-meal; and what with his mill, his distillery, his coopering, his farm, and his river-trading, Richard Magoon held an important position in the community, and was looked upon as one of the best, most discreet, and large-hearted men in the land.

Who thought a "Still-house" a bad thing? Nobody but Elder Peters,—and he was "kind of crazy." Of course he was! It was considered rare fun to cheat the old man, and make him drink his draught of pure water from the tin cup that was used to measure whiskey, because he refused to drink from a glass tumbler lest it might have held the obnoxious beverage.

Deacon Hill, and Major Brant, and Squire Falconer, and Capt. Wilson, were getting rich. They built fine farm-houses; for a man could build a house easily then, by exchange of trade. They had built a good church, too, and a comfortable school-house; and none had been more earnest, active, and self-sacrificing in all these good works, than Richard Magoon. To be sure, whiskey had helped him to build church and school-house; had drained his land, tilled his fields, turned his mill, supported his family; but he prospered, or seemed to, and no one thought of charging him with blame for the way and means of his prosperity.

If Truman drank up all his earnings, if his wife had to spin for a little corn-meal, and his children

ran about the neighborhood begging to share with
(the pigs the skim-milk and butter-milk of the dairy,
if they had no shoes to wear to school in winter,
and no fit clothes in summer, whose fault was it?
Why, not Mr. Magoon's, surely; for he was "*very
kind* to poor Mrs. Truman;"—he sent his team to
haul her wood in winter; let the boys have all the
apples they could carry out of the orchard, pick
roasting-cars from the corn-field, or dig potatoes from
the patch, in summer; he gave her now and then a
fleece of wool, and allowed her to cultivate a half-
acre of flax across the brook, on his hill-land. Yes,
he was "very good to the poor;" and Richard Magoon *meant* to be a good man.

The neighborhood prospered: so everybody thought.
People were getting rich. Farms were enlarging and
multiplying; houses were being built, while the old
steam-engine, in its shady nook under the hill,
shrieked on, and the poor and the needy, the wives
and little ones of the many, very many drinkers,
suffered and groaned in their cabins. Indeed, the
wives were fully convinced in those days, as so many
still are,—that it is a man's privilege to get drunk,
and spend his earnings in self-indulgence; while it is
his wife's highest duty to hide his shortcomings from
the world, with a mantle woven of the beautiful
threads of woman's love and patience.

But in the houses of the rich, too, as, by comparison,
they were called,—in the houses where prosperity
had set her seal,—the shadows of the old "Still-
house" sometimes fell, with dark and fearful portents.

Mrs. Deacon Hill had to tell her "man" more than once, that "he'd got to jest let his bitters alone, 'cept of mornings when there was a fog; for jest so sure as he took a dram before breakfast, he had to have another arterward, and another before dinner, and a good half dozen before bed-time; and then he was always a-cutting up, and telling yarns to the boys, — which was *very unbecoming of a deacon of the church.* 'Fore he knowed it, he'd be getting as drunk as Truman, or Sheldon, or the rest on 'em; and she was n't agoing for to have it."

The Deacon was a mild man, and knew that discretion was the better part of valor; so he listened to the voice of Sarah, his wife, and did as she bade, indulging only of "foggy mornings," — which invariably made foggy days for the Deacon, and ended with storms at nightfall, that kept the atmosphere clear for a week or two afterwards.

Major Brant, too, who bore himself so gallantly on muster-days, — who made the speeches on Fourths of July, and harangues at the political gatherings, — grew rosy and flushed, even purple on the end of his nose, as his poor wife grew paler and sparer.

Squire Falconer, who had gained his title by being justice of the peace for a few years, had lost his election, simply because he was generally too good-natured in the morning, and too cross in the afternoon, to do justice to the litigants. So Richard Magoon, the people's favorite, now held the dignity of Squire in Smithville.

Thus, the men were seemingly prosperous; but

many an aching brain pressed the uneasy pillow, and many a bright eye grew dim with tears over the fatal effect of the old " Still-house."

Where, all this time, was Elsie Magoon? Has she forgotten her vows, and gone over to the help of the wicked?

Let us look in upon her for a little. She is paler than five years ago. Deeper lines are on her brow. The table is set; supper is waiting; and she, weary with her day's work, has thrown herself upon the door-stone of their fine new home, to wait the coming of her husband.

"Little Elsie," now nearly six years, is standing behind her mother, weaving a wreath of roses in her hair; while the two boys, one older and one younger than Elsie, are at play beside them, occasionally making a boyish attack upon the little Alice, and the babe who sits upon the mother's knee. It is a happy picture! Yes, all look happy, but Frank, the eldest, now eleven years, and his mother. Shades of sadness may be seen on the faces of these two, that betoken hearts ill at ease. It is Saturday night—the latter part of May.

"Won't your father be in soon, Frank?" said Elsie, with an effort at cheerfulness.

" I don't know, mother. It's been an awful week, this. There have been a half dozen fights, and half the hands have been drunk every day. Father said Monday, he was going to have all the corn in this week; and we've had pretty nigh thirty hands at work all the time, and they have just been drinking and frolicking right straight along. Kit says they've drunk more than their wages, every one of 'em. Wilson, and Sheldon, and Truman, are all down in the field now, drunk as they can be, lying on the grass in the fence-corners. Jenny Sheldon came over a bit ago, to tell her father to bring home some meal and meat for Sunday; and there he lay on his back; and the poor girl is standing by him, crying, and coaxing him to go home, and he just swears at her. — Mother, I wish that old 'Still-house' was burned down! I do so! I don't believe father will be here this hour; for they had to send for him to come to the 'Still-house.' Mike Dugan and Kit were having a real fuss. Kit would not let Mike in the 'Still-house,' and Mike was throwing stones at the windows and doors; and so it goes all the time."

The boy's tears were falling. The mother leaned her head upon her hands, and buried her emotion in the folds of her apron. Little Elsie let fall her roses, and sprang to her brother's side, begging him not to cry, though she could not understand his sorrow.

"We must be patient, Frank," said the mother, with a choking voice. "I hope these things will not always be so." And she drew him to her, and pressed a kiss wet with the sad dew of tears, upon his sun-burnt brow. Then with a quick effort at self-control, she caressed the little ones who clung about her, and with pleasant loving words and sports beguiled the hour until their early bed-time.

CHAPTER V

LATER in the evening, Richard and Elsie sat alone, in the same place. The full moon shone brightly upon the door-stone, and the soft air revived the weary ones, as it came to them laden with the fragrance of the roses that circled the door.

Richard looked sad and perplexed, and his wife's heart was full to overflowing.

They were both silent a long time.

"Well, Elsie," said Richard, at last, "another hard week's work is done."

"Yes; but not a very profitable one, was it, Richard?"

"No. There's the worst set of men about here, I believe, that ever were called together in any one place on the face of the earth! They have half of them been drunk all the week; and, for my soul, I can't keep 'em straight. I have got to have a real overhauling among the hands at the 'Still-house,' too. Kit is not fit to stay there: he drinks just enough to make him devilish, quarrels with everybody, and, they tell me, uses his wife shamefully. I saw him whipping his little Nelly this morning, like a brute. His wife undertook to get the child out of his way, and he gave her a kick that sent her staggering against the side of the house."

"Kicked his wife!—kicked Abigail, in her condition!" said Elsie. "Oh, Richard! is there no way for us to live but by that 'Still-house?'—by making whiskey, to blight the happiness of the whole neighborhood? Frank has been telling me to-night about things at the Still. I have seen, too, for myself; and it grows terrible, Richard! Only think how the wives of all these men must suffer! Every day I hear of things as bad as those you tell me you have seen to-day; and it is awful to me—awful to think that *we* are helping to make all this wrong and crime among the people."

"I am sure *we* are not responsible for their foolishness. No man is obliged to drink, if he don't wish to. I never asked one of my hands to take whiskey in payment for a day's work in my life; and you know, Elsie, no man hates this whole matter of dram-drinking worse than I do. Besides, I don't see any use of always looking at the black side of the picture. There are some drinking-men hereabouts, but where would you go to find the place where there is a better society of people, or where greater progress has been made, than here?"

"I know the neighborhood grows—that wealth increases with many: how can it be otherwise, in such a beautiful, fertile country? But would not genuine prosperity increase as rapidly without your distillery? Are not all these outrages against decency and sobriety, just so many blemishes upon our community, that should not and need not be? And, Richard, to be candid now: *Is* the 'Still-house' making *you* rich, among others, or are you sacrificing *yourself* in this work? Aye, Richard, sacrificing yourself, and the poor, the weak, the misguided, and their helpless families, to make a market for other people's products?"

Richard dared not answer directly—so he turned to another phase of the subject.

"Something must be done with corn. If *I* don't use it up, somebody else will. Pork, they say, is going to bring a better price this fall than it ever has. I intend to buy all the hogs I can, and fatten them for the Eastern market."

"For the love of Heaven, then, Richard, give them the corn in its natural state; and if there is a devil in it, let it enter the swine, as of old; do not extract it, to make swine of your neighbors. I tell you, Richard," added Elsie, impatiently, "there are not ten men about here who are not becoming the victims of your 'Still-house'; and if it goes on five years longer, we shall have a terrible neighborhood. Just think what schools we have now; what rowdyism; what wild young men!"

"There it is again! Every time we sit down for a chat, up comes that same old story—as if my 'Still-house' were the cause of all. I tell you, Elsie, it's no use talking; I have invested all I'm worth in it, and it *must* go on. If people will be fools, it is not my fault; and I won't bear to be taunted and reproached, day in and day out, about what I can't help. You can hunt up old Father Peters, to talk your nonsense to, if you must talk."

Elsie made no reply. A thought, a revelation, that burnt into her very soul, came to her with those harsh words, and she was deliberating with herself whether she should speak at all, or leave him to his own reflections, when they were startled by a shriek from the nearest cabin.

"Help, help! murther, murther! help!" came in shrill screams upon the evening air.

Richard sprang to his feet. "Pat is whipping Nora again," he exclaimed. "Curse the drunken beast! I expected nothing else when he filled his gallon-jug to-night."

Again came the cry, "Help, help! it's choking me to death, he is!"

Richard waited for no second summons, but bounded away to the help of the suffering woman. Elsie, in her excitement, followed after.

Patrick Sweeney was one of the best stone-cutters and brick-masons, in the country. When sober, he could out-work and out-wit the best. About once a month he indulged himself in a spree, as he called it, in which his good wife Nora never failed to take her full share. Pat demanded the best wages, and as such workmen as he were scarce, found no trouble in getting them.

Nora was as shrewd and as witty as her husband,— never at a loss for a joke, and generally more than a match for Pat—particularly if he was much "in liquor," as she called it.

When Richard arrived at the scene of action, he found them in a fight, around a stump before the

door,—throwing stones, chips, bits of wood, fire-
brands, pots and kettles—anything they could seize,
Nora all the while screeching and hallooing, "Murther,
murther! help, help!" Pat was a large man, and
Nora the merest little creature in the world, scarcely
the size of a full-grown child of ten, slender, and of
a delicate constitution, as one would judge from her
fair complexion and smooth, soft hair.

Just as Richard came up, Pat had seized her by the
throat.

"Och! but I've got you now, my lady; and it's
a stop I'll put to your scraaching, like a blind owl in
the midnight."

This gentle speech was cut short by Richard, who,
seizing him by the back of the neck, laid him prostrate, and was about to pin him down with a strong
hand, and exact a promise of peace, when he felt himself suddenly assailed by a set of wiry fingers in his
hair, which dragged him, despite his efforts, away
from the fallen enemy, and half around the stump,
while the same shrill voice that rang in his ears,
"Murther, murther!" now saluted him with no
loving epithets.

"I'll tache you, Richard Magoon, to be meddlin'
with my husband! What bisiness have ye, I'd like
to know, intarfarin' a-tween man and wife. Hasn't
yer good Book tould ye, ye ould sinner, what God
has fixed thegither, never let man be a separatin'; and
now, ye dirty-faced spalpeen, how dare ye be violatin'
it? Never a hair I'll laave in the head of ye, if ye

5*

don't be after trating us both, like a gintleman, to a nice dram of yer best."

Pat was by this time upon his feet, and came to the relief of his assailant.

"Och, woman! what are ye doing now? Sure it's the Squire yer making so free wid. Lit go his hair, Nora, darlint. You'll be forgivin' her, Mister Magoon, for that same. Faix, a wife would be no wife at all that would not be taking the part of her husband! It was just a bit of a play we were havin', for love's sake, in the moonlight, sir. Not the laste bit of anger in the world, sir—not the laste. But, walk in, Mr. Magoon,—walk in, my leddy. I'll thrate ye to a nicer toddy than iver you drank afore, since the day that your mither gin ye a wee drop, for yer stomach's sake, in the morning."

Richard turned with disgust from his drunken familiarity. Had his own spirit been less disturbed, he might have laughed heartily at the Irish wit, and the ready tact that could, on the instant, turn a drunken fight into a "love-play in the moonlight." But now he paused only to threaten Pat with his magisterial power if any further disturbance occurred, and turned, with Elsie, to retrace his steps.

The sound of a galloping horse was heard in the distance, and, in a moment more, a man rode up, who proved to be the constable of the township. He came with the news that Mike Dugan, on his way home from the "Still," had met young Harry Falconer, in company with his sister; that Mike had insulted Ellen, and Henry had repelled the insult by calling him a "drunken wretch." That Mike had then rushed upon the boy, who was without means of defence, and beaten him with his hoe, until he had cut and bruised him horribly. Ellen had run, screaming for help; but before any one could get to the spot, Henry was dead. That Mike had been taken, and the Justice was wanted immediately.

"Oh, my God!" cried Elsie, "what will come next? Is there to be no end of these terrors? Poor Mrs. Falconer! her favorite son killed,—*murdered!* And Mrs. Dugan's *only son a murderer!* The wretched mother of such a son! Oh! I would rather all of mine were murdered, than that I should live to see one of them guilty of such a deed!"

"It was liquor did it, ma'am," said the constable, respectfully. "Nothing but the liquor. Young Falconer had n't a better friend in the township than Mike Dugan, before he took to drink. He was engaged to Ellen, they say, and she turned him off after he took to drinking. It is a pity, I think, that the Squire ever let him have that situation under Kit, in the 'Still-house.' It's been the spoiling of him. He was the smartest boy in the town when his father died, two years ago."

"Yes," said Elsie, her face white as marble, and the great sweat-drops standing on her brow; "yes, and it was to help his mother—that good, noble mother, who gave up even her widow's dower to her husband's creditors—that he took the position. Oh! he asked of us bread, and we gave him a stone."

"Go home to the children, Elsie!" said the magistrate, in a tone of authority that brought the blood back again to her cheeks and lips. " I shall not probably be back till late." So saying, he turned abruptly from his wife, and went his way.

She watched their receding figures till they were lost in a turn of the road, and then, folding her arms across her breast, walked firmly toward the house.

But who shall tell the agony of that fearful hour, when the horrors which she had so vividly foreseen from the erection of the fatal " Still-house," seemed thickening about them ?—when that most bitter dreg was added to her cup of torture, the suspicion that the husband of her youth and love, the father of her children, was not only in the sight of God and man responsible for the most fearful of evils, the ghastliest of crimes, but that his own self-respect and manhood were falling under the power of this curse. " Oh, God ! oh, God !" she cried, as she strode rapidly on in the deepening twilight. " Oh, God ! my cup is full to overflowing—have mercy, have mercy, I pray !" And she pressed one hand violently upon her breast, and the other over her mouth, as if she had already quaffed deeply of the bitter draught, and were re-pelling what remained. Then bursting into tears, she sobbed out, " Oh! Richard, Richard! better, far better, that we should have struggled on in poverty, toiling day by day for bread, than that we should have made wealth at so fearful a cost! But I must be calm, and let no word or look betray my terrible suspicions. I must work, work, work! But oh, my God! where, where shall I begin?"

Having reached her home, she seated herself on the doorstep,—she *could not* venture in until she was calmer; and the quiet stars looking down from their far heights upon her, seemed comforting in their serenity and peace. And there beneath them, she renewed her vow to work, by day and by night, against the monster that was filling so many hearts with anguish, so many homes with desolation and death. Aye! so many homes!—was not *hers*, would it not also be one of them? And by an instinctive movement she leaped to her feet and turned sharply round to see if even now the flames had not seized it, or some frightful calamity overtaken it. There it stood! the home of her beloved, free from all apparent evil; the star-light clung lovingly about it, the tender vines hung their festoons of beauty and grace upon it. But through all this vision of its peace and loveliness, she saw fearful shadows threatening it,— fierce fiendish shapes closing about it,—until, to shut out all, she sank again upon the step where *he* had so often sat with her beneath the holy stars, when their hearts were as peaceful and unclouded. She wept long and bitterly, but less for herself than for others — for the woes which one dearer to her than her own life, was indirectly inflicting upon the innocent and helpless. As she wept, her soul grew calmer, and strengthened against the future; and at length she arose, went quietly in, kissed each of the dear ones who were sleeping the sleep of unconsciousness amid all the evils which menaced them,—although each kiss smote her with a spasm of pain as it wakened the memory of those other sorrowing mothers,—and, tearing herself unwillingly from them all, she went to her lonely chamber to cast herself anew upon the bosom of Infinite Love.

CHAPTER VI

THE funeral of Henry Falconer was a solemn scene. But the most solemn feature of it was the presentation of Deacon Peters' temperance pledge. Years had whitened the old man's locks, and bowed his frame, and deepened the furrows upon his brow; but it had not deadened the fire and energy of his heart. His words were measured and slow, but their force was unabated. He spoke to the multitude in earnest tones, and begged, with pleading tears, that the young should come forth and pledge themselves to abstain from the beverages which had brought such woe upon the people.

The old men bowed their heads under the influence of his fervid appeals, the women gave their emotion vent in quiet tears, while the young wept openly in the fulness of their feeling. But not one of all the crowd dared turn at the old man's entreaty, and come forward to sign the pledge of " total abstinence from all that can intoxicate."

Once, twice, thrice, he repeated the call. He besought them by the blood of the young man, sent to his last account without a moment's warning; by the agonizing sorrow of the murderer, whose fate was even more terrible than that of him who had fallen by his hand. He portrayed the woe of the aged and

(59)

doubly widowed mother; for her son had stood in
the place of his father till the power of temptation
had overcome him.   He spoke of the probable punishment.   He glanced over the past five years of misrule
in the neighborhood.   He alluded to the burial of Scott.
"Even then," he cried, with tones of honest feeling,
"even then I would have gathered you under the
wings of temperance, as a hen gathereth her brood;
but ye would not.   Oh! will ye wait until your
homes and hearts are all made desolate as these have
been, or will you come now, and thus bring peace
and quiet to your souls?   Is there not one here to
join with me in this self-denial — *not one? not one?*"

Slowly, in the back of the house, but in full view
of the congregation, rose Elsie Magoon ; and, with
face pale as marble, but with firm step, approached
the altar behind which the old man stood, and taking
the pen and pledge from his hand, turned, and placing them upon the coffin, between her and the people,
deliberately signed her name to the pledge — a pledge
that required her not only to abstain from the use of
ardent spirits herself, but "to use all reasonable means
for its exclusion from the neighborhood."

When she had written her name, she lifted her
head, and, looking at the people, said in a clear voice,
"I have done what I believe to be right; if every
one here would obey the voice of conscience, my
name would not stand alone."   Mrs. Col. Parsons, a
beautiful and good woman, rose partly from her seat;
but the strong hand of her husband was laid upon
her arm, and she shrank back again.   In another

part of the house, a young wife rose, and advanced a
step, when the husband caught his hat, twitched her
sleeve and left the house. No others dared come forward; and Elsie, looking over the audience, pronounced solemnly the words, "Alone!—I can stand
alone," and returned to her seat.

Richard was not at the funeral. His duty as a
magistrate had kept him in the village, where the
examination of Mike Dugan was going on. At
about the same hour that the body of Henry was
lowered to its last resting-place by the weeping
family, Mike Dugan was thrust into the dark and
loathsome cell of the heavy log-jail, there to await his
trial before the court, which would not hold its ses-
sion for three months.

The mother of Henry laid her son to his rest with
wild and uncontrollable grief. But the mother of
the murderer saw her child led away to a doom more
fearful than death; where the body must suffer and
the soul writhe in torment, and the good name, the
reputation, be for evermore turned into a by-word
and a curse. But no tear dimmed her eye, no sigh
heaved her bosom; no word of complaint, no moan
of despair, passed from her crushed heart.

"He'll be sure to be hung," said Bill Briggs, who
sat whittling a stick to a point on the fence beside
the office.

"You may bet high on that," answered his burly
companion. "D—n him! he ought to be burnt
alive. Henry Falconer was a right good feller."

"I'd pile sticks to burn old Magoon's 'Still-house,'

6

and that mighty quick, if anybody would help me," said Fred Wilson.

"It's no use laying the blame on the 'Still-house' or the liquor," said Deacon Hill, who was standing by. "It's no use trying to lay the blame where it don't belong. A man need n't get drunk if he don't choose to, and a moderate use of liquor does no man any harm. It's my opinion that whiskey only takes the hypocrisy out of a man, and shows you just what he is. If Dugan had n't had murder in him, it would never have come out of him; and I consider that a man has no more excuse for doing a thing because he's in liquor, than he has when he's been eating hoe-cakes and molasses for his dinner — not a jot."

"Them's my notions precisely, Deacon," said Briggs, the landlord of the village inn. "If a man is a mind to be a fool, why he kin, whether he gits whiskey or not; and it's my 'pinion that Dugan will be hung."

"I think he will. Such an example is very necessary in these parts," said the Deacon pompously, just as the wretched mother passed by. She caught the words, and the already chilled blood froze at its fountain. Her heart ceased to beat; her knees gave way under her, and she fell at the Deacon's feet in a fainting fit.

In a moment, a dozen of the idlers were at her side. They lifted her up, brought water, bathed her temples, rubbed her, and very soon — ah! all too soon — she was restored to consciousness. Opening her eyes, and fixing them on Deacon Hill, she said to him:

"It was you, Deacon, that first put the accursed cup to the lips of my boy. You told him 'to drink and be a man — that he was too big to be hanging to his mother's apron-strings.' If he dies, his blood be upon your head! He never disobeyed me till you succeed at his integrity, and taught him to despise my counsel."

The Deacon shrank back; and Sam Briggs, whose heart was really not bad, insisted upon helping her home. But she waved him away, and calmly and silently went her way to her desolate house by the wayside.

The ceremonies of the funeral had ended, and our heroine returned to her home. Richard was moody and silent at supper, and she did not tell him what she had done. The neighbors did not report the scene at the church, and it was some time before Richard knew that his house was divided against itself before the world, as it had long been in secret.

Meanwhile Mike Dugan had been lying in jail awaiting his trial. Now the day drew near for the final settlement of his case. Mr. Falconer and his family had great influence in the neighborhood, and their sorrow had created great sympathy in their behalf, and an equally strong feeling against the young man who was wearing out his life in the prison-cell.

We have hinted that Michael Dugan and Ellen Falconer had been warm friends, in the days when the young man's father, who had been reputed a man of wealth and character, was still living. He, too, had been given to the habit of the times, and had fallen a ready prey to a violent Western fever, which

seldom spares its victim, if addicted to intemperance.
After his death the estate was found wholly insolvent.
The widow might have claimed her portion, but she
refused to do so; saying that those who had trusted
her husband in good faith should in good faith be
paid to the uttermost farthing, if there were means to
do it. But means there were not; and when the
mother and her only son left their home, and went
into the cabin on the hill-side, and she took to her
spinning-wheel for a living, while he went out to
labor upon the farms, everybody admired her sterling
honesty, and was ready to give her a helping hand.

Squire Falconer, while he was willing to assist
the widow, peremptorily forbade Ellen to have anything more to do with the son. Ellen, for the most
part, obeyed the father's mandate, although her heart
rebelled; hoping that ere long her lover, by careful
industry, would become reinstated in her father's good
opinion.

In the mean time, Michael went to work with
Deacon Hill. He was laboring under the double
affliction of his father's death and the downfall of his
fortunes; and in addition, was made to believe, by
Henry Falconer, that Ellen had of her own free will
discarded him, because of his altered fortunes. It
was under this pressure of adverse circumstances and
feelings that the Deacon had persuaded him to drink
"just a drop," from time to time, to cheer himself.
One step taken seemed to require another. Mike was
a jovial, true-hearted, earnest boy. His father's Irish
blood, mingled with his mother's Puritan stock, had

laid the foundation of a rare character. All the advantages of a new country he had enjoyed; and now,
with an ardent love for his mother, and a hearty desire to work his own way honestly in the world, he
was ready to labor wherever he could win for himself
the means to bring comfort to her.

First, then, in Deacon Hill's field he had been
tempted; next, as a clerk in the great establishment
of Richard Magoon, surrounded on all sides by
tempters and temptation. But never, until the fatal
Saturday,—although in his thoughtful moments his
cheek had often been reddened with shame over some
coarse word or indiscreet or unkind action into which
the stimulus of whiskey had led him,—had he become so far under its influence, and lost to himself,
as to do aught which should wring his mother's heart
with sorrow, or his own with remorse.

In the Distillery, as manager, was a man familiarly
called Kit, who seemed possessed of a demon;—a
deep drinker himself, but never entirely overcome, it
seemed a matter of exultation with him to entice and
break down every man, young or old, who came
within the sphere of his influence. He hated young
Dugan, moreover, because he had several times, in his
capacity of clerk, detected defalcation and wrong-
doing in the distillery, and called him to account for
it;—because too, he had reported, at last, his shortcomings and abusive treatment to his employer, and
thus subjected him to reproof. On the Saturday on
which the murder had been committed, Kit had made
a bet with young Dugan, the loser to stand a treat ⋅

6*

of egg-nog, and both to drink a pint. Kit had lost the bet, as he knew he should, and had mixed the egg-nog to suit his diabolical purpose. He knew well that a pint of egg-nog would completely upset young Dugan; but, to make assurance doubly sure, he made it as strong as the beverage would bear— little less than a half-pint of the raw liquor.

Dugan drank off the draught, without discovering how he had been deceived. In a few moments he was wild with exhilaration, and very shortly a disturbance arose between the two. All the afternoon, Kit enjoyed the demoniac pleasure of chafing the irritated nerves and feelings of the young man.

Once or twice they had come almost to blows; and Mr. Magoon was sent for to settle difficulties. Finding Michael in a state of total inebriety, he dismissed him at once, ordering him out of the "Still-house."

On his way home he stopped at the corn-field, staggering, singing, and shouting. Here he found a new vexation. The boys began to jeer and laugh at him about Ellen. "He was a pretty fellow to be looking after the smartest and handsomest girl in town. No wonder she gave him 'the sack' with both ends open."

Each one fabricated a tale to suit himself, only to deepen the agony of the poor wretch. He drank there again, and when the time came to leave the field, and he started off alone, he had thoughtlessly hung a hoe over his shoulder. On his way he met

Henry Falconer and his sister Ellen, just returning from a neighbor's, where they had been on a visit.

Mike was yet smarting under the taunts and sneers of his comrades; and, drunk as he was, he remembered the hard sayings which they had jokingly put into the mouth of Ellen, and determined to be revenged; so he stepped up to her, and, with an insulting remark, attempted to kiss her. This of course aroused Henry, who called him a drunken fool, and struck him a severe blow, at the same time declaring that if he spoke to Ellen again he would beat his brains out.

Mike did speak, and approached Ellen as she stood by the road-side, trembling with terror. Henry sprang between them, at the same time dealing a second blow. In an instant, the hoe of Mike fell with all his force upon the head of Henry, striking him down. Blow followed blow, and ere three young men, who were in the field near them, could come to the rescue, the fatal deed was done. Mike was hurried to the village and committed to jail. In the morning, when he awoke, he had a dreamy consciousness of what had happened; but it seemed only a dream. He had quarrelled with Mr. Magoon, had a dispute in the corn-field, and an awful fight with Henry Falconer.

Wild was his terror, and fearful his grief, when told that his dreams were realities, and that he was indeed the murderer of Ellen's brother. And still more terrible was his agony when his beloved mother pressed his cold hand in hers at the trial on the Monday morning following the murder.

"Mother, do not reproach me," said he, in a low, husky voice. "I do not ask you to forgive me, either. O! I would die, or live a life of lingering torture,—no word, no murmur should pass my lips, —if I could only bring the dead to life, and, with him, peace again to your heart and *his!* Mother, pity me,—pray for me. No! no! forget me, but pray God to take that curse of all curses out of the neighborhood,—that 'Still-house,'—that entrance to hell,—which is luring so many into its ravenous jaws. Strive for that, mother, and let me die the death I deserve. Do not talk to me,—I can't bear your voice,—it pierces me like a dagger. Oh, mother! mother! why was I left to curse you so?"

The mother folded him convulsively in her arms, and clung to him in silence until he was taken back to his cell; and then, as we have said, she went away to her own home, and through the long summer days lived alone. Few saw her; for all sympathized with her, and none dared intrude upon her privacy. But there was one who spent long hours with the heart-broken mother,—one who, true to her woman's nature, showed her sympathy in two homes, and comforted the sorrows of two mothers. Ellen Falconer had loved Michael Dugan deeply and truly, and she felt· that when misfortunes came, her love should, most of all, have sustained him. But a father's stern command had controlled her generous nature. She had however written to Michael, telling him how matters stood at home, and assuring him that if, at the expiration of her minority, which would be in a few months, her father still continued his dislike, she should assert her own independence,—if he (Michael) remained true and firm amid his trials. But this note Henry had not honestly conveyed to its rightful owner. On the contrary, he told Dugan that Ellen herself had spurned him, and that she was engaged to, and would soon marry, James Watt, a young lawyer from the village. Michael had always made a confidant of his mother; and in the long, lonely visits made by Ellen to the widow, she had been informed of Henry's treachery.

Public opinion, as we have said, was strongly set against young Dugan. The general conviction was that he would be hung; for the rumor had been circulated that he had threatened the life of Falconer *before* the late quarrel; and, moreover, capital punishment was not then so abhorrent to the people as now.

The mother of the prisoner was allowed to visit him once a week. Elsie Magoon also had asked, and been once or twice admitted to talk with him. One Saturday afternoon Ellen called on Elsie, and, taking her aside, asked the loan of a bonnet, a shawl, and dress. No explanations were made. That evening, Mrs. Dugan and Mrs. Magoon sought the jail in the dim twilight, and remained an hour with the prisoner. After they left, a keen eye might have discovered a heavy butcher-knife concealed in the straw of his bed. Three weeks after, on the day set for the trial, when the sheriff entered the prison, he found the cell empty. The breakfast of the young man remained untasted, and his bed so arranged that the jailer, in the dark, had taken the old clothes, the knee of the pants stuffed with straw, and an arm of the coat ingeniously arranged, for the prisoner. The young man had always been moody and silent, and therefore the jailer thought it not strange that his face was covered, or that he refused an answer when his food had been placed inside the door. Under his pallet of straw was found a hole in the floor. The prisoner had dug his way out beneath the underpinning of the logs, where friends were waiting with garments and money to send him on his way; and, with many a prayer, many a blessing, and many tears, he fled from the terrible doom that seemed to await him.

Not until Ellen had entered his cell, did the hope arise in his heart to escape, what he believed just— an incarceration in the penitentiary. This he expected; and the years of solitary thought and suffering—the bloody, lifeless form of Henry ever before him—were to him more horrible even than the idea of the gallows; and he fell into a mood of sullen despair in view of his probable fate.

But when *she* entered his cell—when she knelt by him, and wept her bitter tears, and bade him escape the felon's doom,—to be strong of heart, and resolve in the future to redeem the past; when she, child as she was, bade him live and be a man, for the world's sake—for his mother's sake—*for her sake ;*—when in the fulness of her young love she pressed his pale forehead with her lips, and the electric current sped to his desponding heart, to warm and vitalize it again into life and action,—then he sprang up, and with the force of one just wakened from a frightful dream, he promised her that he would do as she wished; that he would be all they desired; and that a day should come, if God would but spare him, when the world should be willing to forgive, if they could not forget, *that one* maddened hour of his life.

CHAPTER VII

THE escape of Mike Dugan caused great excitement in the quiet village of Smithville. Efforts were made to arrest him, but it was more than half suspected that the Sheriff and his deputies took no special pains to overtake the fugitive. Indeed, public opinion seemed — as public opinion often does — to undergo a sudden revolution.

Ellen Falconer, who, in consideration of her deep grief at the time of the first trial, had not been called upon as a witness, had since given her deposition; and the statement that Henry had struck Mike twice before Mike had made the assault, put a new face upon the affair altogether; for the young men had all testified that they knew of no quarrel between the two, and had therefore believed the attack of Mike to be unprovoked.

Then, too, the treachery of Kit ——, the falseness of young Falconer — his deception in telling Mike that Helen had spurned him for his poverty's sake, also became known, and there were few who did not rejoice at the escape.

The old log-jail passed under review by the commissioners; it was unanimously decided that a new one was needed; and forthwith a new one was built.

Mrs. Dugan and Mrs. Falconer had met, and with

many tears, and kindly condolences, had renewed
their early friendship; and Mrs. Dugan had soon
after left, to join friends in the far East.

The harvests ripened — the autumn fruits fell, and
were gathered in — winter swept over the fields —
and spring gladdened the old door-stone with blos-
soms. There were births, marriages, and deaths —
change, perpetual change — even at the Old Still-
House; which yet groaned and puffed, and puffed and
groaned, under the hill.

Change — aye, there was change. Deacon Hill was
fast losing his respectability, as he had already lost
his position in the church. Squire Falconer never
came home from the village sober; Major Brant was
going the downward road as fast as an ungovernable
passion could carry him. Twenty others, men of
character and means, might be counted, who never
went to a raising, a shooting-match, an election, a
militia training, or even a school-meeting, without
forgetting what was due themselves as men.

All things were changing, and all for the worse —
and Richard Magoon among the rest. His farm was
running down; his barns and fences were out of repair; his stock ill cared for; his home neglected.
Debts were eating up all the profits of the farm and
Still-house; for with bad management, and bad men,
there was but little profit anywhere. And that early
debt — that five hundred, to pay which the Still-house
was built, remained uncancelled, and the wily old
step-father held a mortgage upon the whole estate.

As Richard went down, our heroine seemed to rise

7

in strength and courage. Terrible was the grief that
was tugging at her heart-strings, but she braced herself bravely against it.

"Weepings and wailings will not give me strength
for my duties," she would say to herself; "these loved
ones must be cared for and educated. Who will lead
them in the true path, if a mother's love fail? The
waters of bitterness may roll over me, but I must not
sink." And so she toiled on, patient and strong,
striving to her utmost to rectify her husband's mis-
takes; to think for him and plan for him—working
earnestly for the good of all, conscientiously believing
that what was for the happiness of the neighborhood,
was for the happiness of her own household. Hence,
she was often compelled to take a bold stand against
what seemed to be the immediate interest of her husband.

Five years had again sped by, since the escape of
Mike Dugan, and great preparations were being made
in the neighborhood for a Fourth-of-July celebration.
The gathering was to be held in the grove near the
new brick church. The Declaration of Independence
was to be read, songs sung, and Richard Magoon to
address the people; to be followed by a dinner to be
provided by the ladies from their abundant stores.

Elsie Magoon was chosen superintendent of the
ladies' department; and a meeting was held in her
parlor, three weeks before, to lay their plans, and to
ascertain who were able and willing to volunteer for
the work. There were twenty, or more, present; all
were animated and enthusiastic, and tongues ran glibly,

while hands worked diligently with knitting-needles, and the hereditary " patchwork." The items of turkeys, pigs, ham, beef, veal, mutton, squirrels, venison, rabbits; the bread, biscuits, cakes, pies, tarts, custards, puddings, and all the etceteras of a country festival, had been duly discussed and arranged; the tea and coffee, the sugar and cream, attended to; every one knew her part;—when Mrs. Enson let fall the remark, that they would need other drinks beside tea and coffee, and that she had some nice currant wine to offer; another had peppermint cordial; a third had blackberry syrup; a fourth, as good cider as ever was tasted; a fifth would furnish eggs and sugar for eggnog; a sixth would give nutmegs; and so on,—if Mrs. Magoon would furnish the whiskey.

" My friends," said Mrs. Magoon, after their rapid proposals were ended, " you have, with one voice, voted me your superintendent. If I take any part with you in that festival, I shall insist that neither wine, egg-nog, nor toddy shall be introduced upon our tables."

" Why, Miss Magoon, how you do talk !" almost shrieked Betsy Lake; " we could n't have any Fourth at all, if we went to work that way. Every young man in town would be a-laughing at us; they 'd never come nigh us, if it got out."

" I can't help that," was the calm reply. " Any young man who comes to the grove only to get something to drink, would probably be an annoyance while there, and had better be allowed to stay away. I shall insist upon this arrangement, or, upon giving up my charge."

"La, now, Miss Magoon, don't go fur to be perctic'lar; you know folks allers have had, and allers will have such things," said Mrs. Tim White, the blacksmith's wife.

"I know that well, Mrs. White; but can you tell me of a single instance where *they have had such things,* that evil did n't come of it, since the days when Noah planted a vineyard and became drunken?"

"Did n't Christ make wine out of water, I'd like to know?" piped out Miss Ferrill.

"Yes," replied Mrs. Magoon; "and if any one at our party can do the same, I shall not object. But I take it, the wine that Jesus spoke into existence had none of the properties that produce intoxication, for we do not read that any of that wedding-party became intoxicated, or that the wedding ended in a fight." ·

"No more they did n't," said Mrs. Deacon Hill; "and I'm for Mrs. Magoon; I know just how it'll be. Last Fourth the Deacon went down to Smithville and they got to toastin' and speechifyin', and the Deacon he stayed and stayed, and he never got home till 'leven o'clock at night, and he driv the old mare off the bridge, and come pretty nigh breaking his neck." ("Pity he did n't: he's an old goose anyhow," tittered Miss Lake to Miss Ferrill, in the corner.)

"What's that you was saying, Betsy Lake?" said Mrs. Deacon Hill.

"Oh! nothin'; me and Jane was only talking."

"Well, I'm agin the liquor anyhow," rejoined the Deacon's wife.

"I am fully with Mrs. Magoon," said Miss Mor-

timer, the school-teacher; "I have noticed that many
of our young men drink too freely, even at our parties; and, talking to Judge Icors the other day, he
laid the blame upon the young ladies. Now, let us
all unite; and if we can have one party without it,
and keep sober, perhaps we can have another, and in
the end exert a permanent influence. I have heard
that these things are being done in other places."

"Exert a fiddlestick!" said Betsy Lake. "I tell
you now, there'll not be a beau there, if there's no
fixins of that sort."

"Miss Mortimer will have her beau, and she don't
care for the rest," chimed in Miss Ferrill. "*Parson
Jones* has come out on old father Peters' side, and
don't touch a drop—won't eat apples if they ain't
sweet; so folks say."

"I wish your friend, Ben Allen, was as conscien-
tious," replied Miss Mortimer, while a blush of conscious love and pride mounted her fair brow.

The blush seemed contagious, for Miss Ferrill's
face was as red as a peony, and she reached out of the
window for a sprig of the honeysuckle that drooped
over the casement.

"If I might venture a remark," spoke Mrs. Falconer, in a low voice, "I should say that Mrs. Magoon
is in the right; but how will the gentlemen bear it?"

"We'll make 'em bear it," said Mrs. Deacon Hill;
"and as for the youngsters, if they don't like the girls
better than toddy, let 'em stay away, I say; my girls
can git along without 'em, I reckon."

"Well, for my part," spoke up a little fussy woman

7 *.

in the corner, with a voice very like a screech-owl,
"I think it's meddling with things that don't belong
to us. If the men want whiskey and drinks, let 'em
have whiskey and drinks, and enjoy themselves. It
looks mighty like takin' away people's liberties — on
the Fourth of July too! — my man would never consent to it, I know, though he is as sober a man as
common, I dare say."

Poor little Mrs. Piper! she did n't know that every
one in the room knew that her man was "unco'
happy" seven days in the week, and twice on Sunday.

"Let us put it to vote!" cried out a voice.

"No!" said Mrs. Magoon; "no! — you have made
me your manager. I stand here, ready and willing to
take the responsibility and bear all the blame. If you
will help me this once, I will do all I can to make
the day pleasant to all parties. The young ladies will
doubtless remember their last dance — the shame and
mortification that wrung their hearts at having to go
home alone; of leaving their lovers and fathers too
imbecile to get out of the hall. Some of my married
friends too, have surely not forgotten the trials of the
next day. I will not act, if I am to superintend the
dealing out of the withering curse that spoils all our
enjoyment, and turns our neighborhood peace into
madness and confusion. I shall put another vote,
how many are desirous still that I shall superintend
the arrangement."

The consciousness of doing right, the boldness of
the undertaking, the trial that she knew awaited her
— all conspired to flush Elsie's cheek and brighten
her eye, and her calm, resolute soul shone out in every

feature of her face, as she stood among them with folded hands awaiting their decision. Beautiful and strong she looked. Every one knew her true to her purpose, as the magnet to the pole, and the advocates of drinking were rebuked and subdued before her. Not one raised a voice against her. After a moment's silence, she resumed the subject,—

"No one here will accuse me of a desire to hold the position assigned me. It will be a labor and care that I have not sought for, but which have been forced upon me. I have seen how the demon of alcohol has degraded us in years past. I know my husband makes it: would to God he did not!—For years I have striven to prevent its use in all private ways,—now I am ready to take this bold, public stand;—those who still make me their choice, will lift the right hand."

As if a spell were upon them, every hand was raised. So all-pervading is the influence of one strong heart in the cause of right. Few know their own power, or the influence they may exert over others. A resolute, determined "I can, and will," has often saved a neighborhood. The bold, fervid spirit leads on the mob, and the same spirit by its subtile magnetism can subdue it.

However much Betsy Lake and Miss Ferrill agreed to disagree with Mrs. Magoon, they held their hands high in air, and one would have supposed them the sworn friends of prohibition, in the past no less than the future.

The party of ladies separated in hearty good-humor, and our heroine, elated with her success, went to her work with a more cheerful spirit than usual.

CHAPTER VIII.

THERE was not in the whole country a more expert washwoman than Nora Sweeney. Little as she was, she had a vast deal of physical force, which, united to her extreme activity, enabled her to do a large amount of work. Soon after the quarrel related, Nora was called upon to wash for Mrs. Magoon, who thought there could be no better time to attempt her reformation than when she called for her dram, as she always did about ten o'clock in the forenoon.

"An' sure, Misthress Magoon," said the spirited little washwoman, "you're not going to let a puir body wash the livelong day, with niver a dhrop to warm and comfort them, is yez?"

"Well, Nora, I think I shall. I have made up my mind that it is wrong to give such things to people, and in future no one will get anything stronger from me than a cup of tea."

"Ye'll jist be suiting yersilf, of coorse, Misthress Magoon," was the laconic reply; and the little red arms flashed through the foaming suds at a vigorous rate. But not a word more was spoken, until Mrs. Magoon, who felt as though her duty would be left undone if she did not make an attempt to impress the woman with the necessity of keeping sober, again took up the subject.

"Nora," said she, "why is it that you will continue to drink so much, when you see the trouble it brings upon you? You have little children depending upon you for support, and you have nothing comfortable in your house, only as you earn it; for Pat spends nearly all his wages for whiskey. Surely, it is bad enough for him. Men, you know, think they must drink to make them strong. But I don't think women need it. Now tell me candidly, do you?"

"Troth, thin, since ye've axed, I'll jist say I'm thinking it's as much a need for the one as the other."

"Yes, I know what you mean, Nora. You think that both men and women would be better without it, and so do I. But it really does seem worse for a woman to drink, and fight, and do such things, than for a man. You could get up a first-rate character, if you would only let drink alone, and keep sober; for there is not such a washwoman in the whole town. Then you are so cheerful and happy when you are sober—so witty, too—and you never deceive us, or break your promises. If you would but agree to let the liquor alone, you might in time lead Pat to keep sober. But if you couldn't do that, you could at least keep yourself comfortable, and set a good example for your husband and children."

"Is it me ye're spaking to, Misthress Magoon?" said the little woman, straightening herself to her full height, and dashing the foam from her glowing hands; "me ye're spakin' to, mem, biddin' me be settin' good examples, and makin' fine resolves, and tachin'

my husband good manners? Indade, thin, it's the
same ye may be takin' to yerself. It's mighty few
fine dresses and the likes your leddyship would be
gettin', if somebody did n't be drinkin' the hell-broth
your man is makin' all the year round.

"Bad enough for Pat, you say! and faith it is, and
too hard intirely; for when it's drunk he is, it's *two
dollars* a day that's losin' to me and the childer, for a
betther boss niver tinded the puttin' brick in the
wall; but when I get drunk, it's only your beggarly
quarter-dollar for a long day's work, and grudged
me at that! Strength, is it, it gives to the men?
And which needs it most, thin, I'd like to know —
Pat with his great stout frame, and a fist that would
send me skirting a rod if he liked; or me, that weighs
but a hundred pound, and am only four feet six in
the slippers my mither put on me? Strength it
gives, does it? I'll tell ye the strength it gives.
Did n't he come home last Saturday night as drunk
as a baste? Well he did. And had n't I the beautiful supper for him? And what does he do, the first
thing, but throw my tay-pot beyant the back-log? I
was n't to be put by, so I sint his brown jug to keep
it company. Faith, but it was wroth thin he was, and
up he gets in his strength, and puts me out of the
door, a-shtaggerin' all the while, and bangs it on me,
lavin' the childer screamin' like mad. But you
know, my leddy, I'm spry as a cat; so I jumps in at
the back windy, and jist while he's settled hisself on
the stool ferninst the fire, I switched it from under
and laid him a-sprawlin' on the floor, flat on his back;

and he was jist that strong with his whiskey, he could n't get up at all, at all. And did n't I set the table over him, and dance the beautiful hornpipe a-top, in spite of him? Troth, I did; and I can do it again whenever he gets the strength of the whiskey in him. That's the strength it gives, my leddy — I know;" and Nora chuckled with delight at her own exploit.

"Yes, but if you had n't been sober, you could not have managed Pat in that way. Now, will you not promise me that you will not drink any more? Let the men drink, if they will; but we women will keep sober."

"Niver a bit will I do the likes o' that for yez, Misthress Magoon. It's fools ye 'Merican women are makin' of yerselves, sure. You jist lit the men do as they like — drink and swear, and chew, and smoke, and fight, and whativer else seems their pleasure — and ye niver ask to share a bit wid 'em. Now, if there's strength in the whiskey, none needs it more nor I. If there's comfort in the baccy, I'll take my share; and if an oath relieves a body's conscience, I'll out wid it, — if there's fun in a fight, I'll take a hand. Now, by your lave, my leddy — and it's askin' your pardon I am for spakin' so freely to you — if it's not right for *me*, it's not right for *anybody*. And, Misthress Magoon, don't be for askin' poor weak bodies like me, to be takin' the pledge."

Old Nora was roused by her own logic, inconsistent as it was, — and thus went on in her mixed brogue, between Irish and Yankee:

"Don't be callin' on *me* to keep sober.   Just let your lavin' off, Misthress Magoon, begin at home. What's to become of yer trade, if somebody don't drink the divil's broth your man is so busy a-makin' from Monday mornin' till Saturday 'night, all the year round? And sure, is n't it out o' that ye get yer livin'?—out o' the blood and bones of us poor wretches that knows no betther?

"Don't ye taste the tears of widow Dugan in yer tay, and hear the sighs of the puir weeping and desolate Mother Falconer, in the flut'rin' of yer ribbons? Och! if it be a sin to be drinkin' the liquor, ain't it a wickedness to be *makin'* it? It's a long, long reckonin',, my leddy, will come to the likes of Richard Magoon whin the Good Father calls him to a sittlement; for he is rich and larned, and has been well raised, and can read his good Book, and knows better than to be settin' a thempthation before the ignorant and wake, to lead them into the dark purgatory in this world and the world to come. No, no, Misthress Magoon; draw yer own kith and kin out o' the scorchin' fire, before ye try to preach the likes of us poor creatures out o' the embers."

Nora turned vigorously to her work. Her heart was stung to the quick by Mrs. Magoon's reproof, for, of all the neighborhood, there was not one she loved so well. And now that she had said her say, she wept like a child. Hers was a good, kind heart; and could she have cleansed it of the impurities of a misguided life, as easily as she could purify the linens in her hands, it would have been washed as white as snow.

Elsie had been foiled in her first attempt, yet she did not despair. The words of the excited Nora rang in her ears as she went-about her household duties: "Don't ye taste the tears of the Widow Dugan in yer tay, and hear the sighs of the desolate Mother Falconer in yer fluttering ribbons?" One by one she called her children to her, and, in the secretness of her own chamber, poured out to them her thoughts and sufferings, under the unholy work out of which came their bread. The boys promised to abstain from all contamination; they had not yet drunk a drop, and pledged themselves never to do so.

Let not the reader wonder that the work of reform went so slowly forward, when upon almost every mind, except Elder Peters', was impressed the idea that the temperance movement was one of sheer fanaticism, if not infidelity. Even the minister stood in his desk and preached his sermon upon moderation, taking the text from Paul: "Drink no longer water, but a little wine for thy stomach's sake, and for thine often infirmities." Scarcely a man could be found, who had not an interest, either directly or indirectly, in the "old Still." Yet the one act of Elsie Magoon, in standing alone in that congregation, and signing her hand to a temperance pledge, had aroused the neighborhood to thought.

Many said "It was wrong; no woman should thus injure the interest of her husband;" others, that it was "unladylike" and "unchristian." Deacon Hill quoted St. Paul again: "That wives should ask of husbands at home," and learn their duty there. Most

8

of the women, and many of the men, condemned her
for the act, while others defended her; and discus-
sions, long and earnest, were had all over the neighborhood.   Talking and thinking are very apt to elicit
truth; and more than one of the good men, who stood
high in authority, found, before they were through
their argument, that there were really some pretty
strong points on the other side of the question.

Amid this talk, which amounted almost to slan-
derous persecution, the strong-hearted woman walked
on, unswerving in her duty; though every passing
day, darker and more threatening clouds gathered
about her.

Day by day, as the weeks rolled by, she saw, with
feelings amounting to terror, that a direful work was
being done in her own household.   The flashing eye
and the irritable temper of her husband confirmed
her suspicions that he too was becoming a victim to
his own fearful trade.   Yet, as her trials grew more
terrible, her spirit grew stronger in its resistance.

Elsie, the younger, now a beautiful child, budding
into early womanhood, was busy one evening setting
the tea-table for the harvesters, who would soon be
in from their work.

"Mother, is n't Ellen Falconer pretty?" said the
child, artlessly, as she laid the plates upon the long
table.

"I think she is, dear, because I love her; some
persons think she is too sad.   But what made you
think of her just now?"

"Oh, because Betsy Lake and Susan Ferris were

talking out there, in the garden, under the honeysuckle arbor, all about lawyer Danvers wanting to
marry her, and how Ellen would not have him; and
they said she might better, because he was rich and
knew so much; and that he would go to Congress some
day, and that he would make her such a nice lady, and
all that; and that she need n't be so afraid of folks
because they got a little the worse for liquor, sometimes, for her father got high every day; and that her
brother Tom was as bad as lawyer Danvers. And then
they began to talk about your not having any toddy
at the Fourth of July,—and then they saw me and
stopped. It was something about the old 'Still-house'
they were saying. Oh! mother, I hear folks say *so
many things.* Won't father do something else some
time but make whiskey?"

"I hope so, dear."

"Mother, when I get a little bigger, I mean to go
away, teach school, or do something, somewhere. I
won't stay here if he don't quit making whiskey, for
all the girls now call my father the 'old whiskey-
maker,' and I can't stand it. And Mary Truman said
to-day, that if my father did n't make her father a
drunkard, she could have a new dress and shoes to
wear Fourth of July, as well as me; and she said it
was my father, too, that made Mike Dugan kill Henry
Falconer, and that was what broke Ellen's heart, and
made her look so sad; and, oh! I don't know half
she said;" and the poor child buried her face in her
apron and sobbed bitterly.

"Elsie, my dear," said her mother, "there 's your

father coming from town; dry up your eyes and help
me get the supper; we will hope that these things
will not always last; perhaps pa will not always keep
the 'Still-house;' I think *something* will make a
change.

Richard discovered, on entering the house, that Elsie
had been weeping, and ordered her abruptly into the
other room: "she was too old to act like a baby, and
have her face in that condition."

The mother saw in an instant that he was in an
excited condition, for, like all drunkards, in proportion
to his manliness and tenderness when sober, were his
unreasonableness and severity when intoxicated.

"I have something to say to you too, madam,"
said he, with menacing tone; "they tell me that you
have set up your authority, and decided that no liquor
is to be drunk at the celebration. Is that so?"

"The ladies gave me the place of superintendent,
and I told them, that, if I occupied that position, I
should exclude all intoxicating drinks. I left it for
them to decide whether I should take the office. They
knew my principles."

"They know you are a canting, hypocritical fool!"
said Richard, almost stamping with rage. "I'll let
you know, madam, I'll not put up with interference
with my affairs, any longer. I'll see if there is not
liquor to be drank on the Fourth of July, because a
snivelling Methodist says there sha'n't be!"

He had never been so boisterous in her presence;
and though her knees trembled, and her heart almost
ceased to beat, she controlled herself, and went on

with her work. Her quietness seemed to exasperate
him. He was determined to provoke her to a reply.
He muttered the most terrible curses and threats; followed her out to the well, then down into the cellar,
and into a dark vault within, where choice food and
fruits were kept.

He stood near her as she filled a dish for supper,
and, as if to show her his power, knocked it from her
hand, and shook his fist in her face. By an adroit
and quick movement, she passed him, stepped out,
and in an instant closed the door, and locked him in.

Sudden shocks often for the moment recall drunken
men to their senses, or awaken in their minds at least,
a dim consciousness of their condition. So, with
Richard. He seemed to comprehend the whole, and
his pride would not allow him to cry out. He sat
down to await his release; soon, drowsiness overcame
him, and he fell asleep.

A woman of less resolute and determined will
would have yielded in an hour, and released the
offender from his confinement.

Elsie was wiser; and bitter as were her feelings, she
resolved to bear the worst that might befall.

Trembling from head to foot, she returned to her
work, saying to Elsie the younger, "Be quiet, and do
not let Frank know that your father is in the house."

It was Saturday night. The men came in to supper
—the meal was eaten—the workmen dispersed, the
children retired; still the sad wife plied her needle.
Again and again, she went down and listened at the
door; but his breathing told her that he was asleep.

8*

"Ah," thought she, "will he ever forgive me — to leave him all night locked in this cold cell? Better by far, to have it thus, than that he should waken in a felon's cell, with the terrors of a guilty conscience hanging over him; and so perchance our children be worse than orphans."

Slowly and wearily wore the hours away. It was near morning when the heavy sleep of inebriety passed off.

"Elsie," was his first word, as he threw out his arms, groping for her. "Elsie! where are you?" His hand fell upon the edge of a shelf. "My God! where am I? In the cellar-vault? Yes, I remember it all now — I threatened her — followed her down — I remember that; swore at her; fool! beast! madman that I am! No wonder that she turned the key!"

As if a new thought had come to him, he ceased speaking, and knocked upon the door. Elsie had slipped noiselessly to the top of the stairs, and now came down, unlocked the door, and the two, without a word, ascended the stairs. A cup of refreshing tea, and a bit of toast, were made ready for him by the kitchen-fire; and with as much kindly affection, and as little embarrassment as if he had just returned from town, she begged him to eat. He sat down, drank a cup of tea, and ate a few mouthfuls of toast. She ate with him.

As they rose from the table, both walked to the door. The cool breeze of summer fanned their burning brows. The eastern sky already bore the gold-

and-crimson tints of morning, and a lark sprang from his grassy bed, and uttered its cheerful cry as it darted upward. He passed his arm around her waist —her head drooped upon his shoulder, and he whispered, in his own gentle voice, in her ear,—

"Elsie, my own dear wife—I thank you."

Not another word was spoken. She had conquered!

CHAPTER IX

SHE had conquered; that strong-hearted woman! Not by the force of prayers and tears; not by accident, or by fainting, and failing, and dying; but by following her brave humane instincts, and doing the right thing at exactly the right moment—just as a resolute, wise man would have done under like circumstances.

She knew Richard's temper — she knew his pride. Though good-natured almost to silliness to others, when intoxicated he was invariably harsh and petulant to her. She knew this to be a very natural result of wrong; we would rather all the world should know our shortcomings, than those we love best; our pride rebels at the idea that a wife, a mother, a father, or sister, has become cognizant of our sins—and the deeper the love, the more galling the exposure.

Thus, of all others, Richard most disliked the company of his wife, when he had drunk too deeply. Too proud to acknowledge the wrong; too proud to bear patiently the look of deep mortification and anguish written upon every feature,— spoken in every tone of her voice,—every glance of her eye,—even manifested in the motion of her body, he felt impelled, by his pride and remorse acting together, to speak to her in cold and unkind tones, and often to treat her with

contempt and scorn. It is a fearful thing for a man
to feel that the wife, whom he must respect for her
many virtues, must lose her respect for him; that he
has fallen from that high estate which first secured
her love and esteem, and which alone can continue it;
to see her love waning day by day,— to feel that his
sins are only tolerated and borne with, from a sense
of duty. Many of the thousands of instances in
which wives have met a violent death at the hands
of their husbands, may be traced to this cause,— this
love turned into maddening hatred in the hour of intoxication, through the accumulated fury of mor-
tified pride and unendurable remorse.

Elsie was not ignorant of this reaction of wrong-
doing upon the wronged and innocent,—she had not
walked with closed eyes through life, — and she had
noticed with keenest pain for many months past, that
Richard's language to her was less polite, less even
respectful than formerly; that he had often threatened
her, although never had come to personal violence.
But in even his sober moments he had grown malicious, and improved every opportunity of wounding
and disturbing her; and she felt that under the stimulus of liquor he was becoming dangerous to them all.
She had felt compelled, therefore, to put it beyond
his power to do them any harm, and she was gratified
to find it result in even a temporary success.

It was now several years since Elsie had signed her
name to the Temperance Pledge on the coffin-lid of
the murdered victim of the old "Still-house." And
she had labored day and night in behalf of the cause,

during all that time. For when the day's duties at home and abroad were ended, she retired into a quiet nook of her own, where none intruded, and wrote far into the night the thoughts that burned and plead for utterance, within her. A friend in Smithville had shared her secret, and given her articles to the public through various journals. Many of these were re-printed and sung throughout the land, from the pine forests of Maine to the flower-wreathed shores of the Gulf of Mexico.

Now and then, and as if by magic, scenes of rowdy revel and horrible brutality, enacted around and within the old "Still-house," were detailed with graphic minuteness in the "Smithville Luminary." None knew whence they came; and many a one who thought his secret safe, began almost to think that fairies were abroad telling tales as in days of yore. The distiller could not read, and he was one of them-selves; therefore it could not be he who wrote them, or gave information; besides, he had sworn a solemn oath that he knew nothing about the matter!

Dan, the chore boy, also solemnly protested his innocence. Mr. Manford, the minister, denied their authorship, and he was believed without an oath. Nobody suspected Mr. Magoon, of course; and as to Mrs. Magoon, none dreamed that she, the hard-working farmer's wife, the best housekeeper in all the country round, the woman who was ever at her post, often with the sick, the afflicted,—and whose whole round of "wifely" and motherly duties was run with exactness and care,—could ever find time to scribble for the papers! Nobody ever suspected such a thing; and so the "Sketches from Life" remained a marvel to the neighborhood.

An article, severe in satire and truthful in detail, had just been published, and met the eye of Richard for the first time in Mr. Compton's grocery, where he had called to get a dram. His wife's father-in-law was there on the same errand; and at least a dozen more, of like character, all intent upon cooling the outward by heating the inward man.

"I say, Magoon," said lawyer Varnum, "who do you keep as Recording Secretary up there at your 'Still-house?' They must take things down in short-hand."

Richard bit his lip, and his face flushed with excitement.

"I'll be —— if I know," he replied; "I'd give a round hundred to find out."

"Well," said his step-father, "just hand over the cash, if you've got it, and I'll tell you."

"What do you know about it?" was the short and crusty rejoinder.

"I know that them pieces in the newspaper ain't written nowhere only in your house," said the old miser, with a sneer; "that woman of yourn used to scribble cute things long afore you knew her. She could take off anybody, and write a story, when she was a gal, as well as any Philadelfy lawyer."

"Oh, you would not pretend to say, Mr. Porter, that Squire Magoon's wife would write such things to destroy her own interest, and that of her husband, do you?" said Varnum.

"Well, I didn't say anything about his wife, *in*

particular," said the old man, with a chuckle, as he saw how Richard was writhing under the new suspicion that was finding its way through his muddled brain.

"It's false as the devil!" exclaimed the latter, as he lifted another glass of the waiting liquor, and tossed it impetuously down.

"Well, maybe it is; but if you've a cool hundred to spare *on a bet, maybe* you can just settle this little account," said the old Shylock, handing him a note, which was due for interest on that *old debt.*

Not one cent of the principal had ever been paid, and little of the interest; but instead, sum after sum had been loaned at the same place, until both farm and "Still-house" were under mortgage to the old sharper.

"I can't do it, Mr. Porter. You'll have to wait till I thrash out my wheat, or get in my fall crop."

"Well, I reckon I've waited about long enough; it's nigh on to fifteen years I've been a-waiting, and that's about as long as it becomes a man to be patient. So I'll just hand it over to lawyer Varnum here; maybe *he* can get it, if I can't. But I want to give you a word of advice: if you don't want more on 'em to get into a lawyer's hands, you'd best stop that woman of yourn from signing temperance pledges, and talking about temperance all over the country;— she's a-ruining your business with her canting. Why, she's set the hull of the women folks up that they won't have any whiskey nor nothin' down at the grove on the Fourth. Pretty doings that, for a stiller's wife! Bedad! if she was my wife, I'd stop her tongue, or I'd make her take the breeches,—one of the six. What do you say, Major?"

"I say, if she was my woman, and run round as *she* does, spilin' my business, I'd let her know what was what," replied the drunken blacksmith, who had just stepped in. "Mr. Compton, fill us a glass."

Richard was in a terrible excitement. He was not sufficiently intoxicated to be lost to a sense of his degrading position, in hearing the name of his wife bandied about upon the tongues of those low, revellers in a grog-shop. He almost reeled with dizziness. He stepped to the counter and drank another dram; then turning to the company, broke forth with a vehemence that no one of them had ever before heard —threatened to horsewhip the first man who spoke again of his wife as the author of those articles,— shook his fist in his father-in-law's face, and defied lawyer Varnum's power to collect the debt; took another drink, and rushed out of the store.

"It's a great pity," said Varnum, "to see so fine and good a man as Magoon making such a fool of himself. I don't want to prosecute this claim, Porter; for, if you begin, his creditors will pitch upon him and hook him up. They will strip him of every cent."

"Can't help it; I want my money."

"But you are in no special need of it, are you?"

"Every man is in special need of his own, ain't he?"

"Darn'd if *it's your own*, old skinflint," said the

9

drunken blacksmith; "I know'd you when you was n't worth a copper, and could n't get yourself a glass of grog, and did n't have a second clean shirt to your back; and when you married the Widder Stockton, you just set your heels up. Now, supposing she'd a never had ye, every acre of that grand old farm over yonder — the best one in the State — would have fell to her daughter there, Mistress Magoon. But she married you, and you got it all; and now you're going about to set a cussed lawyer to work, to take that home from the dead mother's child. And how long, I wonder, do you expect to hold on? You're nigh on to the groaning time that the Bible tells on, now; and then who'll get it all? You haven't a chick nor child, and it'll all go to them stuck-up brother's children, that hate you like pizen; and won't they scatter it though? — won't they! he! he! he! — Won't they though!" and the old fellow, who had once been generous and noble, chuckled with delight as he saw the torture he was inflicting.

"Oh! here, take back this note," said Varnum; "wait a little; Magoon will pay it as soon as he can. I don't like to bring distress upon him nor his family, and his creditors won't let you sue alone."

Slowly and silently the old man took the paper, put it into his pocket, and walked away.

Richard mounted his horse, and rode home at a furious rate; and the scene in the last chapter followed.

CHAPTER X

FRANK," said his sister Elsie, as they sat in the moonlight side by side, " you 're 'most a man now; what are you going to do when you are twenty-one?"

"That's just what I was thinking about, Elsie," said the brother, winding his arm affectionately around her waist. "If it were not for leaving you and mother, I'd ask father now to let me go away to school, but I don't know what mother and you would do if I were gone."

"Oh! Frank, you must go; though I don't want you to leave us. George don't think as much about me as you do; he don't help me, and when I feel bad, he don't comfort me; he don't let me lie upon his shoulder so. I believe he thinks it's a shame to be loving to his sister."

"Oh, no! Elsie; he's like other boys, — thinks he's more like a man, when he don't seem to love anybody, and talk pleasant to folks; — George would n't cry for any thing, he thinks that's babyish, —and so he thinks it is to love you, and kiss you sometimes just as I do," —and the young man pressed his lip to the rosy cheek that lay so confidingly near his own.

"I say, Elsie, if all the boys had such a loving, kind-hearted, and good sister as I have, to kiss once

(99)

in a while, they would n't be writing love-billets to other boys' sisters, would they?"

"I don't know; I don't love anybody, Frank, as well as I do you. But, Frank, see here, don't laugh at me! now, and I'll tell you. I love you, oh, so much! and I shall miss you every day, and so will mother too; but what of that? I don't want my brother to grow up a big man and not know anything—and be a great booby, like Sam Briggs, or Dick Hall, and such fellows; and now harvesting is almost done, maybe mother, and you, and I, can persuade father to let you go to school. I am getting large now; I'm *twelve*, you know; and I can help mother a great deal; and when you are gone, George will think more, mother says, and we shall do nicely. Willie too is such a good boy, and Alice and Kate begin to help a good deal. Oh! I shall hate to have you gone; but then, Frank, I'll be thinking all the time about my tall, good brother, that will be so smart and know so much, and write stories and poetry for me. Oh, Frank! I *know* you'll be a genius"—

"A what! who ever put that notion in your head?"

"Oh, dear! can't I have notions, I wonder; did n't I read, this morning, in the paper, how Webster went to school and turned out such a great man; and how Dr. Clarke did not know his letters when he was seventeen, and then learned to write such big books; and James Stone learned his letters after he was thirty; and Shakspeare turned out such a great genius —and I was just thinking all the time, if you would not be a genius too some day, and make us all proud of you."

"But, Elsie, I don't see how father can get the money for me."

The child was puzzled and silent, for a few moments, and looked at the moon, as if reading in its broad face the destiny of her brother. At last she said, very earnestly, "Why, Frank, *you can earn the money for yourself.* You know they wanted you to chop over on that new farm of Major Falconer's, last year. Can't you go to school a while, and then chop that wood for him and pay for it? You're big and strong, Frank. You can work for your board in winter, you know; and I will spin harder, and help make your shirts and clothes, you know; and that will save something."

"I *don't* know, Elsie; I don't believe I can do it," said the boy, despondingly.

"Yes, you can, too, and you must and shall! *I* would; and we'll all help. There are Emma Wright, and Mary Truman, and Martha, coming down the lane. Let us run and meet them."

The celebration at the grove, where no liquor was to be drunk, was the topic of conversation for miles around. Deacon Hill declared it was usurpation on the part of the women, and said *he* wouldn't go. But when Mrs. Deacon said, "Yes, you will, too," he only replied,—"Wall, wall, I 'spose I must."

Major Falconer thought Mrs. Magoon might have let things gone on the usual way. But his wife's allusion to past trials stayed any further objection.

9*

But Tom Falconer declared in favor of an opposition party being got up in Smithville, under the head of "The Young Men's Club;" and the word went forth, that all the whiskey, the music, the flags, the banners, all the gunpowder and military, and all the fun, were to be at the "Independent Celebration;" and all the women, and tea and toast, and ministers, at the "Petticoat Celebration!" Party spirit ran high.

The death of Henry, and the consequent low spirits of Ellen, had, as the colonel asserted, induced him to send Ellen back to old Massachusetts, among his friends, to be educated, and to wear off the effects of her sorrow. She had been three years absent; and had returned, an accomplished and dignified woman, only a few months before the celebration.

She decided for the grove, and quietly made her biscuit and cake and pies. Lawyer Danvers sent her an invitation to the "Independent Celebration," got up with a great flourish, in red and blue ink, on a sheet of the best paper; but it had no influence over the pensive girl. She respectfully declined.

Amid all the confusion and gossip, one thing revealed itself to the whole neighborhood, to their great astonishment. Richard Magoon had kept sober; and the distiller reported that something had come over the old boss, for he had not drunk a drop or sworn an oath since Sunday three weeks.

Elsie made her arrangements with so much precision and energy, and so much, too, of good-nature and cheerfulness, that no one thought of deserting her ranks, except the very lowest class,—those who love

rowdyism and vice for their own sake, and instinct-
ively shrink from the companionship of the virtuous,
the orderly, and the good. Even Betsy Lake, who
had a kind of off-hand shrewdness and activity that
made her no mean help in time of need, had not only
grounded her arms of opposition, but run up Mrs.
Magoon's colors, and declared vociferously for cold
water and home-brewed beer,—loudly asserting, "that
it was a *plaguey* mean set that was going down to
Smithville, anyhow,—they would n't catch her there;
if they did, they'd catch a weasel asleep afore sunset.
She'd just made up her mind, and determined as long
as she lived never to go to a party again where people
drinked; nothing good ever cum to nobody from
liquor-doings."

The conversation of the brother and sister, though
so abruptly broken off, was often renewed, and the
desire for education gained strength daily, while deeper
and firmer resolves were shaping themselves in the
minds of each.

But how were they to be spared from the great
farm, with its complicated work, to which were added
the distillery and the mill, making more calls for
labor than could be supplied in this new country?
Every season seemed a busy time, from the Christmas
holidays to the fading away of the beauty and brightness of the autumn.

In the spring, Richard would put Frank off by a
promise for the summer. He could not be spared in
ploughing-time. In summer, haying and harvesting

required every hand; it was not possible then. In autumn, the wheat must be got in and arrangements made for the coming season; and in winter, wood must be prepared for the distillery, the corn must be husked, the butchering done; and so Frank was put off till he could bear it no longer.

Each busy season without, brought its corresponding busy season within. The labors of the wife and mother were heavy to be borne. No cooking-stoves simplified the labor of the farmer's kitchen; no spinning-jennies or power-looms relieved the weary day's works of the wife and daughters; no sewing-machines, with fairy power, gave the aching hands and eyes rest. The tasks of spinning, weaving, and making the garments of the household, were added to the labor of cooking, washing, ironing, cheese and butter making; and life was a round of unceasing toil from year to year.

"Oh, this wool!" exclaimed Mrs. Magoon, one June morning, "how is it to be turned into cloth? We must have some new blankets next fall, and I did hope to get a carpet made for the parlor; it would look so comfortable and save us so much trouble. Then the boys must have new suits all round, and father a new overcoat, and all us women-folks, dresses, besides the shawls we have been threatening to make these two or three years. I wonder if I could get Maria Goodhue to spin for us through the summer."

"What does Maria charge a week, mother?" asked Elsie.

"Seventy-five cents. Little enough, if she would

do her work well; but she can't be trusted, she is so careless, and the last time she spun for me, she cheated in her count; and when the web was in the loom, I had to stop in the midst of my apple-drying, and sit up nights to spin and color."

" Mother, Alice and I can spin it."

" You and Alice! Bless me! it will take nearly a hundred yards of cloth to do us all this winter; and you must go to school."

" I mean to go to school; but I can spin my day's work and go to school too; and Alice can spin half a day's work. Don't hire Maria. We'll save the money and board, and send Frank away to Athens. He wants to go so much. I talked with him about it last night, and he almost cried. He says father will put him off till he is a man and ashamed to go among those that know so much more than he does."

" Frank must go; but I don't think you and Alice can help much."

" Yes we can, yes we can! Let us try," answered the resolute sister.

" I will tell you how we can fix it, mother," said Alice, as she deposited a large cheese on the shelf. " I will give Elsie all the time out of the kitchen. May and I will milk and do the churning; and so we will all help."

" Well, we will see," answered the mother, proud of daughters so willing to increase their own toil for their brother's sake.

A few days later found the summer arrangement being punctually carried out. Elsie spun her twenty knots before going to school, and often twenty after, beside helping Alice with the milking.

While she spun, her book lay open on the window-sill in front of her, and her lessons were thoroughly learned as her feet flew cheerily to and fro. The shirts were made in school under Miss Martin's eye, and the socks knit with busy fingers while she was reading; and when autumn came, Frank found himself fully equipped in fine rich homespun, for a six months' stay at college.

Major Falconer loaned him some money, for which he was to clear a piece of woodland the next summer.

It was a sad morning when Frank left them. Elsie ran up-stairs for a good girlish cry, and the mother lifted her apron to her eyes more than once as she watched his receding figure down the lane, till it was lost behind the stalwart trunks of oaks and maples.

But these tears were not all of sadness. They rejoiced in Frank's escape, and were made happy by the consciousness that they had helped to bring about his emancipation from unrequited toil and continual disappointment.

Weeks will end, and so did these weeks of preparation. The glorious Fourth was ushered in with boisterous shouts, with firing of cannon, martial music, the tramping of the military without, and busy preparation within.

Ten o'clock was the hour of gathering. A cooler, balmier, and more delightful day never made the hearts of patriots glad; a rain the evening previous had cooled the air, laid the dust, washed the flowers, paved and hardened the streets, and smoothed the dancing-spot in the grove.

The good farmers' wives were up "*by-times*," as they used to say; cows were milked, cheese taken care of, butter churned, house put in order, and all things prepared against the hour of the celebration.

"Lord a massy, gals, where's your pa?" said Mrs. Elder Jones, one of the leading members of the church.

"Drot if I know!" replied Pete, as he went whisking round the corner, full tilt after the old mare, that had a notion of spending Independence in the pasture with the colt.

"I'll tell your father, my boy, when he comes, if I hear any more talk like that, sir," responded the anxious mother, looking after the hopeful, as, with bridle in hand, he dodged back and forth in the corner of the yard, where he held the old mare prisoner.

"Tell, then, for all I care.—Whoa, now, stand still there, you old crop-eared varmint!" shouted Pete, almost crying with vexation and fatigue.

"What a boy that is! He'll break my heart yet with his capers. Dear me—dear me! mothers never know what they're bringing their children up to."

"You might a' known, mother," said a bright-eyed, pert-looking Miss of sixteen, who stood before a cracked glass, ten inches by eight, curling her hair with a broken fragment of the tongs, "*you* had the raisin' on him."

"Nobody asked you to speak, Miss, said her sister,

who was beating eggs for a pudding. You'd look
better letting your hair alone, and giving a hand to
the work, to help me get things agoing."

"I can't stand it no longer, nor I won't neither," said
Mrs. Jones. "That man is always behind time. Here
it is nigh unto six o'clock, and we must go by ten."

"*Elvira Jane—Elvira Jane!* come here this minit!
What are you up that cherry-tree for, you good-for-
nothing, you? Go right down to the barn now, and
tell your pa to come to the house this minit!"

"Yonder he is," shouted back the child, who was
sharing with the cat-birds the last remnant of the
crimson fruit in the tree-top.

Just then the Elder made his appearance round
the corner.

"Elder Jones," said his wife, in shrill tones of displeasure, "if you're agoing to 'tend prayers this
morning, be quick about it, or it can't be done; for
it's time we was hurrying up half an hour ago."

The Elder answered the summons, called in the
workmen, bent his knee in a hurried manner to the
good Father above, thanked Him for blessings, craved
His protective care through the day; and in a summary way dismissed the assembled household, hurrying back to give the boys directions to spread the hay
on the creek-meadow, to bring in the oxen, unyoke
and turn them out, and put the black horses into the
farm-wagon.

A merrier meeting never was held than that which
made mirth and music in the beautiful sugar-grove,
on that memorable day. The Declaration of Inde-

pendence was read, original odes were sung, and a fine poem full of wit and satire was recited, that raised shouts of laughter and joy.

Richard Magoon rose above himself. The weeks of soberness, and earnest reflection, had given tone and power to his naturally vigorous intellect; and the people listened with earnest attention to his able address, and sent shout after shout through the old trees and away among the hills. All were delighted, surprised, and instructed,—and all were happy, for the Demon of Disturbance was not in their midst.

Ever and anon the far-off sound of the Smithville cannon was heard; or passers-by called and reported that "they were going on at a great rate down at the village. Lawyer Marvin was so high, he could not speak at all. The leader of the music was drunk, and had had a fight with the drummer about the tunes;" and every one prophesied a horrid time before night.

The dinner at the grove was splendid. The drinking-glasses were filled with rich bouquets of flowers; and those present had never been so happy, for there rested no fears in their hearts to mar their pleasure. Dinner over, the dance began, for those who enjoyed it; others walked through the grove, or played "Philander" under the cool, green awnings of the maples. The little ones formed rings, and

"Here we go, a ring, a row,
In Uncle Johnny's garden!"

added to the general mirth. While the shyer and more bashful boys joined in "Prisoners' base" and

10

"Hunt the Fox." The old men looked on and renewed their youth,—told over the incidents of their
own childhood, or of the early time of the pioneers,—
when they had had

> "The hunt, the shot, and glorious chase,
>   The captured elk or deer;
> The camp, the big bright fire, and then
>   The rich and wholesome cheer.
> The sweet sound sleep at dead of night,
>   By camp-fire blazing high,
> Unmindful of the wolf's wild howl,
>   Or panthers springing by."

CHAPTER XI.

THERE was a matter of great wonder at the celebration, in the shape of a tall young man, with
dark eyes, and a sun-burned face, bronzed almost to
the color of the Spaniard. But for a heavy beard,
which covered his lower face, he would have been
voted a grand fellow, even by the old ladies; but his
beard spoiled him. "How could a man be so un-
reasonable," no lady could see! Beards were horrible!

He was introduced into the society of the ladies by
"Parson Manford," (as Betsy Lake called him,) a
young minister who had not been long out of Yale,
and had been sent on a tour of missionary labor to
the out-of-the-way town of Smithville, which, in the
opinion of the Eastern Missionary Society, was quite
beyond the pale of civilization.

Mr. Delno was received by the young ladies with
a great flutter of hearts. Never had such a specimen
of courtly manners, address, and appearance, come
among them.

After the dinner, the speeches, and the toasts were
all disposed of, the dance began under the trees, as we
have said,—not a ball, but a cheerful dance,—to the
sound of Bob Jones' fiddle. Bob was a blacksmith,
and though he never knew a note by rule, he played
"Muny Musk," "Speed the Plow," "Rural Felic-

(111)

ity," and a hundred more of the same sort, with an energy and spirit that put life and mettle into their heels, and sent the country lads bounding a foot from the ground at every balance step.

Mr. Delno selected sweet Elsie Magoon, the youngest of the dancers, as his partner, and led down a long "contra" as if he had never done anything else but dance. Mrs. Deacon Hill whispered to Mrs. Magoon, "that she'd bet a cabbage that that whiskered chap was nothing more nor less than a Yankee dancing-master;" and she deprecated, in no measured terms, all idea of his being employed in that capacity. "It would be the ruination of half the girls in town, to have sich a handsome feller a-teaching on 'em." But Mrs. Magoon quieted her fears by telling her that he was a gentleman in the employ of some government organization, sent through the country to examine it, and report to the department in regard to its soils, minerals, timber, &c. This satisfied Mrs. Hill; and her fears for Helen all took flight when the "whiskered man" led her out for the next set.

But what was to be done? There were more dancers than dancing-ground, and more feet than fiddles. The married men seemed disposed to join in the sport; and some matronly ladies, who did not like to be considered old, notwithstanding full-bordered caps, with strings under the chin, moved their toes restlessly, as if, should any one ask them, they would like to try whether they had forgotten the winding of "Cheat the Lady," or "Fisher's Hornpipe." But the dancing-ground was full.

"Clear another!" shouted some on the other side of Pete. "No use standing still, while we have all creation for a dancing-floor."

"Said and done," responded a second; and at work they went.

But who was to play for them? Pete's fingers were already blistered: — here was a new trouble; when up the young stranger stepped and offered his hand; and away went the dancers, to the sound of the finest music that had ever echoed through the grove. Every one was delighted. The old men clapped their hands; the old ladies kept time with pattering feet; and while their lips half condemned, went back to their girlhood days, when they "felt just so." Only "times were better then than now;" as times always are to those who look back upon them.

"My stars!" cried out old Col. Falconer; "if that don't beat all; it makes me feel like a boy again. Come, mother, let's try a hand; I can't sit still, no-how. Come, I say, we'll dance 'Haste to the Wedding,' once more, as we did twenty-eight years ago. Come, Lizzy, just this once;"—and the good lady suffered herself to be led out, and though a little corpulent and rosy, distanced all competitors. She had not forgotten her boarding-school training, and tossed her head, as she turned her partner, with all the pride of her girlhood days.

The evening shades began to fall; the whippoorwill piped loudly in the neighboring trees. But the mirth and hilarity were unabated; the new fiddler had

10*

...ed to renew them. Deacon Hill was garrulous w.... while old Squire Peabody, who was now ...ore and five, made a rifle of his cane, and told the youngsters of many a gallant exploit; shot the bear in the tree-top, and brought down the ten-horned buck at his feet, with new power.

Mrs. Dugan, who, after many wanderings, had come back once more to look upon her husband's grave, and renew old recollections and acquaintances, had been persuaded to attend the celebration, and sat quietly by the side of Mrs. Magoon and Ellen, stowing away olden memories in her heart, until it was full to the brim, and ran over at her eyes. "Ah! Ellen," said she, "this is indeed a happy hour, to see so much joy and mirth, and no strong drink to drive them mad."

But the thought, pleasant as it was, saddened the group by the recollection it awakened. Improving the opportunity, the first she had enjoyed since her return of meeting Ellen alone, she turned and asked, "Have you ever heard from Michael since *that* night?"

"Not one word," said Ellen, her face pale as marble.—"Is he living?" she asked, in a hoarse whisper.

"I think he is. I have twice received notes from him, through the post-office in New York, dropped there by strangers; but they gave no clue to his place of concealment. In one, he only said: 'I am ...., dear mother, and well. Think of me—forg.... ...e —and trust me. I will never give you caus.... ...in to suffer.' That was all. In the last, three weeks ago only, he inclosed money to build a monument over the grave of his father, and bade me come here and see it done. Oh, Ellen! if I could only look upon him once more, and hold him to my heart, I should be willing to die. Once more—only once more!" The old lady's tears fell fast upon the hand she clasped in her own; and the shining drops that slid down the face of the fair young girl mingled with them, as with bowed heads they recalled the past. Yet not only in sorrow for the past, but in the excitement of a newly awakened hope for the future, did the young girl weep.

"Alive, alive, and well!" Nothing more! But all possible future joy seemed hanging on those words, all past pleasures revived in them. She lived again their youthful sports beneath the old beech-tree, by the river-side, in the glen where, when they were but children, Mike had piled the turf and stones, over-laid them with moss, made a seat and built an arbor of the hanging boughs, for his little favorite.

She saw again this shady nook, where the wild anemone and blue violet still proclaimed the advance of spring; where the forget-me-nots first dipped their feet in the running stream; where the robin wooed his mate among the bursting buds, and the whippoorwill sang his solitary note in night's solemn hours; where the squirrel garnered its winter store in the lofty tree-tops, and where in later years the youth and maiden had often met to repeat their child-ish loves and vows. As she sat dreaming, her eyes falling indifferently upon the groups which passed before her, she became aware for an instant of the fixed gaze of a stranger among the dancers, whom she had before noticed only in the distance. Now he passed directly before her, and, changed as he was to all others, that glance revealed to her keen-sighted love, the lost and mourned. The discovery gave her a shock of joy which thrilled through all her being, and startled the poor widow who still held her hand.

"Ellen, my child, you are getting chilled; let me wrap your shawl about you," said the good woman, and with instant self-possession, feeling that what *he* had not chosen to reveal, she must not, Ellen yielded to the kind caution of her friend, and suffered herself to be wrapped from the evening air, when she was glowing with warmth and joy.

Lamps were hung under the trees, and the sport went on until nearly ten o'clock, when some of the old men withdrew, with their wives and small children; but not until they had all been called together, and the voice of Father Peters had gone up in earnest prayer, to "God the only good," to continue the work begun, to bless and shield each and every one, until the year should roll round, and the same great call of freedom gather them again in happiness and innocence!

"One dance more!" shouted Richard Magoon. "Come, let us all join in a regular shake-down, in honor of my wife's rebellion against her lord and master. It will do no harm for me to make whiskey, if the women declare you sha'n't drink it. — One more tune, if you please, Mr. Delno, and then you must go with us and spend the night;" and Richard led out his wife for the first time.

All hands joined in that gleeful dance. Even Ellen Falconer suffered herself to become one of the set, and moved gracefully through the figure with Mr. Delno, who had the rare skill to dance and play at the same time.

The figure ended, Richard Magoon seized a glass of cold-water, drank a vote of thanks to the ladies of the cold-water party; then led off in a hearty hurrah, which made the welkin ring again.

Scarce had the shout ended, when the sound of a horse at full speed, was heard; and in another instant, horse and rider dashed in among the affrighted group; and the latter, throwing himself to the ground, called in a voice of terror for Dr. Harvey.

"What is the matter?" was the cry from many voices.

Almost fainting with terror and excitement, he gasped out—"The cannon's bust, and blowed up the powder-keg, and set fire to the tavern; and they are all killed—Tom Falconer and Kit, and Briggs, and all—oh, my God, give me some water! Where's the doctor?—their brains are all scattered about, and Olcott's eyes are blown out, and he's screeching like mad! Oh, don't stand here; where's old Col. Falconer? Tom's a-dying, and calling for his father!"

This, and much more, was incoherently uttered at intervals, by the terrified and almost exhausted boy.

What a scene of confusion followed! Many of
the party at the grove had friends at the village;
and one feeling of horror filled all hearts. The
younger children were sent home with their mothers;
while the men drove with all speed in their trim
wagons to the village. Richard and Elsie sent their
children home with Frank, and took their way to
help the sufferers — taking the elder Falconer with
them.

Mr. Delno, who stood near Ellen, laid his hand
gently upon her arm. "Miss Ellen, I have a light
gig and a fleet horse. Will you not ride with me?
We can reach there sooner than others." Speechless
and tearless, with the intensity of her emotion, Ellen
suffered herself to be carried by the strong arm of
Delno, and placed in the gig. He sprang in beside
her, and drove off at a rapid rate — distancing all
others. "Ellen," said the young man, as the horse
slackened his pace in ascending a steep hill, — "Ellen,
do you not know me? Have I so changed that even
you, while you hold my hand, and listen to my voice,
feel no thrill of emotion, no recognition of days gone
by? Then have I lived in vain — then have I
struggled for naught — and henceforth the world will
be a blank" ——

"Michael Dugan! call not up the past in an hour
like this. Know you? Yes — the first glance of
your eye, the first wave of your hand, the first word
that fell from your lips — I knew you; and my whole
soul has trembled with terror on your account."

" And yet you were calm, and seemed unconscious of my presence ?"

"Only seemed, Michael ! My whole life has been a seeming. Oh, I have learned the lesson well, and at a fearful cost ! "

" Do not recall the frightful past, Ellen, the present has its own fearful terrors. Alas ! that our meeting of recognition should be in an hour like this. But listen a moment, I beg you, Ellen, while I may speak. I have sacrificed feeling, I have braved danger, resisted temptation, struggled against fate, mastered destiny; and return to you, educated, trusted, honored, and the possessor of wealth. In all this struggle—in all these years of trial—you have stood before me, beckoning me onward, and pointing to a higher goal, to be attained before I could be worthy of you—worthy to ask a realization of my highest ideal of happiness in the future. I did not write; I did not make known to any that I lived, except my mother. I wished that you should be free to act, without the knowledge of my poor existence. I find you single, and apparently untrammelled. Let me ask, even in this sad hour, if—if—may I hope—may I dare to plead for favor ?"

" Michael Dugan, I love you ; even as in the days of our childhood. But to-night, how can we speak of this ! Oh, merciful Father ! another brother, another victim, to that 'Old Still-House !'" She covered her face with her hands, and groaned aloud in her agony.

It was a moment of fearful trial for Michael Dugan.
Upon the death of one brother had his hopes been
wrecked for years; upon the death of another, the
future, so radiant before him, is again shrouded in
gloom; and a stronger and more earnest vow than
ever before was breathed in the silent moonlight,
against the foul Destroyer of life and hope.

CHAPTER XII

WHEN the dancers from the grove arrived at the village, a scene presented itself which chilled their hearts with horror. The cannon had burst, the powder blown up, four men had been killed, and a large number wounded. The tavern, which had stood in the centre of a long street that formed the main part of the town, was in ruins. The light summer breeze had swept the fire to the most important end of the street, and house after house was being devoured by the hungry element. The houses indeed were little better than kindling-wood, built of light material, and filled, many of them, with inflammable substances. Little or no resistance had as yet been made; for many of the citizens of the more sober and earnest class, had joined the grove party. Of such as were upon the ground, a part were actively engaged with the dead and dying, and others, too nearly intoxicated to do any service, were running about in wild confusion.

The facts of the accident were soon detailed. After the day's conviviality, while almost every man who had joined the village party was in a state of partial inebriety, and many of them furious in their glee, it was proposed that a gun should be fired, for every

11   (121)

State, as a winding-up of the day's sport; and ten o'clock P. M. was the hour appointed.

"Leave our own State for the last," said Briggs, the tavern-keeper, as they drew the old field-piece up before his door, "and let's give her a roarer! I'll furnish the powder, and stand a treat all round. I'm bound to do something onst in my life for my country!"

A loud shout of approval answered this patriotic speech, and the firing commenced. Nearly every State had its representative, and each clamored for a louder report for his own native land.

They had come to the last round.

"Whoop! hurrah!!" shouted the tavern-keeper. "Our turn now, boys! Let's blow up all creation, and wake snakes; none of your pop-guns this time. Here, you Sim Olcott, fetch on them brickbats — fill her full!"

"Better look out, Briggs; the old thing will bust, and kill some on ye," said a voice in the crowd.

"Go to the devil with your prating. Who's afeard of bears?" was the rude response, accompanied by a ruder and more terrific oath. "Ram her down, I say, boys; fill her up chug. Don't leave room for a bullet. That's it. All ready. Hold on!" And, with an oath, the drunken, infuriated father ordered his boy to bring out the bottle.

"Here, you Tom Falconer, give me that torch. I'm bound to touch this one off myself!" and lifting the tumbler to his lips, he exclaimed, "Now for a toast, — hang me, if I know how! — here it goes, though, hit or miss: 'Mistress Magoon, and her breeches! old father Peters and his prayers! Let us blow them all to'——" He paused with a leer as he pronounced the last diabolical word—drank off the glass, and touched the torch, which he held to the powder, while a loud shout went up from the rowdies about him.

There was a vivid flash, a stunning report, a dense smoke,—then cries, screams, groans, and shouts told the fearful tale. The cannon had been blown to fragments, and the little powder that was left, burned at the same instant. When the smoke cleared away, a sight presented itself the recital of which even now thrills the soul with terror. The landlord Briggs, lay a mutilated mass; his head cut from his crushed body, and his face stamped forever with that last demoniac laugh, and the death-struggle, blended together. Two of the men who were loading the gun, Kit, the distiller, and Billy Alison, a workman at the "Still-house," were killed; and an old man of gray hairs, grasping a staff in his hand, was hit by a piece of the flying iron, and fell to rise no more. Tom Falconer had an arm torn off, and his face burned. Blind and maddened with pain, he was shouting and swearing when his parents and sister found him. Sim Olcott, who stood near the landlord, had both legs broken, and was terribly burned with powder. Many others lay groaning and shrieking with lesser wounds; while the shouts, sobs, cries, and moans of the bereaved and affrighted friends and neighbors, formed a scene that beggars all description.

It is never the wrong-doers alone that suffer in a time like this. The good too often share the same fate; and not unfrequently the offenders escape, while some pure-minded and innocent one is made to suffer and die instead. So had it happened. The old gray-haired sire, feeling that there was danger, had risen, and taken staff in hand, to go and plead with the revellers to desist ere mischief was done; and thus the good man—the patriarch of the village—loved and respected by all, met his fate.

A fragment of the gun had entered a window of the tavern, killing instantly a fair young girl, who had retired from the party, with a friend, weeping bitterly that her lover, who had brought her there, was too much intoxicated to be civil to her. The flying missile struck her on the temple, crushing the skull and burying itself in her brain. She fell, and in her fall overturned the light-stand, pitching the candle into the folds of a curtained bed, that was covered with bonnets, shawls, and dresses. In an instant all was in a blaze. The surviving young lady fled to the room above, where the dancers had paused to listen to the sound on the street, and gave the alarm. The dancing-room was the whole size of the building, and on the second floor. There was no plastering on the rooms below, and the revellers had only time to escape through the windows and doors, and save the body of the young girl, ere the fire burst through the floor and spread rapidly through the room where they had just stood. Before the people at the grove arrived, it had fallen in; and the whiskey-barrels, in close proximity to the room where the fire started, had blown up, and added greatly to the fury of the fire.

The dead and dying had been gathered up by the crowd and carried to a large ware-room by the river-bank, as a place removed from the fire, where the physicians could, for the moment, be brought together to see what was to be done in the speediest and best way.

As the party from the grove came up, they saw at a glance the condition of things. Mrs. Falconer swooned at the sight of her mangled child, and was carried away from the sound of his groans to a neighboring cottage, and left in charge of Ellen; while the old colonel fell upon his knees by the side of his boy Tom, and moaned in piteous helplessness.

"What is to be done?" asked Delno, turning with blanched lip to Magoon; "this fire must be stayed, or not a house on the west will stand till midnight."

"But the wounded and dying—they need help now—the houses afterward."

"Leave them with us," said Elsie. "The doctors are here. We women can nurse, but we can't fight fire. Go; we will do all that human hands can do!"

It needed all the calmness and the presence of mind that could be brought to bear to quell the tumult and set those to work who were unhurt. But Elsie had all the qualities the occasion demanded. Sensitive, tender, and shrinking almost to weakness; yet was she strong, resolute, and self-poised in every time of danger and trial. Fully able herself to meet emer-

11*

gencies and conquer difficulties, it took her but a few
moments to organize all those fragments of a great
machine, and put them in working order; and what
was a fearful chaos, soon became at least partial order
under her direction and that of others now at hand.
The slightly wounded were taken home; beds and
litters ordered for others; oils prepared, cordials and
soothing draughts administered; wives, mothers, sisters, and daughters were efficient, now that there was
one firm, controlling mind to guide and direct. Oh!
it was a fearful hour; but all was done that could be
done for the sufferers.   Tom Falconer and Olcott and
Smith were the most mangled of the crowd, and each,
in his own way, vented forth his agony.

"Oh! God bless you, Mrs. Magoon. I know it's
you by the soft touch of your hand; those men are so
rough!   I did not think it would come to this when
I opposed you so. Oh! if I could only die! Oh!
where's *mother, father, Ellen?*   If I die, tell them all
to forgive me. *My mother! Oh! my poor mother!*
She taught me better. Oh! what will she and father
do now? Henry gone, and I"——

Here poor Tom fainted from pain and loss of blood,
and in a few moments breathed his last.

Smith cursed his fate, breathed forth the worst
oaths, and accused Mrs. Magoon, as she held the
cooling draught to his lips, drugged with an anodyne
to deaden his pain, of being the cause of all his misfortune.

"It was you—you—you"—he almost shouted at
her, "that did all this. If you'd a' let us alone, we'd

a-never got up this spree, and now see what's come
of it!"

Even so in all time past, and mayhap it will continue in all time to come, have reformers been accused
of being the cause of the wrongs and outrages committed by their infuriated opponents. It is considered
sufficient to say, "You made us angry. Had *you* let
us alone, we should not have done thus."

While the ministering angels were doing their work
within, let us follow, for a few moments, the efforts
of the men without.

The breeze seemed to gather force with the fire.
The flying cinders lit upon the houses and caught the
roofs. Every man, woman, and child were put in
motion. Lines were formed with buckets to the
river; and the sober, sound men, under the lead of
Delno, worked like giants. The neat little church,
which had been consecrated to the use of Father
Peters, caught from a lodging cinder, and already was
the flame crawling up its steeple like a hissing serpent. Directly beneath stood the parsonage, both a
little back of the other burning buildings. Into this
low cottage Ellen had retreated with her mother, and
was left alone by Mrs. Peters, who ran with her oils
and lints to the warehouse. The fire from the church
soon communicated to the cottage, and before Ellen
was aware of her danger, the roof was in a blaze.
Her mother, who was beginning to recover her consciousness, on hearing Ellen's cry, "Oh, mother, the
house is on fire! Come, come—we must fly!" sank
back again, utterly helpless and incapable of moving.

In vain Ellen strove to arouse her. She essayed to lift her, but the portly form was too heavy for her slight strength.

The flames crackled and roared above; the hot air became stifling. Her mother must be removed, or in a few moments she must die. "Help, help!" shrieked Ellen, as she sprang to the door. "Oh, God, what shall I do!" At that instant the tall form of Delno strode past the alley a few rods distant, followed by strong men carrying a ladder. Ellen flew to his side, and almost hissed in his ear, so terrible was her fright, "My mother will be burned to death — come with me — the parsonage!" and turning was back in an instant. But the flame met her at the front door. She stood transfixed with horror.

Delno was about aiding the men to pull down a small house, as the best means of heading the fire. He paused only to give a word of encouragement. "Down with it, boys! Tear off the roof! Strip the weather-boards! Hurry up the water! Work away — we'll soon conquer! Pitch those timbers over the bank! Work away — work away!" Then with the bound of a young deer, he sprang after Ellen. The house seemed one mass of flame.

"My mother, my mother!" gasped Ellen, pointing into the burning dwelling. Delno comprehended, and dashing through the flame, which was light, driven by the wind, sought the fainting woman; groping his way through the smoke, he soon found her; and rolling her in a woollen coverlid that lay beneath, caught her in his arms, and had just time to

clear the threshold, when the roof and chamber-floor
fell in with a crash; the blaze leaped wilder and
higher, as if in wrath at its defeat, as he struggled
out of its way, and laid his burden by the side of
Ellen.

The sudden motion, the jar, the unrolling, after
such suffocation, the intense heat, and the glaring
light, aroused the poor woman. She regained her
consciousness, and they were able to seek a place of
safety. .

Delno's face was blistered, and his hands seared,
but he flew to his post among the men, nor left it till
his work was done. The fire in the row was checked
by the pulling down of the building. None were
burned that stood back of the row except the church
and parsonage; the others were saved by the perseverance of the women, who stood upon the house-tops,
and did their duty with strong hands, as women can
and will in hours of trial.

CHAPTER XIII

DELNO and Magoon, as soon as they could be spared from their duty at the fire, repaired to the warehouse, to attend to the wants of the wounded, and make the necessary provision for the dead. Old Mr. Falconer was utterly incapable of thought or action, and the Olcott family were, if possible, in a worse condition.

Weeping mothers, wives and sisters; fathers and brothers, with pale faces, which told the inward struggle; little children, crying and moaning, with fear and weariness; groups gathered together at the warehouse and at corners, because they had no other place to go for shelter from the chill night-air. Ruin, desolation, grief, anguish of spirit and torture of body, were on every hand!

Richard stood at the door a moment, surveying the scene, as he entered: his eye soon rested upon his noble wife. She was beside one of the wounded men, soothing the agony of his burns, by laying sweet oil oil over his face and neck, with a soft feather. Curses were mingled with his hideous complaints, and the "Old Still-house" fell upon the ear of Richard; then the soft voice of Elsie stilled the tongue of the railer, while her softer hand lulled the pain.

Lifting his hat from his brow, and wiping the dust

and sweat of the fire away, he turned to another portion of the room, and there bent Ellen with tearless eyes, over her mother and father, who sat near the mutilated corpse of Tom, which rested beneath a sheet, ready to be borne to the house.

We said she was tearless. How could she weep? Hers was a bitterness of sorrow that dried up tears, and left her heart cold and dead.

There are trials of heart, for which nature seems to have made no provision. Violations of the laws of humanity and of right, bring with them punishment that admits of no amelioration; punishment which the heart must bear, until its pangs are washed away by time, and the wound heals with the on-rolling years. So stood Ellen in her anguish. Could she have believed that Providence had thus stricken her, she would have bowed herself at the feet of Him "Who holdeth the winds in the hollow of his hand," and soothed her anguish with the thought, "He doeth all things well." But there was no such oil of mercy to pour over her burning heart. All was darkness, black, and impenetrable. Richard moved toward the group, and spoke to the sobbing, moaning old man:

"Ah, Mr. Magoon!" said the Colonel, — his voice broken with his outpouring grief, — "this is a dreadful business, and I must say it, your 'Old Still-House' is at the bottom of it all."

Richard made no reply, but to press the old man's hand in silence. He passed to the group gathered round Olcott. Some one called the name of Magoon, with almost a shout of defiance. Olcott vowed ven-

geance "on that Old Still," if ever he lived to get
well.

Richard turned away again.

Agony, deep and terrible, was stirring within him.
And yet it was the agony of active, present sympathy, rather than of a startled conscience. "Why
should *he* be so harshly blamed? He did not compel
any one to drink his whiskey; they drank because
they liked it; he was only doing as others did. Strong
drink always had been made, probably always would
be, and there would always be found people to drink
it. Besides, cannons had burst before, would again,
without doubt, whether he made whiskey or not."

So ran the current of his thought. Nor was it
strange. How could any one stand under such an
avalanche of censure, and not strive for escape? If
he allowed himself to feel that these ills were all
traceable to his door, how could he go on? Even
now, while the groans of his neighbors pierced his
ears, and the sobs of houseless, homeless women and
children stirred every pulse of his heart with pain,
his eye was glancing into the future: the gaunt skele-
ton of his debts stalked before him, and with shaking, threatening finger pointed to his own family,
beggared and ruined. How could he give up the
only business that seemed to him of any profit? All
this passed through his mind in an instant—it was
but an instant. The hand of Elsie was laid upon his
arm:

"Richard, we must help get these people away
from here, before the sun gets high. A litter must

be made, and Smith must be carried by hand; so must Olcott; their wounds will not admit of any rougher mode; and if not immediately removed, it will take weeks to restore them so far as to make it practicable."

As she spoke, standing before him, the beams of the morning sun, which was just rising above the trees, fell upon her head. "Why, Elsie," was the exclamation of her husband, as he laid his hand suddenly upon her head, "what is the matter with your hair?"

"I do not know; is there anything the matter?" she replied, looking up at him with weary eyes.

"It is white—almost as white as snow."

"No?"

"It is."

"I have heard of fear and grief turning the hair instantly. But it can't be possible. Yet I know that I can never suffer more intensely than I have to-night. But go; it matters not whether my hair be black or white, these must be cared for."

He passed out, and she tied her handkerchief over her head, lest others should mark and marvel at the phenomenon. Scarce giving it a thought herself, she crossed over to Ellen, to speak a word of hope and cheer to the stricken girl; the poor girl's spirit seemed utterly to have failed her. She was leaning against a post; her eyes closed, and her hands clasped around it for support. She seemed to sleep. It was from exhaustion.

"Ellen!" said Mrs. Magoon.

12

She started, and rubbed her eyes bewilderingly. Then slowly, as they ran over the group, the whole horrid reality sprang into view before her.

"Oh! Mrs. Magoon, if I have one wish above another; one object for which I will toil unwearyingly, one for which I would die,—if by that means I could accomplish it,—it is to annihilate that 'Old Still-house;' that thing of all others that I hate, and loathe; that rises up ever and evermore before me, as wronging the whole people; that calls curses to my tongue, and bitterness to my heart; that has seared and blighted every bright prospect of my existence, and made life, thus far, cold and dead. Oh! if I could carry a brand from yon smouldering houses, and place it where it should do its work, I feel that I should do a Christian duty; and I would do it too, but for my parents. If God is just, a curse must fall —"

"Ellen, Ellen!" replied Elsie, hurriedly, "it *has fallen;* curse us not; our lot is even now heavier than we can bear."

The unearthly tones of her voice, the pale quivering lip, and the despair that shrivelled her fine face, and blanched her hair in that terrible hour, told how fearfully the curse had fallen even on the innocent!

To most persons it is a terrible thing to die; terrible to pass from earth into the sphere beyond; and while the chill fingers of the monster (as death has been strangely called) are kept away, they walk on, unterrified and unchanged.

But it is of far more consequence that men and

women should live aright, than that they should live.
It is strange and sad that family, friends, and neighbors will look coldly on, for days, and months, and
years, and see those whom they love, treading the
path to certain destruction, and yet feel no anxiety or
fear, until the fatal goal is reached; until the doom,
to which with steady footsteps they have been tending,
is sealed forever. Then the wildest fear seizes those
who have looked and smiled with cold indifference,
or perchance have thoughtlessly given a helping hand
to aid the fall.

"Curse us not," repeated Elsie, "we are already
accursed. But join with us — with me, to put the
evil away. I have striven and wrestled for years,
yet who has given me aid? Who has dared stand
by my side? Did I need to see such a scene as this,
to know that such scenes must come? Ellen, Ellen,
by all the friendship and love you have ever given
me, let me implore you, to arouse yourself from this
grief for the dead. Better a thousand times that he
(pointing to Tom) should lie *there*, than that he should
have gone on for years, as he has done for the last."

"Oh! Mrs. Magoon," almost shrieked Ellen,
"spare him now he is gone." Her eye-balls sear and
dry, rolling wildly in their sockets, had warned Mrs.
Magoon to turn the current of her thoughts, if even
with a savage hand.

A light word, a soothing expression, or a common-
place, would not have done the work; a chord must
be touched that should vibrate through the whole
being, and arouse its dormant energies.

She had accomplished her work. Ellen fell upon her shoulder in a passionate fit of weeping, which probably saved her a brain-fever.

Delno at that moment joined them. Arrangements had been made for the removal of the corpses, and Delno seated the still-weeping girl by his side in his carriage, and drove away to the desolate home.

As they parted at the door, he whispered:

"I came here, Ellen, hoping to do a different work from that which must now fall to my lot. No one, as yet, not even Elsie Magoon, suspects who I am. Let us keep the secret for the present. Will you meet me to-morrow evening, under the old beech, by the river-side? I see that our seat is there still."

She assented; and they parted, as the sad procession arrived, with the remains of her brother, and her exhausted parents.

The day wore slowly and fearfully away to the bereaved ones. But in Ellen's heart a new fire had been kindled, from the smouldering embers of other years.

Dugan had saved the life of her mother; would not that wipe from the memories of her parents the olden time,—would not the sin of his boyhood, mighty as it had been, be forgotten, or, at least, forgiven?

They met under the shades of the familiar beech; the summer moon was at its full, and its rays, flickering through the thick foliage above, fell in silvery flecks at their feet; the whippoorwill still trilled its doleful song above; the stream still rippled and murmured over the pebbly shore, and the little wavelets danced and sparkled, and glowed like myriads of diamonds, as of old. All was beautiful and calm. They met, but not as in other days, in the freshness of early youth, with hearts bounding with joy and gladness; for, though young in years, strange and fearful were the trials that had made the hearts of both old—old before their time.

He told her how he had struggled and conquered; how he had won friends and wealth. He plead for his old place in her heart.

"Your parents are now without a son; let me, Ellen, replace, in part, the loved and lost. They are old, and I am told your father is in debt. In my business, as Government Agent—a Surveyor of Western land, I have been able to secure large tracts to myself. Let me have the privilege of making the last days of your parents and sisters as comfortable as possible. They ought to remove from here, where everything will remind them of their lost sons. *I* could not live here, Ellen; every tree and shrub and plant, every field and fence-corner, cries out to me of the past. Let us persuade them away, and then, if a life-time of effort in all that is good; if struggle and self-denial; if giving myself and fortune, to help the poor, to encourage the weak, and to uphold the trembling; to break the bands of drunkards, and to remove every stumbling-block out of the way of the multitude, that my hands or influence can reach; can in any measure atone for the past, so help me Heaven, it shall be done."

"Not now; not now!" was the feeble response of Ellen.

12 *

"No, not now! but will not the day come when I may hope?"

She bowed her head upon his shoulder: "You took the life of my brother; but you have saved the life of my mother."

Let us leave them to their long talk of trust and love.

The fire was stayed; but the dead were never brought to life. The houses were rebuilt; but the broken and distorted limbs were never again made whole and stout. Fortunes were mended; but the blind eyes saw no more light, and the sorrowing hearts never again sang the songs of mirth and joy, as in other days. Sweet Alice Sumner, who will call thy old grand-parents at morn, or waken the echoes of youth for them again, now that thy bird-like voice is hushed forever,—who turn the merry wheel to earn their bread,—who be ears for their hearing, and eyes for their seeing? Thou wast all in all to them; but thou art gone, never to return, and their gray hairs will soon lie low in sorrow!

Aye, thou wert all in all to them. So joyful in thy innocence, so simple and trusting in thy ignorance of the world's vices, so self-sacrificing in thy loves. No wonder the young clerk gave his love to thee, all the love his polluted heart was capable of holding, and won thee away to the village-dance, with vows and promises of eternal fidelity. He would have wedded thee, thou wert so beautiful, hadst thou not gone apart to weep at his weakness and wickedness. Better a thousandfold, sweet Alice, that thou shouldst be the bride of death, than of such a one as he! His feet were already treading the paths of sin, and making swift haste to the gates of destruction.

Another victim, maimed and wretched, is sitting by the vine-covered trunk of the blasted sycamore that once shaded the old tavern-door. It never leaved out again after that fearful night; but some kind hand planted a wild creeper at its root, which in a year or two covered its naked trunk, and hid away its blackness and deformity; and there he sits at the roots of the old tree, in his arbor of vines, that trunk of a man; no legs, no eyes. Since that fearful night, God's sunlight has not been for him. It is Tim Olcott, blind and helpless, stretching forth his hand for charity to the passer-by, singing his home-made ballads, and telling his tale of other and better days to the village boys as they gather round him. He is a temperance man now; and many a story he tells of the terrors of that "Old Still-house."

The other wounded ones recovered. The town was rebuilt; and, as is often the case, of better materials and with finer structures. "It was a great help to it," some said.

A firmer and truer temperance spirit began also to pervade the community; and yet Elsie Magoon was not without censure, as few are who walk boldly forward in the way of right. They may do no great deeds to call out the world's plaudits or censures, yet they cover the hills and valleys with their influence, and waken sweet echoes in mountain and plain, in the shady nook, where the wild flowers grow, and in the crowded village, where the lone wife sits watching beside her cradle, for one whose feet never seek the cottage-gate until the weary hours of absence have wrung her heart with agony.

The thunder-shower startles us into admiration and wonder; we exult in its grandeur and power. But the dew falls upon the earth, the sunshine warms, the gentle showers refresh until the harvest is ready, and the land teems with its richness, and we scarce note its progress as the mighty work is being wrought. Even so the influence of Elsie Magoon spread gently over the country round, until, unconsciously to themselves, the opinions of the people partially had changed. Their bottles were retained, but were only now and then brought out. Whiskey-toddy was seldom given, save to cheer some aged man or woman whose habits were supposed to be invulnerable. And every-day drinking was going out of fashion. But the "Old Still-House" still sent up its dark, dense smoke in the valley, and groaned and shrieked as of old.

Richard, after the great fire, was a sober man for a time. But troubles came thick and fast. Debts accumulated, trials followed, and he became worse than before. Every one in the neighborhood seemed to feel Elsie's influence in some form, except her husband, who should, most of all, have felt the power of one so patient and so good.

If woman's influence is so potent as our theorizers declare it to be, why is it that we so frequently see the most gentle and beautiful wives—living long lives of agonizing endurance; bearing insult, neglect, tyranny, even personal abuse; and dying without ever having brought the husband to realize their worthiness, or to yield one gross appetite, one whim of fancy, or to control one burst of passion for their sakes?

With men of drunken and beastly habits, a wife's influence is almost always nullified by the mean, base fear, that they shall be considered "as being ruled by a *woman.*"

To good and true men, the thought never comes. They need no ruling, and the gentle influence of a wife over such a one, and his over her, is that of mutual restraint and blessing, giving higher life and purer happiness to both. No two human beings were ever so nearly perfect as not to require in the marriage relation mutual concession and mutual forbearance. These Richard and Elsie had given each other in faith and love for years after their marriage. But when the time came that he ceased to *respect himself,* — when his own heart became, day and night, the bold accuser, — then he grew irritable, morose, jealous, repulsive, abusive. He might still have gained something, could he have been found sober long enough to have come to his old standpoint of reason and judgment. But that time now never came. Every night he retired excited with drink, and ready to become furious with the least provocation. He was never wholly imbecile, never wholly sober. It requires weeks, even months, to restore the brain to a state of perfect coolness and reason after years of constant indulgence. Hence it is that so few, so very few, inebriates ever reform.

It has taken years to overturn wholly the throne of reason, and it will take years to lay the foundation again, and build it strong and firm enough to stand; it can never be fully restored.

The neighbors pitied Richard very much. "Poor man, it was too bad for his wife to turn agin him so. He'd 'a' never drank so, if she had n't a-set up to pull down the "Old Still-House." So the more he drank, the more the good souls pitied him, and condemned her. It was as great a crime then, as now, for a woman to dare think for herself—particularly if she made her thoughts tell upon the public.

So, on, on, on, walked this heroic woman in the path of duty; her family of children looking up to her for all their counsel, support and strength. Few knew how she suffered; none knew, except Frank and Elsie, the extent of the indignities put upon her.

With unfaltering footsteps she still walked her daily round of household cares, providing for hourly wants, preventing wastefulness, teaching the younger children; cheering and counselling the workmen; doing good everywhere; watching and waiting, but never fainting or failing. And much as the town-gossip condemned what it had no power to comprehend—yet her nobleness had kept the crushing hand of the law from her husband's head during all these fearful years.

On, on, on she walked!—head, hands, and heart full—and pouring out of that fulness large draughts for suffering humanity. Yet every year her prison-house and chain became narrower and shorter.

But, like the prisoner of Chillon, she walked to its extreme length, until at last her feet had worn deep channels in the old marble of habit, custom, and prejudice. Many a young boy of the neighborhood was saved by her power; and many a mother's heart made strong for home duty through her counsel.

Frank, who, for loving and reverencing his mother, became hated by his father, had been harshly turned from home and his mother's counsel. He went to school and to college, working his way with manly independence, and coming forth at the end, strong and well-equipped for life's battle. He was now working his way as an educated mechanic in a neighboring city.

She had done all for Elsie that could be done, and she was now a teacher in the Smithville Academy — an earner and learner at the same time. George, always impulsive and headstrong, was learning a trade; while the younger ones were being trained for the future under her wise oversight.

But the "Old Still-House" still groaned and shrieked in the hollow; and its burning stream rolled on.

CHAPTER XIV.

IT was a cold blustering March day—seven years and more, after the horrible catastrophe at the village—that Elsie Magoon the elder, and Elsie the younger, sat together before a cheerful fire, in the old house. If the fire was cheerful, it was almost the only thing that could be called so about the premises. The whole farm was out of repair; for Richard Magoon had not risen from his bed sober for three years. His active, energetic, managing wife could not set things right, for she was "only a woman," and the law gave her no power to manage or control even her own earnings; and yet as matters grew worse, through his neglect, the weight increased on her already over-burdened shoulders. With unwavering patience and perseverance, she had managed, however, to keep the children in school a part of the time, and to teach them herself, by diligently studying or reading, at late hours, when others were asleep, that she might have some new lesson or thought for the morrow. The labor of her own hands even was not her own, to spend or use as she thought expedient. The butter and cheese she made, went to pay the hands that labored about the distillery. A large family of work-men on the farm required her constant toil in the kitchen. Richard, moody and cross, often abusive,

(144)

refused to say anything to her about his money-matters.

Frank had been gone two years; he wrote that he was doing well,—and his mother, in her replies, gave him good advice and words of love, but did not tell him how much she had to encounter. Elsie still taught, but her salary was little more than enough to support herself. George remained on the farm and did all he could,—which was mainly to keep things together. There was no advance: it was impossible, under Richard's misrule.

So things stood at the beginning of this chapter.

The mother and daughter sat before that cheerful fire, with tearful eyes. Elsie, the elder, was industriously patching her husband's coat, while the other plied her needle with busy fingers over some other useful garment.

"It's no use to weep over it, my child; it must be done, and perhaps it's for the best. Let us drop it now, and think of something more cheerful."

"I cannot, mother. This old home, that you and father have toiled upon so long, to be put under the Sheriff's hammer,—and for such a debt!"

"If it cannot be helped, my dear, is it not better wisdom to submit? A thing that can be helped, should never be patiently borne, although it cost trial and struggle, and even antagonism; but I see no help for this. Mr. Porter has waited a great many years: it is now twenty-five since your father borrowed that money."

"Which *should have been yours*," said the young
13

girl, with indignation. "Mother, the law is a bar-
barism — it is *monstrous* to give a man *all* the property
of his wife, *all her labor, all her mind and soul.*"

"Women must be careful how they marry, then,"
said her mother in reply.

"Careful how they marry? rather they must not
marry at all, mother. How can any woman know
who or what she is marrying? Could any foresight
or any care have told *you* that our once noble father
would have ever been what he is now? Oh! with
what pride and love I remember him, as I used to fly
to him, ten years ago, — when he wound his arm round
me, and lifted me up for a kiss — great girl, as I was.
He was so noble, so good, so sensible, so loving! And
see what he is now —"

"Elsie, my child, he is *your father* still."

"I know it, mother; but my heart must pour out
its fulness now, this once, if never more. Next
week, our home is to be sold; and you, what will
become of you and all of us? You have toiled here
for twenty-five years; and were the butter and cheese,
the woollen and linens you have made, piled up before
you, they would pay for the farm. You have educated us all; you have washed and cooked, carded and
spun; you have dried the fruit, made the garden and
become the market-woman; anything, everything,
that we might be clothed, and have books, and be
brought up respectably; you have never made a bad
bargain; have never been drunk; never neglected a
duty: all that human hands, human ingenuity, and
human patience were permitted to do under the law,

you have done. And now, what have you to show
for it? Without a word or explanation, this terrible
effect comes upon you, from causes which you have
struggled, day and night, to avert! I ask again,
what have you to show for all your labor and self-
sacrifice—what individual right do you possess?"

" *I have my children*, Elsie, and I hope and trust
that I have built a home, and stored up wealth in their
hearts, that the Sheriff will not be able 'to put an
attachment upon. If I am bankrupt *there*, my child,
I shall be poor indeed. I know the law is unjust;
I know that women hold, under it, an inferior and
degraded position. . "Could I," said she, speaking
with fervor, "be permitted to keep the farm, and
manage it myself, I have no doubt that I could in a
few years pay all the debt. I love the old place, —
every shrub, plant, and tree is a part of myself, — it
is interwoven with my life, with all that is dear, and
all that is sad and sorrowful, too; — I do not love to
see it go; but it must." .

"It must not, it shall not, mother; there *must be*
some way; I will move heaven and earth, but I will
save it for you."

"Elsie," said her mother, with deep emphasis,
laying down her work, and looking directly into the
face of her child, — "are you strong? able to endure
patiently — to take up a cross and walk under it *for
years*, for the sake of a great good? For the sake of
redeeming your father, would you be willing to toil
as I have done, — if you could put out the fire under
that boiler, and still the shriek of that engine, which

has since your childhood haunted me like the cry of
damned—"

"Yes, mother", said Elsie, returning the steady
gaze without flinching. "Ready to toil, and endure;
to sacrifice ease, self-enjoyment, *everything* but virtue
and ⬛ if I could but accomplish what you suggest, ⬛ ⬛ *ther.* Oh! mother, if I could do
that, we ⬛ be saved!—And mother, I have
a plan ⬛ ne; I will tell you mine, and
then I will hear ⬛ You know Mr. Delno and
Ellen came last n⬛ When they were here last,
Ellen told me about his being Mike Dugan, and how
much you did to help him out of jail. He is so rich
now, and so noble, I thought I would go to him;—I
am of age, you know, and if a wife cannot own property, *a woman can;* and I can be a woman and no
wife a long time, if I choose;—I am almost sure he
will ⬛ me money, and buy the place for me, and
then ⬛ see what we can do. George is not of
age, b⬛ he will stand ⬛ every emergency. I
will give up ⬛ sch ⬛ home and live with
you, aid you, a⬛ d⬛ and I fancy I can do
more than you think. ⬛ uch an end to be attained, I feel equal to any effort.

"You are a brave, blessed child, Elsie! and your
plan is what I had in my own mind. I wrote to
Frank, and had hoped he would be here, but it is too
late now; and I was almost in despair, when ⬛
last night that Mr. Delno had come; but sti⬛
not know just how to manage. The farm ⬛
ours, not his, or father will not yield. George⬛

be brought into all our plans, I think,—and then we must hold your father to it. Together, I feel that we can accomplish this work, formidable as it seems. Elsie, *your father must be redeemed; he must not, shall not die a drunkard.*"

And the strong-hearted woman bent her head upon her daughter's shoulder; the silvery hair—silvered over in that one night of horror—hung in shining folds beside her pale cheeks; her attenuated hands were clasped convulsively together. She felt that she had found a brave young heart, that would lovingly share the weight of that burden which had so long pressed upon her own.

George was called in, and agreed to put himself under their guidance, if the farm could be saved.

Elsie, the younger, then sought her friends. Mr. Delno readily agreed to bid off the farm, make over the deed to her, and to wait any length of time for his money. He was only too happy to have it in his power to return many unforgotten obligations.

Old Porter had intended to bid off the farm,—there was no one else heartless enough to do it. But as almost every neighbor was a creditor to some small amount, and none were friendly to him, they had determined to make him pay well for it.

The news of the coming sale had spread far and wide, and the bids ran higher than old Mr. Porter had anticipated. Mr. Delno was in the group, and when the right time came, his voice was heard. No one going beyond him, the farm was declared his, and the crowd gradually passed away complimenting

13 *

him on the possession of the best place in the valley,
when it should be put in good repair.

Mr. Magoon was not as much under the influence
of liquor as usual.   He could always abstain for a day
or two, under any urgent motive, and then the inherent
hospitality and gentleness of his nature returned.

Mr. Delno wished to close up the business at once,
as he had little time to spare, and they all repaired
to the Justice's office, to make the necessary arrangements.   The money was promptly paid down, all
legal claims met, and in a few days the deed made
out.   But that was the astonishment of Richard
when he found the name of his daughter on the deed,
instead of that of the purchaser.   There was a long
talk, which ended with no very kind feelings between
the father and daughter.   But she was firm.

"Father, I have not taken this responsibility
alone.   If it had been possible for mother to hold it
under the law, I should not have been obliged to
stand in her place.   But why may *I* not save my
father from ruin, as well as Frank, or George.   The
farm is now mine—as much mine as it has ever been
yours; for you have never paid the principal of the
purchase-money.   If after years it has to be sold
from under my hand, as it has been from yours, be
it so; but we shall see."

It was early spring—the roads bad, and streams
high—and Frank did not receive his mother's letter
in time to get home to the sale, or he would have
done what Elsie had done,—borrowed the money,
and saved the home.

But it was better as it was; for he was settled in the city, and he felt that she could do better at the farm than he. And as the busy days of April came upon them, she took possession as gently, and with as little demonstration, as if her father were still sole proprietor.

"Father," said she, as he rose from the breakfast-table, one morning, "I wish to talk with you a few moments."

"You are aware, father, that I am, with the judicious help of mother, to carry on the farm; *we* feel that the 'Still-house' has been the sole cause of all our misfortunes—of misfortune to the whole neighborhood. To-day, I shall dismiss the hands, and put a stop to the making of ardent spirits; and the sound of that engine shall never more be heard in the valley."

"You will put a stop to the only money-making thing on the premises," said he; "whiskey never brought so good a price as now."

"That may be—whiskey may bring money; but look over the farm and see *what it has brought with it*, or rather what it has compelled you to lose. If whiskey is so profitable, why am I the legal owner of all you have toiled for so long?—No, father, not another drop shall ever be made on the place."

"What will you do with the fixtures? They are worth thousands of dollars, as much as the whole farm would sell for, without them."

"*Let them rot where they are*," said she, resolutely. "Aye, fall to staves, every hogshead, barrel, and tub, if there is no other way to dispose of them. But not another drop of the accursed beverage shall be manufactured with them."

Mr. Magoon was vexed, and said many unkind words. But it was useless. There was no yielding in the resolute girl, who had taken all into her hands.

Frank gave her the assurance of help, and all pledged themselves to aid as occasion required.

Had she, in a rash impulse, plunged into a stream, braved a fire, or confronted a wild beast, to save her parents from ruin, the world would have declared her a heroine. But she had undertaken a mightier task —to bring harmony out of discord; beauty from deformity; and to let happiness and comfort in upon a household where misery and misrule had for years held almost undisputed sway. To do this, she must sacrifice the heyday of her girlhood to hard toil and earnest thought. She must appear to many of her neighbors as an unwomanly creature, endeavoring to rule and govern her father, and as wanting true sensibility and refinement.

Strange, how little it takes to make a heroine! How much of self-poise, and earnestness, and truth, to make only an "eccentric character!"—or, as the world says, a "masculine woman."

CHAPTER XV.

IT did not cost a great effort to put an end to the operations of the "Old Still-House;" for a cold spring, a hot, dry summer, early frosts, and a long, tedious winter, had reduced the usual amount of corn all over the country, and made the demand for it at · the South so great, as to induce many young men to engage in the Southern trade. Large quantities were sent down the Ohio in flat-boats; what remained was readily sold. The mill still did its work for the farmers around; but it was almost worn out, and ready to lie still with the rest.

All sorts of gossip was in circulation about Elsie Magoon; but the common opinion was, that the bargain was all a sham, to keep the property out of the hands of old Porter; nobody loved him, and nobody cared; for, through Elsie, many were getting their pay. The feeling towards her and her father, may be drawn from the following conversation at Mrs. Hill's quilting:

"Lor's help us," said Mrs. Hunt to the ladies around the quilt, "why did n't Frank take it, if anybody, and not put such a scandalization upon his sister? It's mighty unbecoming in her, to be sure, to be going round about, and doing business after the Still. She does just for all the world like men-folks."

"I reckon she'll be a-turning out one of them there 'Women's Rights' that we hear tell on, one of these days," replied Miss Ferril; "one of them that wants to rule."

"Should n't much wonder," continued Mrs. Hunt; "Elsie is all-fired smart; I know that, and she knows it, too. But I reckon, 'gin she gits through with that scrape of stopping the 'Old Still,' she'll be tired a-warin' the breeches. Old Richard Magoon is a hard old customer, and he's a-getting worse and worse."

"You don't say!" broke in Mrs. Phillips, a very quiet, orderly lady, who was always astonished at anything new. "I thought he'd quit drinking."

"Good gracious! our Dan, who Miss Elsie had up there ploughing for the corn, says he's been ridiculous every day since *he* has been up there."

"He used to be a mighty clever man, when I first knew him," said Mrs. Hunt; "but I raly believe the nicer and decenter and smarter a man is, when he is sober, the worse he is when he is drunk."

"You don't say!" ejaculated Mrs. Phillips.—"Marie Jane, will you hand me the thread?"

"Yes; I believe it. Just think of him—after he has let everything go to ruin as he has, tearin' round like mad, and calling his wife and Elsie all sorts of hard names, 'cause they're trying to fix up things! Why, our Dan says he swears worse than old Street; and *he* was hard to beat, I tell you!"

"Old Street? Who was he?" asked Miss Marie Jane.

"La! dew tell! Never heard of old Street? I

thought everybody knowed him. He was a queer old sneevus, that used to go round about, up and down the country, all tatter and rags—kind a-half crazy—and always begging whiskey. He was a cute old soul—never forgot anything he ever knowed—and when he was a mind, could talk like a book. They say he went to college, way down in Old Virginny—Prince Williams, or something like that—and was counted awful smart; and just as he was a-gettin' through, some gal he was in love with, turned round and got married to some other feller, and so he went kinder beside hisself, and took to drink; and never was anything but a pest afterward."

"Dear me! how romantic!" said Miss Marie Jane, with a lisp.

"I guess you would have thought it was morantic, if you'd a-seen him, sometimes. The women were as feared as death of him. Oh! you never hear'n no critter swear so as he would, when he got mad, in all your born days; and he'd *always* get mad if they did n't give him whiskey; and if they did, there was no telling what he'd do. Did you never hear about Mrs. Brant's giving him a whippin'?"

"No; you don't say?" said Mrs. Phillips again, with a giggle. She always laughed when she spoke.

"You see, Mrs. Col. Brant had a grand party, one day, and had all the *respectable* ladies in the neighborhood. There was me and Miss Magoon, and Miss Ferril, and Miss Scott, and Miss Bill Lake, and Miss Tom Lake, and Miss Uriah Lake, and all the rest of the Lakes, and everybody—a hull room full—and we was all sittin' a-talking: and who should walk right up to the door but old Street!

"'Betsie,' said he, (that was Mrs. Col. Brant, you know,)—'Betsie,' said he, 'give me some whiskey:' and he puckered up his lips, and squinted his little black eyes, as if he was plotting some mischief. He was a terrible mischief, Street was, always.

"'No!' said she, 'I sha'n't,' said she; 'you must just go away with yourself.—March!'

"'Well,' said he, 'I will, if you will give me some whiskey. Just a little, Betsie; I am so dry. Now, if you will, I'll go to the orchard and bring up some sweet 'uns for these pretty ladies.'

"'No, Street!' said she. (Mrs. Brant was a mighty res'lute piece when she set out.) 'You don't need a drop, and you must go away from here.'

"And then you ought 'a' heard him swear! Oh, my goodness! I never did hear the like. And there we was all a-settin'!—so Mrs. Brant, she got up and shut the door—and the first we see, he was coming in the winder, head foremost, with no shirt on his back; and we all set to screaming, for he was awful mad. And Mrs. Brant, she never said a word, but just slipped to the cupboard and took down the colonel's raw-hide, and she gave him three cuts over his bare shoulders, that made him back out quicker. She did not know but he'd kill her for it; but he only looked up,—'There, there! Betsie,' said he, just like a gentleman; 'I'll get out—don't strike again—I'll get out!' And out he got, and walked off, the blood almost starting out of the great welts across his shoulders; and he never troubled her arterwards. Years arter, when he used to come back, he used to say to her,—'You did right, Betsie: you did right; but you struck a *leetle* too hard.' Poor old critter! I 'spect he's dead now. He used to come round once in six mouths, or a year, for nigh twenty years, when the country was new. He was mighty larned, and could figure up anything uncommon; and talk Latin and Greek, and had all the histories, ever since Christ down, at his tongue's end; and he knew all the ministers and lawyers, and so the people used to let him stay to hear him talk, poor old soul; but I guess he's dead now!" And the good old lady stopped, out of breath.

"It's my opinion," said grandmother Lake, "that if more of 'em had the cow-hide taken on 'em when they are in their mad fits, it would be better for 'em!" and the old lady bit off the end of her thread spitefully.

"To be sure it would," said Miss Ferril.

"I tell you, if I had a husband," said Mrs. Styles, "that knew as much as Magoon, and could be as smart and gentlemanly when he was a mind to, and then cut up as he does sometimes, would n't I?—would n't I?"—and she gritted her teeth, and tried to look daggers. It was evident she had a husband who sometimes provoked her.

"They say he treats the women folks arful," said grandmother Lake.

"I do expect he does, from what I can hear, 'specially since the Still-house has stopped; and

14

our Dan says, Elsie won't allow a bit of whiskey on
the premises, only what he gets on the sly. They do
say that she let out barrels and barrels in the Old
Still; and he has to buy every drop he gets now.
She says there sha'n't one mite go into the field this
year; if the corn can't be planted without, it must
go unplanted."

"Good for her!" shouted Miss Ferril; and in the
attempt to clap her hands, she ran her needle into
her finger.

And so ended the chat over the quilt; and such
was the gossip of the town. As Mrs. Hunt said,
Richard grew worse rather than better. He felt
himself broken down and worthless; the very force
that was arrayed to save him, drove him to madness.
As had been said at the quilting, no whiskey was
allowed on the premises; and hands enough were
found who would work without it. Indeed, temperance societies were becoming popular; many young
men joined, who were ready to work without stimulants.

The farm had been put in better order; fences
repaired and built. And now that the laborers were
not called off to take care of the distillery and its
surroundings, everything went on nicely.

The fields were planted in due season, and the
crops seemed likely to be abundant. Except the
conduct of Richard, there was a manifest improvement everywhere.

Mrs. Magoon and her daughter had just finished
folding the clothes after a large washing, one Monday

eve, when one of the little Truman girls ran in, crying bitterly, and said, — " Mammy is dying, and Mary wants you to come right over, quick."

The two women put aside their work hastily, gave directions to Alice about the morning duties, if they should not return, and hurried away.

They found Mrs. Truman, who had been ill a few days, breathing her last. She was not old, not over fifty-five, and that should be life's meridian, and yet her face and form would have proclaimed her " threescore and ten." Her eyes were heavy and dim, care and toil and weeping had driven them back under her furrowed brow, and bleared them with sorrow; till she was old, oh ! how old, and worn and weary !

And what a life she had lived ! The early years of it had been spent by the side of one who, when he married her at fifteen, was good and industrious, and meant to do all he promised. She was a pretty girl then, with a heart full to the brim of tenderness and unselfishness. But she had grown, in the course of these toiling, suffering years, hard and petulant, and vixenish, often almost matching him in violence and abuse.

Yet, after all, she had been as good a mother as one plunged in her very childhood into matronly cares and duties, from which there was no escape or rest, not even long enough to learn to accomplish them aright—could well be. And what had she to encourage, or lift for an hour of her long, wearisome pilgrimage, the burden of her destiny ? Truman, kind-hearted and jovial when sober, silly and fawn-

ing when half sober, and a very demon when fully
drunk, had made life to her a fearful thing for thirty
long years. She never went from home; but washed
and ironed, and spun and wove. Day and night,
year in and out, was heard the click of her loom, or
the buzz of her spinning-wheel; and as an accompaniment, the clack and running of her tongue. She had
scolded in the beginning, because she thought scolding would mend matters. Because a troop of children, full of life and mischief, who had nothing to
do, and nothing to do it with, were always doing the
very things they should not; and because she had no
time to reason with them, and did not know how to
do it, if she had,—she strove to govern by screams
and threats.

She loved her children, toiled for them, saved for
them, denied herself everything for them. And her
husband, "Drunken old Truman," as all the neighborhood called him, always had a clean, whole suit
for Sundays, no matter how poor and old it might
be; and if she scolded some to get it on, it was love
that stirred her tongue, pride, and a lingering hope,
that struggled against all hope, that she could still
make the husband of her youth, and the father of
her children, a little bit respectable.

And those twelve children, that for these many
years have hung upon her, while she struggled, and
toiled, and wept, and scolded, and suffered,—those
twelve children—the drunkard's children—every
one of them bore, in some form, the brand of the

father's sins — every one, more or less, the impress of the mother's trials and sorrows.

Oh, ye men of our nation! who measure your duties to humanity by codes, "constitutions," who dare not prohibit the use of ardent spirits by law, lest you take away some man's *liberty* to make a beast of himself; have you ever paused to think what opportunities you give him to destroy the liberty and peace of *others?* to entail upon offspring, one by one, unnatural appetites, debased habits, polluted tastes, and diseased conditions? The power you give to man to crush out the life of the wife whom he has sworn to "love, honor, and protect," by long years of torture, or the quick frenzy of an hour? To compel her to exhausting toil, not only in her own support, but to make amends for his unfaithfulness in the support and protection of their children, and, worse than all, to become the mother of those who must both inherit and perpetuate the curse which has blighted their life? Can the wife and mother, whose spirit is broken, by seeing her youthful hopes prostrate before her, who with every passing hour feels the burden of another's sin,—whose very soul is steeped in despair,—can she give birth to beings harmonious and beautiful? No matter how noble her own spirit,—no matter how amiable and gentle, how pure and true she may have been,—if her husband is a drunkard, the "trail of the serpent is over them all." And the truer and higher her nature, the more fearful will be its antagonism with that curse; that is pressing the iron deeper and

14 *

deeper into her soul, blighting those dearer to her than her own life.

Ah! if the woes of intemperance fell only upon the guilty, we might be patient and *logical* over them; but alas! who can measure their height and depth, their length and breadth?

But now the mother of these twelve children lay dying.

As Mrs. Magoon drew near the bed, the sufferer looked up; a ghastly smile of recognition flitted over her face; then her eye ran around the circle, as if in search of some one not there, and she asked in a husky voice, "Where is he?"

"He is gone out, mother," said Martha, the eldest, who lay weeping on the pillow, holding the damp, death-cold hand in hers.

"Yes, gone out!" and then a low deep groan burst from the panting breast; "gone out — yes, I know — gone for a dram. Bring him in once more, oh! Reuben, once more before I die! Let me see him.",

This was said to her son, a young man, who stood before her at the foot of the bed. He went out, and soon led in his father, too drunk to walk steadily, and seated him beside the bed. He took her hand in his, and seemed to realize partially the scene before him.

"Don't go to dying now, Nancy," said he. "You mus'n't; I can't stand it. Come! cheer up, old woman, and I'll try and do better; I will; I swear I will!"

"Oh, father! don't, don't!" almost shrieked poor Martha, at the coarse words and tones so at variance with the occasion; while little Jane buried her face in the bed-clothes, and smothered her sobs as best she could.

"Truman," said the dying mother, as her breath came labored and long, "I must die; won't you promise me now, before Mistress Magoon and Elsie, that you won't drink when I am gone? Promise me; do promise me!"

He did not answer; and she lay silent, and with her eyes partly closed, for a few moments, his hands clasped in hers. With a great effort, she turned her eyes to him; he was fast asleep—nodding stupidly, and almost ready to fall upon her.

"Take him away, Reuben," whispered Elsie; but the words, though low, had caught the ears of the dying wife.

"No, no, no!" said she, with strange, deep earnestness, "let him stay; I loved him once—yes, once, once! I love him still. But it's whiskey, Elsie, you know—yes, *you* know; it's whiskey, Martha—Reuben. Take care of him when I am gone." She was silent a moment from exhaustion, and then a strange smile flitted over her face; her eye brightened, and her voice seemed stronger.

"I loved him once; he was so handsome and good, and he loved me, too; I was happy—once—once! Wait, mother, I am coming—*he* will come directly; *I loved him so!* Mary—Reuben—Alice—Jane—where are you all gone? Who put out the light? it's cold here. Mrs. Magoon, go to the fire—I loved him once; the birds sang and the sun shone so bright that morning! Mother, wait a little; I'm almost ready. Nellie, tie this white ribbon round my waist; there —so. I loved him"——

The strange smile was playing over the features; her hands were lifted up, and she seemed to be meeting friends. For a moment there was a struggle, and then she fell back upon her pillow. The eyes lost their light, the smile became fixed—the heart ceased to beat. The tried spirit, in that fearful hour, had stricken out the long weary years of suffering and sorrow, and had linked itself with the freshness and purity of its early youth; to that day and time, when her soul was nearest heaven—when Nellie fastened the emblem of purity over her beating heart, and led her away to become the bride of one whom she loved with all a woman's true devotion. What might have been her life—how much that is good and beautiful might have budded and blossomed in so true a soul— had he walked by her side in soberness and good faith to the end!

It had taken twenty-five years for that "Old Still-House" to crush out the life of that strong, brave, though erring, woman. Erring, did we say? Will the recording angels set down against her the sins of so tried and tempted a spirit? No; rather will they say at the last, "Well done, thou good and faithful servant; thou hast been more true, amid thy manifold trials, and greater in thy resistance to evil, than they who, having no temptation, have stood afar off, saying, 'I am holier than thou!'"

Will God, when he makes up his jewels, find no diamond amid the rubbish of such a life,—where faith, and hope, and labor, linked all the hours of a quarter of a century with unfailing love?

CHAPTER XVI

LOUD were the wailings of grief that went up from those stricken ones in that solemn midnight hour. She was their only hope and comfort, and if she had sometimes been stern and fretful, it was forgotten now; they saw only her long life of devotion and love, flecked here and there by flitting shadows, when her poor, weary and tired heart could bear up no longer.

They had forced the husband from the bed, when they found the cold stiffened fingers released their grasp, and the tongue ceased to say, "Let him stay; I loved him once." He seemed unconscious, muttered a vile curse, and stumbling into a bed in the next room, was soon fast asleep, while the sorrowing children still sobbed and moaned over their dead mother.

"Indeed, indeed, Mrs. Magoon," said Martha, "I don't know what *is* to become of us now; *he* never does anything to help us, and she has worked so hard —oh! mother! mother! mother!" and the poor girl broke forth afresh in weeping and lamentation.

"He has not done a day's work for four years, only what he has done for your folks," said Reuben bitterly; "and in all that time he never came home

(166)

sober or without his half-gallon jug full, and she working so hard !"

"Only last week," said little Jane, " while she was 'most too sick to keep up, and Mrs. Ferril sent her home two dollars by me, as I went from school, for washing her carpet, and she was going to buy medicine with it, he took it away from me right out by the gate, before her face and eyes, and went off down to the corner, and he and old Randall, the blacksmith, were drunk there two or three days, — and now she's dead; and he killed her ! I know he did!" and the child sobbed aloud.

"She is *at rest*," said Mrs. Magoon, with a choking voice.

"Yes, she is," said Reuben; "and I would n't, if I could, bring her to life. We shall miss her; but it is best as it is." And the great untrained boy, who was ashamed to weep, dashed the tears from his cheek, as he looked upon her cold, still face, with that strange smile lingering about it.

"Yes, better as it is, Reuben; and may God shield you and all her children from the sorrows she has borne. Remember *what* has brought them upon her —"

"Mrs. Magoon," said the young man, earnestly, "never a starving man longed for food as I long for, and love, strong drink. It is a desire that haunts me day and night. It makes my nerves quiver and my tongue burn to see or smell it. I can drink it now, and not hurt me. But if I thought that I would ever come to such a fate as *that man there*, or bring a woman to suffer as *she has,* I'd never touch the stuff again while I live. Never, so help me God; I'd die first."

"Reuben, is it not better to give it up entirely now? If you go on, thinking you can stop when you like, you will never stop, till you begin to suffer; and then you will have lost the power of self-control. Look at your mother, as she lies there, and think of all she has had to bear. Yet when she married your father, he thought himself as safe as you are now, and she did not doubt him any more than Ruth doubts you. Will you not promise me, here, for the love you bore her who is gone; the love of your brothers and sisters who must now look up to you; the love of Ruth, and last of all, the love I know you feel for me, will you not promise me now, Reuben, to drink no more?"

She led him to the bed-side. "Here, Reuben, let your promise go up to heaven with the passing spirit, and it will bless the vow!"

The young man dropped involuntarily upon his knees, and throwing one arm over the body of his dead mother, cried with intense anguish:

"I will never taste the accursed stuff again; never! never! Oh! mother, help me, and keep me from temptation!" Then overcome with emotion, he rushed from the room.

Mrs. Magoon and Elsie closed the eyes and folded the hands of the weary sleeper. Other neighbors hearing the news dropped in, and when all was done that could be for the family, they returned home.

Sad were the thoughts of the mother and daughter as they wended their way homeward in the deep stillness of the night, after that solemn death-scene.

Memory was busy with the past, and with the future, and they walked for some distance in silence.

The mother spoke first.

"We have seen a sad sight to-night, Elsie."

"Yes, mother."

"And I could not help thinking of what might happen in some other home."

"Mother," and the young girl grasped her mother's arm convulsively,—"you must not die!"

"I was not thinking of that, Elsie; but you have no doubt seen that your father is more given to his habits than ever?"

"Yes, mother," answered the child, mechanically. A vision of horror was before her eyes. She had scarcely ever had the thought come before her, seriously, that her noble mother could die. But the words had awakened strange feelings, and brought out before her fearful phantoms, of what might be; and she clung to her mother, without daring to say more, lest she should pour out from her full heart curses upon him whom she must call father.

It was late at night, or rather it was nearly morning; the full moon was sinking, and casting the long shadows of the tall trees along the path; the whippoorwill, which always sang his melancholy strain by the river-side, and was answered from every grove in the neighborhood,—kept up his wail. The owls down in the glen spied a storm for the morrow in

15

the low black clouds which skirted the horizon, and they laughed, and howled, and hooted, as owls only can, in a most terrific manner. It was lonely, fearfully lonely, as the two walked towards their home. Elsie clung closer than ever to her mother, and they unconsciously quickened their pace. At length Mrs. Magoon asked, "Are you frightened, Elsie."

"Frightened! why, mother, I was never frightened in my life, when I could see no danger."

"What makes you walk so fast, and breathe so hard; and you have only answered me, 'Yes, mother,' since we started?"

The dread vision grew more dim; the blood coursed through her frame more warm and rapidly, and she answered, —

"I am weary and nervous a little, and I could not shake off a strange feeling that the incidents of the night have thrown over me. Mother, look down there into the valley; was there ever more beautiful corn? And along on the hill-side, the wheat looks grand; the orchards are loaded with fruit, and the dairy is doing wonders. Everything that we have done, since we took the charge, has prospered; Providence seems answering our prayers everywhere but in that one place, where of all others we most earnestly seek for a blessing. Oh, mother! what shall we do next for *him?*"

"I have prayed, my child, and *I know that the time will come.* Yes, I know it; and my heart is ready cheerfully to bear and suffer, until the hour arrives."

"*I* am ready to bear, mother; but not cheerfully. I cannot cheerfully see my father sinking lower and lower every day."

"You know what I mean; to fret and wear faces of gloom would only waste our own energies, and take from the courage of the rest. *We* must keep up, or all is lost."

"I fear we shall have a scene to-night when we get home. *He* (when she spoke of him as an inebriate, she *could not* use the words '*father*' and '*husband*') has been down at the town all day; and you know he always comes home furious from there; and when he finds us both gone, and no warm supper prepared for him, he will be the more so."

"And we forgot to tell Alice!"

"Yes. And she is thoughtless."

The new fear made them quiet again; and as at last they reached the house, the sound of angry altercation reached their ears. The voice of Richard, raised to a high pitch, seemed to be accusing George for some remissness of duty.

Lights were in several of the rooms, showing an unusual commotion at that hour. The two women trembled.

"I *am* frightened now, mother; there is something to frighten in the sound of that voice," said Elsie, the younger.

"Hush—what is he saying?" They paused. "Oh! what curses he is pouring upon the heads of those poor children. Listen:"

—"You're a set of devilish brats, just like your

mother, every one of you, and I'll —— if I'll stand
it.   Here I come home at night and find her trapesing
off to the neighbors, and no supper.   And——I'll
kill her —yes I will! I'll put her where Truman's
old hag will be turned now, about six foot under
ground" —

"Oh, father!" screamed Alice.

"Shut up; nobody's going to hurt you.   But just
let *her* show her face" —

"Richard, I am here," said Elsie, stepping up to
him—thinking that her presence would quiet the
tumult, or at least relieve Alice and George.

Richard had just returned home from the village,
where he had been carousing with a gang he often
met, whose delight it was to stir up his wrath against
his wife and daughter for the part they had taken
against the 'Still-house;' for the influence of that act
had touched the pockets, if not the morals, of every
dram-seller and drinker in the country round.   He
had stayed late, started home in his little wagon, become languid and sleepy; and his horse, wiser than
her master, had drawn the carriage safely home, and
walked up to the stable-door where she stood quietly;
while he slept soundly, curled up in the bottom of
the vehicle, where he had pitched down when he first
left the village.   When he awoke, he was stiff and
cold, and cramped with his uncomfortable position.
As soon as he knew where he was, he scrambled up
and took a heavy drink to warm him up; then tum-
bled out, and began unharnessing his horse, which
had stood there so long, and was so furiously hungry,

that she angered him with her impatience. He could not find the buckles, so he drew out his knife and cut his way through. The stable-door was locked, and he knocked and hallooed for the key, till he was more enraged than ever; and in the meantime had taken another dram. His shouts and curses at length wakened George, who went to him; and who, when he found half the harness hanging around the horse, cut to pieces, could not forbear saying in most decided terms what he thought, giving his father some words of advice that were, to say the least, not respectful, and worked him into a state of perfect frenzy. He went raving into the house; called up Alice; ordered everything he wished put upon the table, and stood by it, with a butcher-knife in his hand, when his wife entered.

He did not wait an instant, but sprang towards her with a maniac's fury. The three drams taken so closely together had not had time to stupefy, only to infuriate him.

"You old devil, I'll teach you to tell your brats to talk to me as that imp has to-night."

Elsie sprang back again out of the door, and he started after her; but George, who was strong, seized him from behind and pinioned his arms to his ribs, while the younger Elsie took the knife from his hand, and by their united strength they held him until the liquor had completely overcome him, and then he dropped upon the floor, unable to rise again. He was soon too stupid to make any resistance, and they then carried him into a small room used by him as an

15*

office, laid him on a lounge, and, locking the door, left him there.

It was near morning, and the family gathered to consult what could be and what ought to be done.

"He will certainly kill you, mother," said George, "if he goes on in this way; he is perfectly mad when he is as he was to-night."

"I never knew him so furious before," said the wife, in sad tones.

"But you will see him so again, and he has threatened you so often, that I feel there is danger; and we cannot afford to give you, too, a martyr to the demon Intemperance," said Elsie.

"No, nor any of us," said George; "the cattle and horses are not safe either. He is the biggest brute of them all."

"Hush, hush, George; you must not speak so, my son. Let him be what he will, you can still be respectful."

"I feel it, mother, and I can't help it. He struck Alice to-night; oh! such a blow. It would have felled her to the floor if I had not warded it off. Look at my arm." And the boy showed the bruise upon his arm, that, had it fallen with all its force, would nearly have killed her. "*I* say, go and swear your lives against him," said the impetuous boy.

"And what good will that do? It will only spread our disgrace; and besides, he has nothing to pay a fine, and anybody in the county will go his bail; he is so good and noble when he is sober, nobody will believe us if we tell them how badly he acts at home," said Elsie, the younger.

"No!" said the mother. "We must not talk of such a thing. What is done must be done here at home. Alas! can we do anything?"

"Nothing, unless we can get father thoroughly sober, which he has not been for months, even years. If we can accomplish that—can keep him from drink, in any way, long enough to have his reason once take possession, I believe we could save him; and it shall be done," said Elsie, the daughter.

CHAPTER XVII

ELSIE arose deliberately, took the jug from the corner of the table, and emptied its contents out of the window.

" He will kill you," said Alice.

" He will not," was the calm reply. " Mother, go lie down and rest till daybreak. Go, Alice and George. Oh! what a night this has been!"

They obeyed her as one having authority; for beautiful and grand she stood in that hour of trial, ready to brave all things for the sake of those she loved.

" If I can keep him where he is till he gets duly sober," said she to herself, "and then reason with him, I am sure he will yield. He will not dare expose us again to such dangers as he has to-night. But how can I come face to face, and reason with *my father* over his shame and madness? I cannot. But I can write."

She went to her room, and, taking her pen, wrote out the strong emotions of her soul in a pleading prayer to her father to abstain from drink. She recounted the death-scene of poor Mrs. Truman, and then his fury and diabolical attempt against the life of her mother; his blow aimed at Alice; and the fear that in some moment of frenzy he would accomplish his threats, and justice would fall upon him, and not upon him alone, but upon them all; for with his deep disgrace and punishment would come to them,—who were innocent,—a sorrow that would crush them as well as himself.

"Oh! my father," she continued, "there *is* a suffering that goes even beyond the misery of the crime and sin of the one who inflicts it. Could you see dear mother as I see her, defending your name and honor, pointing us back to the time when you were the sun and glory of our home; could you see her tears of sorrow now, her nights of suffering, hear her pleadings of hope, and with how strong a spirit she resists despair, you would, for her sake, if not for your own, turn aside from that path beset with devils, which you have chosen. Oh! by the love you once bore us, be a man again; be as you were when I used to climb on your knee and kiss your lips,—which had not then cursed me,—as when I stood upon your knee, and with tiny fingers smoothed out those silken curls, that now lie sodden and matted upon your brow, because no hand of love dare approach you. Oh! be again as when you used to sing your beautiful songs, at twilight, upon the old door-stone, till my little heart melted in ecstasy, I scarce knew why, upon your bosom, and swelled out in thankfulness to God that he had made me the daughter of such a father.

"Do not curse us that we have turned the key upon you; it was love—the love of children for their father and mother, that prompted us. Reflect that you have been a maniac for months, and that, unless

you can be induced to let your brain regain its true
temperature, and your reason return once more, you
will never be free. Suppose the heavy blow, which
has so bruised George, had fallen on the head of our
dear, delicate Alice, as you designed. Suppose that
knife—used for years to cut the bread that supplied
the household-table—had reached the heart of our
mother, as you intended it should,—a key would have
been turned on you, a more inexorable jailer would
have held it—than any of those who now only wish
to save you for themselves and for yourself, can ever
be. We would rather yield our own lives if by so
doing we could make yours pure, than to see you live
out a few more shameful years *a drunkard.* Oh! my
father! my father a drunkard! To save the farm;
to save my mother from beggary and ruin; to preserve the younger children from being scattered, as
outcasts over the earth, I have dared to do what many
women would have thought impossible. But with
God's help I will pay for it all, asking only as a
recompense, that my father, in his old age, shall live
under the trees he has planted, and eat the fruit of
the vines which in his stalwart manhood he trained,
an honored and respected man."

Her letter was written, and blistered over with
many tears. When done, it was directed, and fastened
to the handle of his empty jug, and set inside the
door of his room, while he yet remained in his stupid
sleep.

When she arose in the morning, she repeated to
her mother what she had done; and as the family

came from their slumbers, one after another, they were hushed into quiet, that his sleep might be prolonged as far as possible.

Fear rested upon the whole household.. George did not dare go away to the field; but the younger ones were sent away as far as possible. It was near ten o'clock in the forenoon before Richard became sufficiently aroused to seek for his bottle. They heard his mutterings, heard him rise; and come to the door, lift the jug and set it down with a growl; then all was still.

This little room, or study, as he called it, had long been his *sanctum*, into which he retired when he wished to avoid observation. It was furnished with a settee, on which he often slept for hours; his pitcher and tumbler always stood upon the mantle; and here he often shut himself for days. There was no word spoken inside, and all was quiet without, and so the day passed away.

Towards evening, Elsie opened the door cautiously. He seemed slumbering on the settee; and she placed a tray, with a bowl of hot coffee and other food, upon his table, and left the door unlocked. The night passed; and if he left the room, no one knew it; and so for three days he continued his voluntary imprisonment.

What were his thoughts, what the trials of his spirit during those three days, no one on earth will ever know!

On the fourth morning, he came out and went as usual to his work. At breakfast-time, he took his

accustomed seat at the table.   There was an evident
awkwardness and restraint—a choking down of emotions—a turning away from the crowding, suffocating
thoughts, that were thronging upon him.   But gradually, little by little, the conversation glided into the
ordinary stream of family talk.

After breakfast, Richard went out with George, to
the barn.   The old harness hung over the gate in all
its fragments.   Richard took it down, carried it into
the tool-room ; and with patient care it was soon
mended.

Then he sought the garden ; looked around for
some light work, and finally came in, just before
dinner, laid himself down upon the bed, covered his
face, and slept.

For many days he went patiently and quietly about
his work, his old gentleness and cheerfulness seemed
returning, and great joy came upon them all.   Elsie's
voice was heard at early dawn, like the song of the
morning-bird ; the step of the mother grew lighter,
and her cheek and eye brightened with every hour
of hope and comfort.

It was the custom to go once a week to the town
in the family carriage, to take the butter to a particular customer, and do any shopping that was needed
for the family.   The usual day came ; the horses
stood pawing impatiently at the gate.   Mrs. Magoon
was ready, and only waited to lay her beautiful rolls,
rich and golden, in the basket with her own hands,
when Richard emerged from the bedroom, with a
clean shirt and his best suit on, and said quietly, " I

believe I will go with you, Elsie; it's a long time since we have been down together."

Elsie's heart beat quick and hard. "You have no objection, have you?" said he.

"Certainly not," was her quick reply. But Richard had caught the troubled glance that told the fear within. She had no objection, only the fear that he was not yet sufficiently strong to resist the temptations that would beset him.

They walked down the path together to the gate, he carrying the basket, as in olden time. She was happy, oh! how happy! for the returning kindness and affection. But would he not fail? She dashed away the doubt, sprang into the carriage, and they drove off.

The day passed on as usual. The errands were done; and at evening they turned the horses' heads homeward. Proud and happy was she; for "Richard was himself again." He had not drank a drop; but he seemed restless and uneasy; his eyes were heavy, and his face flushed. It had been a hot day. He complained of chilliness, which was followed by fever, and reached home, severely ill. His long course of excess, his exposures, and his sudden abandonment of stimulants, had induced a slow typhoid fever; from which he arose, nearly six months after, weak and broken,—blessing heaven every day that his two children, George and Elsie, had been able to do so well in managing the farm, and providing for the family; and more especially, for the care and tenderness of his wife, which had, as the

16

doctor every day told him, raised him from the grave.

It was at the beginning of harvest, that he was taken sick, and it was in the dead of winter, when, for the first time propped up with pillows in the big arm-chair, he looked out upon the fields covered with snow, and saw the comfort and thrift that seemed to surround him. The barn had been weather-boarded, and the cattle housed from the wintry blast. The hay-stacks, capped with snow-wreaths, looked thrifty and picturesque. His mind, which had been sadly bewildered through his sickness, seemed to be gathering up the fragments of the past.

"Elsie," said he, "Mrs. Truman died just before I was taken down; what became of the family?"

"Oh, they are doing finely. Truman promised me, at his wife's funeral, that he would not drink any more; and Reuben made the same pledge over the dead body of his mother; and they have not drank since. They worked for us through harvest, and did well. You know they are both good hands when sober; and not a drop of anything stronger than water, went into the field to tempt them."

"Thank God for that!" said the weary invalid.

"Elsie rented them those twenty acres over the run, you know, and they have girdled and cleared it off, and raised a fine crop of late pickles and turnips. The boys all work. I have persuaded Mr. Truman to let Israel learn the blacksmith-trade, with Randall."

"And is Randall sober enough, nowadays, to teach a boy a trade?"

"Yes, indeed. After the 'Still-house' went down, a new state of things arose from its ashes. Randall seldom drinks any now.

"Israel works well; and Thomas is learning the shoemaker's trade in Smithville. Martha and Jane manage nicely at home. Susan has learned to weave, and makes a good many dollars that way. They had no hope while the old man behaved so badly; but now they all seem willing to work. The house has been repaired, and they are really comfortable."

"Who keeps the district school this winter, Elsie?"

"Why! don't you know? Elsie has been teaching it these two months. Alice and Kate get along nicely with the work; so Elsie took the school."

"Big boys and all?"

"Yes; big boys and all. And she has not had one bit of trouble. Ned Brant and Steph Ferril obey orders like two little girls. She has seventy scholars, and could have twenty more, but the house won't hold them."

"I thought I missed her sometimes, lately, through the day; but she seemed to come in often; and I am so weak, I don't remember. How are all the neighbors?"

"Oh, they are all doing nicely. George Brant was married, last week, to Susie Underhill."

Richard looked up with surprise.

"You thought he was thinking of Elsie; and I did too, for a time. But it was all a mistake. He liked her, there's no doubt; but she has no wish to marry, and I think, will not, for years to come."

"Maybe so!" said the invalid, with a faint smile

of incredulity. "One question more: What has become of Slidell, and Vanhorn, and Bell, and Samson, and the others who lived over the creek? Now the 'Still-house' is done for, how do they get liquor?"

"Bell and Vanhorn have moved off, nobody knows where; and the others have joined our Temperance Society, which meets once a week, at the school-house."

Richard bit his lip.

"Oh! there *has* been a great change in the neighborhood, I can tell you. We inquired for the poor and needy last Tuesday night, in our Temperance meeting, and found that there was not one in the township. The whole people have become temperate. We have all cause to thank Providence for the change."

"Thank *Elsie Magoon and her daughter first!*" murmured Richard. "If that 'Still-house' had gone into the hands of Porter, what would have become of the town?"

The sick man was overcome with the thought; and covering his eyes with his emaciated hands, the tears trickled through his fingers.

"There!" said Elsie, springing to his side; "I have talked too much. Dear Richard, don't weep! let by-gones be by-gones. Come: let me help you into the bed; you must go to sleep now."

She led him to the bed, adjusted the snowy pillows beneath his head, smoothed back the hair from his pale forehead, and as he murmured a "God bless you!" she laid her lips upon his, and answered back the prayer.

CHAPTER XVIII.

YOUNG Elsie Magoon, whom we found sleeping in her cradle at the commencement of our story, now comes before us a beautiful and graceful woman. The stern discipline of her life had only served to bring out more strongly the best points of her character, and to fix in her mind the determination to give heed only to the highest and holiest impulses of her nature.

By her adroitness in the different branches of labor assigned to the females about the farmhouse, she had been able to pay for a substitute to take her place in the kitchen at home, while she attended the Smithville Seminary for young ladies, and acquired some of the accomplishments as well as the more solid studies of the time.

To her intuitive mind, a long course of hard study under teachers did not seem necessary. She grasped the key of science offered by her teachers, and went forward opening such doors as suited her, taking possession of the priceless treasures within; and while other girls in the neighborhood wasted their hours of leisure at parties and balls, Elsie's candle flickered in the west chamber and threw its gleams over many a page that even the minister of Smithville, who had brought his sheepskin embellished with blue ribbons

16*   (185)

from the classic shades of Yale, thought quite beyond the comprehension of *women-folk.*

Elsie's mother was a close reader and thinker, and could help her daughter in all her studies; but with all her mental power, Elsie remained the generous, cheerful, frank country girl, whom the maidens round about loved as well as if no superiority of effort had lifted her mentally so far above them. Nor was this admiration confined to those of her own sex. Many of the young men found their hearts warming towards the merry maiden.

George Brant, who had been to college three whole years, and had returned with clustering chestnut curls about a fine face, and who bade fair to be a marked man among them as a merchant's clerk at Smithville, was among the number of her admirers. There was much wondering among the gossips; but they could decide nothing. Elsie met him without blushes, laughed and talked with him without visible emotion, until he married Susie Underhill, and put an end to all speculations on the subject.

Half a dozen others had been known to call at Farmer's Castle, or to ride home with Miss Elsie; but she was so genial and kind, and withal so entirely proper, that not a dish of rumor could be concocted from these occasions. Some people have a wonderful faculty of

> "Keeping something to themselves
> They scarcely tell to any."

And so had Elsie Magoon.

Mrs. Deacon Hill, who was the head of the house

up on the bend, and who has been on several occasions introduced to the reader, deserves a more explicit notice.

"There's the Deacon and his wife going down to the ford," said Alice, one day, as she saw the well-filled market-wagon rolling by, in which were seated the pair alluded to.

"Troth! thin, it's different you should be saying it," said Hitty Talford, who was busy shelling peas for dinner. "It's Mrs. Hill and her man; for sure it's. herself will make every bargain, from the butter-rolls in her tin bucket to the white calf that's tied to the back end of the wagon."

"Maybe she can do it better than her lord and master," answered Alice, with a cheery laugh.

"And, faith! she does that. Lord and master! Why, bless ye! it's niver a thought he gets into his head only from stubbornness that he does n't be taking from her. Not that I'd be saying the Deacon's not good enough, in his way; but it's a wonderful smart woman the Deacon's wife is, if she ha'n't got no larning. She's only ignorant on the outside; for, saving your mother and Miss Elsie, there's not her match in town. Och! but she's a great hand to make money, and more nor that, Miss Alice, have n't I knowed her these twenty years, and thin niver a word could she read in her Bible, and now she can talk with the ministers like a book; and that Fred of hers is the natest young gintleman I've seen in this country, and, sure I am, Miss Elsie here will not be disputing me there."

Elsie, who had just entered the kitchen, blushed scarlet, and old Hitty's keen eye caught the signal; but Alice saw nothing.

Indeed, so full of generosity and kindly gallantry was Fred Hill, that he had become a universal favorite, whom yet they only thought of as the very best and brightest boy at all their parties and merry-makings; the one whose music and mirth infused all the rest with joy and gladness.

But Fred Hill and Elsie Magoon had been especial friends since the days of their childhood, and at length, unsuspected by any, so quiet were they in their demonstrations of affection, and so universal in their kindness to all, a deep and abiding love filled their hearts to the exclusion of all other guests.

But Fred had left the neighborhood years ago, and gone to California or somewhere, nobody knew where, nor did anybody know exactly why. There were rumors afloat of a quarrel between him and his father; for, as old Hitty said, the Deacon had one point in his character as unyielding as a knot of live oak,—stubbornness. When he had once taken a position, a thing he did not often do, he adhered to it as if to convince the world that he could have a will of his own sometimes; and the more Mrs. Hill tried to change him, the more persistently he refused to be changed.

Something was certainly wrong between the Deacon and Fred; for the former always flew into a passion when mention was made of the absent boy. The workmen told of a spiteful quarrel, and that Fred had struck the old man; but who could believe such a story of one so far above his fellows in morals and manners? For, though Mrs. Deacon Hill did hold the reins usually, she drove with a steady hand, and there were no better boys and girls than those she had disciplined.

Fred's disappearance had been but a seven days' wonder, and scarcely that; for half the boys in Smithville had gone, and mothers were too full of anxious care about their own to talk much of others.

If Elsie's heart was sad, no one knew it. Her life was full of duty and earnestness.

CHAPTER XIX

" ISN'T she magnificent?"

" Rather so; but I fancy I have seen girls just as fine-looking; that old flame of yours, for instance, who used to gallop by your side so splendidly, on the beach .at Newport last August."

" Pshaw! that pale, die-away beauty? she's not a circumstance—should n't be talked of in the same day with this flying 'Die Vernon.'"

" I presume this one will wear the ribbons till another turns up, who will probably as far surpass the present meteor as this one does the star of last season."

" Eliza Wetherell was a beauty, no mistake; and when well dressed in the height of fashion, with the glow of excitement and emulation on her brow, she was not to be treated with contempt. But hers was a languid beauty, that won your—what shall I call it?—pity comes too near contempt."

" Won your tenderness, and made you feel protective."

" Yes, that 's it exactly; I used to love to feel the pressure of her pretty foot on my hand, as I lifted her into her saddle, like a fairy bird; and then to ride by her side holding her rein, and ready to take her under my arm, and screen her from all harm, if her steed but dared to step awry. I tell you, Walters, there is a kind of soft, sentimental pleasure in the society of a woman who never has a will of her own, and who seems to hang upon you as if you had in your hand the power of giving and taking life, or happiness, at will. But there is a bold up-springing joy, that stirs my whole manhood into a kind of idolatrous enthusiasm, when I see such a woman as *that.* See how she rules that high-mettled steed! By George! I wish I knew who she is."

"Here are our horses, and if you are so extremely anxious, you can make chase, and follow 'the Lady of the Black Plume,' till you find in exactly what lofty castle she hangs her chapeau, and how many bold retainers wait her bidding."

"Agreed. And, by the way, she is going our road: so let us be off."

The foregoing conversation was held between two young men, who stood ready to mount their horses, at the Smithville hotel, one pleasant Indian-summer afternoon, in the year 18—. The person who had elicited so much admiration from Albert Lincoln, was a tall, finely-formed lady, who, in a long, gray riding-skirt, and hat of the same shade, surmounted by a black ostrich plume, emerged from a dry-goods store across the way. Her habit was gracefully gathered in one hand, while the other held a light riding-whip. She stepped to a beautiful black steed that stood pawing the earth, nearly opposite, and taking the reins in her left hand, and laying the right upon the horn of her saddle, she sprang into her place as easily as if she were stepping over the threshold;

adjusted herself neatly on the saddle, and with a snap of her finger to a splendid greyhound that lay near by, horse, rider, and hound dashed away at a rapid pace up the steep hill that skirted the village, when the two friends, Albert Lincoln and Charles Walters, mounted their horses and followed the same path.

They were to remain in town over Sunday, and had called for horses to enjoy a ride up the valley.

The two young gentlemen were travelling agents for large firms in New York, one of dry-goods, and the other of hardware ; and were, just now, spending a few days at the *town* of Smithville, as we may now call it, having outgrown that stage in which the Westerner would call it a village.

Both were sons of members of the firms, well educated, and well-bred, and were for the first time enjoying a trip through the rich and rapidly improving States west of the Alleghanies.

As they reached the top of the hill, which they ascended more slowly than did the charger of the lady, they looked off down the main road, but could see nothing of the object of pursuit.

"Lost! lost! lost!" said Walters, running his eye along the level road as it skirted the river's brink for two or three miles, in open view.

"Turned into some by-path," answered Lincoln. "Keep an eye out your side the road, and I will mine; for I am bound to follow."

They paused, to look on the landscape that lay beneath.—The water wound away, like a line of

silver, for miles, amid large farms, cultivated corn-
fields, and well-trimmed forest, interspersed with orchards and rich green meadows, which frequent fall-
rains had kept in spring-time beauty. The corn was
cut and gathered in shocks, all along the bank of the
stream, while the high hills that rose beyond, stretching their tops almost to the sky, were one bright blaze
of crimson and gold. There is no more beautiful
sight than our grand old forest-hills of the West, when
they put on their gorgeous hues at the touch of the
fatal frost.

Off, in the distance, but in full view, along the
winding of the stream, lay the rich and well-tilled
farm of Richard Magoon. His large white mansion-
house, which years ago had crowded away the cabin at
the door of which he and his wife sat when we began
our tale,—loomed up amid the surrounding forest,
like some old ancestral hall. The lines of dark ce-
dars along the garden-walks, the great weeping-wil-
lows at the gate, the huge barns, and the long sheds
for the sheep, which lay near them, looking in the
distance like huge white lilies, amid the green of the
pastures, made a scene enchantingly beautiful to the
young travellers.

"What a magnificent landscape," said Walters.
"Now, if we could spy your beauty somewhere in
the midst of it, and make her the queenly mistress
of yon 'Farmer's Castle,' we should have a romance
of the most enchanting kind."

"Ah! yes—provided I could in the meantime get
up an excuse for a call, and worm myself into an

17

invitation to spend the Sabbath under those willows, instead of sulking round all day in that abominable hotel," replied Lincoln, still peering into the deep forest that closed in the road at the foot of the hill — hoping to spy the path that had carried with it the object of his interest.

"The easiest thing in the world, Lincoln. Do you see that noble flock of sheep? Let us ride up to the farm-house and make inquiries for our friends of Philadelphia. You know they bade us keep an eye out for them, among the wool-growers."

"Good! as far as it goes, Charley; but an inquiry as to sheep may not win for us an invitation for a Sunday's tarry."

"Let me alone for that; these Western farmers are whole-souled, noble men,—touch them in the right spot, and they are at home with you at once. Tell them straight out you don't like towns and cities, are out on a journey West, to ruralize, and would like to make yourself at home a day or two, and, my word for it, you'll find yourself one of the family for as many days or weeks as you please."

"Yes, and find yourself *ten miles* from the '*Belle of the Forest*,' with nothing to repay you for your rashness but the company of a man, who will bore you to death about his crop, chew tobacco by the handful, and be-spatter the porch-floor for a yard around, whip two or three white-headed urchins to bed before sundown, and be yourself, nine times out of ten, invited to take a hand at paring apples for the old lady to string, in which employment you will pass the long evenings, and he made acquainted in the meantime with all the village gossip and neighborhood scandal for miles around."

"Where did you learn so thoroughly the minutiæ of a Western farm-house visit, pray?"

"Oh! from the newspapers; you know our Eastern travellers are fond of writing of Western adventures. But see here," and his horse was brought up so short, that he reared upon his haunches. "Here away, into the dark forest, has sped our beauty. Do you not see the tracks of her steed, as she turned here into the wood?"

The path which had nearly been passed ere discovered, turned almost at right angles with the road, and was screened by a clump of tall pawpaws, which interlaced their branches overhead. It led off into a dense forest, dropping back from the river to the hill, at the foot of which ran a bubbling, fretting little brook, that came dancing down, now running over pebbly bars, now hiding away among the brush, and then foaming and dashing past the little rocky falls, that here and there let it drop a few feet at a time, until it reached the bank of the river, and mingled its clear waters with the silvery stream.

Up this bridle-path, overhung with wild grape-vines, had the mysterious lady of the black plume evidently gone. "Westward ho! who'll follow?" shouted Lincoln to his companion, who had now shot several yards ahead, as he turned his horse into the path, and dashed off at a rapid pace.

"Hang the fellow!" exclaimed Walters. "He is

perfectly beside himself, with that fast young lady. However, I may as well follow;" and wheeling round, he soon came up with the determined pursuer.

They journeyed on, as nearly together as possible, chatting gayly of their adventure, and the unrivalled beauty of the forest-path, which was almost as dark, with its interlocked trees and running vines, as if it were closely roofed over; crossing and recrossing the little brook, till at last, after a ride of a mile or two, they emerged suddenly upon a clearing of about an acre. The brook in front of the clearing leaped down a pretty waterfall of some four or five feet, and then circled round a tiny garden, made almost an island, amid the forest. In the centre of this garden, hemmed in by a rude bush-fence, stood a still ruder log-cabin, so completely covered with and held together by a wild mountain creeper, that one might have fancied it of marble, as its whitewashed walls glistened here and there through the green. The bush-fence about it was completely covered by a drapery of sweetbrier, bitter-sweet, and grape-vines. The golden bells of the bitter-sweet,—the scarlet pods of the sweetbrier, contrasting with the rich clusters of wild grapes still ripening in the early frost, all blending together, formed a picturesque hedge, which answered a threefold purpose, as a fence, an ornament, and a protection to the cottage from the bleak winds which swept down the valley in the winter days. The sun was sinking low; but just where it went down behind the hill, and where a deep ravine parted the earth, the tall forest-trees had been cut away, and let the glow of departing day fall full upon the garden. It was not laid out after an elaborate plan, yet it was full to the brim of beauty and use, and its very want of exactness and style rendered it attractive; its walks without a weed; its borders of violets, pinks, and primroses; its varied brightness in its rich profusion of autumn flowers; its vines, its rustic arbors, and, not the least, its well cultured vegetables, made it a thing to be looked at again and again with admiration. The young men involuntarily reined in their horses, and stood still, in wonder and amazement at the unexpected vision, as it lay there glowing in brightness; the sun falling upon it, through the break in the hill, gave it warmth and cheerfulness for nearly an hour after the rest of the valley fell into the shade.

"Upon my word, Walters," exclaimed Lincoln, in a low voice, as the horses stood side by side, "we are in luck this afternoon; this is worth going ten miles to see."

"Aye, and more too," answered the other, dropping his voice still lower, and looking over the hedge to the other side of the garden. "For if I mistake not, there is the 'lady of the black plume.'"

As the words left his lips, the lady in question emerged from a grape-vine arbor made of rude poles, with her hands full of rich clusters of grapes, followed by an aged woman. The latter was of medium size, with a face full, round, and rosy as sixteen; but the snow-white hair upon the brow, and the deep lines upon the face, told the story of her years.

The pair did not discover the strangers on horse-
17*

back, and kept on their chat as they neared the house, and sat down on a bench under the protecting shade of a fine apple-tree, that stood in full bearing before the door.

"Now, grandma," said the sweet voice of the young lady, "you must lend me one of the little straw baskets that you braid; they are just the thing to lay my grapes in, and I can hang it on the horn of my saddle, and take them home safely to father and mother."

"And sure I'll do that same for ye, darlint. There's niver a basket in the cabin, but ye should be as welcome till it as the sunshine to the corn in a cold June morning."

And the old lady entered the cottage and brought out a straw basket, made by hand, and neatly stained with barks and berries.

"Oh! not that one, grandmother; that is your very prettiest. Let me have one that is older and plainer; one that you have not taken so much pains with."

"And shouldn't I be bringing out my best? for sure the best is not good enough for the likes of ye; for it's yeself that saved my Willy from the dead ruin that was coming upon him, and turned the black purgatory that was yawning upon me, till a blessed heaven upon earth;—and God's blessing presarve ye for that same, to the longest day of your life."

"Oh! it was not I grandmother, that saved Willy; you must thank the great God above, for that."

"And true for ye, I do. There's no hour of the day goes by, but I'm muttering the prayers to Him. But sure it was yeself that he set to the work. Och!

Miss Elsie, darlint, it was many a lang, lang night, I lay here in my bed, twenty years gone, and heard the 'Old Still-House' screeching and groaning, down there in the valley, and its voice went through my heart like a sharp knife, for I knew *he* was there; and then I would go in and hear poor Betty a sobbing and groaning in her bed, all for him; but they 're gone now. Oh! darlint, it is hard, when them we love best takes to bad ways; and sure I 'd none then to love but the two that I brought over the salt seas wid me."

"Are Willy and Jenny all you have left?" said the young lady, endeavoring to change the current of the old woman's thought.

"It 's the truth ye 're spaking, my sweet lady. They 're all that 's left me here; but I 've a company of them in the bright heaven above. But as I was saying, darlint,—Betty used to lie rolling in her bed, and Willy down at the holler, and the little ones without bread, mores of times without shoes and stockings till their feet, and he a-drinking. Och! Miss Elsie, but ye made Better Days for us all, when ye put out that fire, and poured that devil's-breath into the creek. True for ye's, my leddy, if there 's a better seat in heaven than the rest, it 'll be God's will ye should fill that same, for giving the sunshine of life and peace back to throubled hearts, here on earth."

"I see you keep the spinning-wheel going, grandma; you spin your day's work these pleasant autumn days." And again Elsie tried a new theme.

"Oh! yes! as long as the thread of life is spared me, I'll be drawing the flax from the distaff; if all the cuts I have rolled and lopped since my head was white as the blaze on the rock, were linked thegither, it wad make a rope that would swing me back, all the long way across the ocean to the banks of Bally Shannon. Ten childer, Miss Elsie, twice ten grand-childer; and poor ould granny has outlived them all. I have none left me now but Willy and Jenny;" and the old lady bent her white head, and wiped the fast-rolling tears upon her checked linen apron; and then, as if ashamed of even the appearance of complaint, she started up, with a glow of cheerfulness upon her face.

"It's your pardon I should be asking, shure, for giving way; for have n't you scattered all the throubles and let down the sunlight into my heart; just as Willy's axe let the sunset thro' the ould forest there, to cheer me in my bit of a garden.

And stooping, the old woman filled her basket with grapes, all the while talking garrulously of the past in her own graphic style, between the Irish and the Western dialect. The young men were in close proximity to the speakers, and could see and hear them, but, unless the pair turned directly round, could not be seen; and they now cast about them, by signs and winks, for a place of retreat.

Two or three cows straying leisurely homeward, enabled them to turn their horses without being heard into the shade of a great tulip-tree, that overhung the waterfall, just in time to escape the notice of Elsie as she left the cottage.

"No, no, grandmother, you must not come down the path to-night, to see me mount Barney,—you will be tired. There! not another bunch in that basket; you must save them for yourself and Jenny, in the winter. Come, Clo," she added, again snapping her finger to her greyhound.

"Indade, indade, Miss Elsie, you must let me see ye spring into your saddle, for my ould eyes have never seen the likes since I left swate Ireland. Och! but the fine leddies that usen to come over from 'merrie England,' (the quality, you know,) to go a-hawking and hunting over the old manor, could do the likes; but it was never a one of them, but wad 'n' hid the light of her eyes in yer presence."

"Oh! grandmother, you flatter me—comparing me to the grand lords and ladies of noble blood."

"Niver a bit, niver a bit, Elsie, darlint; it's no blarney to be calling ye the noblest of them all."

And the old woman leaned over the stile, and clapped her wrinkled hands in an ecstasy of delight, as the maiden again sprang into her saddle, and with a wave of the hand to the kind old creature she was leaving, bounded out of sight, down the winding path.

The gentlemen immediately left their cover, and prepared to follow; but seeing granny Alison still at the stile, they turned to her and asked the favor of a few grapes.

"As many as ye likes, as many as ye likes; providen ye don't be tearing the vines, which would anger the young lady mightily, for it's a big spot in her heart the place holds, to be sure."

"And who may that young lady be?" asked Lincoln.

"And sure it's only a stranger in these parts, wad be asking after the name of Elsie Magoon, the angel next to Mary Mother hersilf, in kindness to the poor and needy."

"Indeed! mother, that is high praise. Does she live here about?"

"Only over the brook there away, where ye see the fine white house upon the hill. And but for her mother before her, there would never be a better creature than she in the world."

"May we ask what she does that is so wonderful?"

"And ye may thin; for my ould tongue will niver be weary waggin her praise while I stay. Who was it but her that stopped the croaking of that old 'Still-house,'—who but her and her mother, who are like the blessed Trinity, one and the same—that led ould Truman to be sober,—who but her found places for Tony O'Brien's orphans,—who but her that got up Sunday schools, and temperance-meetings? Lord love you, gintlemen, it's mysilf that would walk to the village in a January night, to hear her plading with the young men to let the bottles alone. Wasn't it the black throuble the people were all in, her father none the best of them,—and hasn't she let the bright day in upon us all? Och! it's not a callant you can meet in ten miles roun', but will tell of Elsie, the darlint, who has made for us all the 'better days.'"

The gentlemen received the grapes, and offered her money, which she indignantly refused, asserting that as long as she got freely, she would give freely to any one that would ask her "dacently." With a promise to call again, they followed the path the maiden had taken, and after a ride of another half mile, came again into the main road, just by the fine avenue of sugar-maples, that led up from the gate under the willows to the noble farm-house once owned by Richard Magoon.

We say once; for although another five years have flitted by, since Elsie became the owner of the fine old farm,—although the debts are paid, and Richard is again a sober, noble-hearted man,—he has never consented to become the owner, or to hold the deed of the farm.

From the time that Richard Magoon had lain so long prostrate with fever he had never been well. Year after year wore on, and still he was weak and tremulous, often entirely prostrate from diseases resulting from his long-continued excesses. Hence he felt no disposition to take from his wife or daughter the power of controlling the estate, in case a sudden death or emergency should carry him off. Yet his counsel had always been asked, and his wish and will were sacred. Elsie had grown to be a staff to him in his old age; and the quiet young girl, who up to the age of twenty had been known only as a modest maiden, at her post of duty in the household, had become to the whole neighborhood a model of strength and wisdom, walking side by side with her mother in an earnest and useful life.

As the two young men rode leisurely up to the house of the Magoons, Richard was in the lane, driving a flock of sheep to their shelter for the night. As Lincoln attempted to force his horse through the flock, the foremost of them commenced leaping the shadow of an oak that lay across the road. The horse took fright, and wheeling suddenly, became unmanageable. Richard sprang forward and caught him by the bridle. A conversation ensued, and ended in an invitation to enter, which was gladly accepted.

Tea was waiting for Elsie and Richard, and the strangers were cordially invited to partake.

" We have plenty, my friends, such as it is, in our farmer's way;—don't mention your horses.—Jack, put away the gentlemen's ponies, rub them down well, and give them plenty. Make yourself at home, Mr.—what shall I call you?"

" Mr. Walters,—Mr. Lincoln."

"My wife, Mrs. Magoon,—Elsie, my daughter,— Alice, Mary,—George,—all Magoons. Gentlemen, be seated; what might have been a misfortune to you, may be a pleasant piece of good-fortune to us all."

And so, in the most friendly manner, the young men were made welcome.

CHAPTER XX

A H, gentle reader! Don't think we are going to plunge you into a love-story, full, to the end of the last page, of trials and perplexities, odd happenings, and the most curious things coming to pass just at the right instant, because we have introduced two city gents to our beautiful girls: for we shall do no such thing; we don't like stories all love, a bit better than we should like a dinner all preserves and cream.

Love, to be worth having at all, should come in the natural way, on common-sense principles, and made firm as the everlasting hills, on some substantial basis—such as goodness and usefulness—not upon the set of a plume, or the shape of a bust; and though we have let our young gentlemen follow the dashing lady to her house, through the wild paths of the green-wood, we have no more idea of dashing Albert Lincoln head and ears into a love scrape than we have of giving Charley Walters a douse in the same subtle fluid.

"Falling in love!" What does it mean? Do people come down, tumble headlong into a vat or pool, from which they have to be drawn, heels foremost, to save their souls and bodies? Wish somebody would tell us, why to be infused with a tender and ennobling passion, should be called "falling" into

the thing.   But nobody will tell us, so let us follow
the fortunes of our new-found friends.

Happy they were to receive, and ready to accept
the cordial invitation of Richard Magoon : and soon
found themselves enjoying, with infinite zest, the
wholesome, home-made luxuries of Mrs. Magoon's
tea-table.

She was as naturally a good housekeeper, as she
was naturally a noble, thoughtful, orderly woman ;
and though her whole life had been full of other duties
to her neighbors and the world, she had never dreamed
in her philosophy, that she must therefore desert any
of those interesting and holy cares which become life's
richest blessings to the true heart.

"You are strangers in this neighborhood, I think,
gentlemen?" asked Richard.

"We arrived at Smithville this morning, sir, and
as we had business that would detain us a few days,
we were trying to pass time as pleasantly as possible,
reconnoitring in your pleasant valley, and were out
on our first trip of observation."

"And how do you like us?" asked Richard, in his
blunt way.

"Your farms are splendid, and I own I am surprised at the progress and cultivation I see all about
me."

"We were new and wild thirty years ago, gentlemen, when I felled with my own hand the first tree
in those broad meadows below.   But I dare say we
have made some improvement since then."

"We have always heard the West spoken of as a

new country," said Walters, " I was not prepared to find it so nearly on a level with good old New England."

"The West," answered Alice, with a silvery laugh, "the West is ' over the hills, and far away;' — *we* are '*way down East*'— here, on the Wahoo. Smithville is only an offshoot of Boston, and should be as near like it as the son is to the father. It is only when you get out on the plains, that you find the natives."

So went on the pleasant chat until the meal ended; the young ladies led the way to the farm-house parlor, which was brilliantly lighted, disclosing an open piano in the corner, some fine old pictures upon the wall, a well-filled book-case, and a brilliant carpet, of home-made stripes, upon the floor. It was a cool September evening, and the motherly care of Mrs. Magoon had laid a bright fire upon the ample hearthstone, that scattered the dampness, and made the room still more inviting and cheerful. Elsie had thrown off her travelling dress, and arrayed herself in a plain brown silk, with a small white band, pinned at the throat. Her rich auburn hair hung in wavy ringlets around her rosy, healthful face, and her dark-blue eyes glowed in the fire-light more lustrously blue than usual. Lincoln thought her beautiful; but the fashionable world would not have given the Belle of the Forest, praise. It might even have denounced her as masculine, because there was something about her so self-reliant and strong.

"Masculine?" How can a woman be masculine? Can the face and form the Creator has given her, be

anything but womanly? Are fine, physical proportions, health and strength, to be noted disgraceful?
Are features that bear the stamp of a great soul to
be derided, because they are those of a woman?
Shall such a woman be called *masculine?* — as if to
manhood belonged all the strength and glory of the
human race? Oh! captious, sneering, tyrannical
world, how hast thou wronged and made to suffer
the truest and best womanly hearts. The taunt of
masculinity has subdued many a girlish genius, and
made her sink into listless indolence, rather than
brave the odium of being thought mannish, while
she possessed the power of performing works that
would do honor to the sterner sex.

Alice, the second sister, was beautiful at first sight,
but so soft and tender in her expression of form and
face as never to jeopardize her reputation. And yet
she was strong and brave in her own way. Mary
was a very fairy,— with her soft blue eyes and golden
hair, and her form light and agile as a sylph. One
could see at a glance that hers was not a heroic nature,
that she was not even self-sustaining, and needed
the protecting care of a stronger hand and heart.

Such were the three sisters as they sat before that
pleasant evening fire in the old farm-house, — each
fitted to fill a distinct mission in life, — neither
promising the power or capability of filling the place
of the other.

Elsie's mind took in at a glance the far-off as well
as the near. She knew in the spring time the needs
of the harvest, and read in the necessities of to-day

the possibilities of to-morrow, of the next year, of fifty years to come. Strong-hearted and strong-handed, she yet bore within herself elements of the tenderest and kindliest emotions. She loved to plant the rose-tree, to prune and nurture it into beauty, and to drink in its dewy fragrance; to bend over the wild violets in the spring time; to hunt the forget-me-nots in the meadow, and listen to the love carol of the wild bird. She would have loved, as other young girls do, if one had ever met her capable of concentrating the sunlight of her soul upon himself. But now those rays fell like the morning sunbeams on all the creatures of her Father's love and mercy. She knew, too, that strong hearts and hands were needed among women, as well as men, in the thorough-fares of life, and already had she seen and felt that she was fitted for her place. She delighted in culti-vating human souls; even as she would take the wild rose from the forest and graft upon its stem the lux-uriance and fragrance of the cultivated flower; so would she take the heart, bedded in the shadows of ignorance, superstition, or vice, and place it in the genial soil of truth, where the dews and showers of love, the light of reason and thought, might warm and freshen it into a flower of beauty, for society and for God. Was this masculine? Was she less a woman for all this noble thought and earnest action? Less a woman, because she had not made self the motive power of all her actions, preferring that easy life which most women lead, to the work of making hun-dreds wiser and better for all life's duties, through

18*

her ministrations? Was she less a housekeeper, because she was capable of being more than one? Was it wrong for her not to become a wife, while she felt herself uncalled to that post of duty,— while she saw clearly that a greater good could be accomplished *by her*, with untied hands, and untouched heart? Should she be branded an *old maid*, because twenty-five summers had kept the roses fresh upon her cheeks, and the gossips could point to no grave that held a buried love; to no man, who, in his fickleness or pride, had broken her heart? Because she was not willing, like most women about her, to become a fixture in some household, and walk the same round of duty in contentment till the gray hair should silver her brow, and the grave claim its own? Alice — Mary — and a thousand others, were fitted for that calm, loving work. Were there not enough such as these, who had no taste for the duties so grand to her, that the world could not spare one, for the mission which she felt called to fill?.

Oh! World, World, wilt thou never learn that all women were not made for the same duties,—as are not all men?

But while we moralize, the new acquaintances chat on.

"We are to have a little gathering of friends and neighbors this evening, gentlemen, and shall be truly glad to have you among our circle, if not engaged to return to Smithville," said Elsie.

"We have no engagements, Miss Magoon," replied Lincoln, rising as if to depart, "but will not crowd ourselves upon your hospitalities."

"Not going?" said Richard, entering at the moment; "by no means; you are welcome till Monday; and, honestly, I believe we can make you as comfortable as they can down at the 'White Horse'; your ponies shall be returned to their stable; so make yourselves contented."

"But your daughters are expecting friends," interposed Walters.

"Only a little gathering—a society—a something, I hardly know what. In old times we had chopping-bees, log-rollings, squirrel-hunts, spinning-bees, apple-cuttings, husking-frolics, and quiltings, to bring the folks together once in a while, to keep up neighborhood sociability, and the boys and girls out of mischief. But since the introduction of parlors, pictures, and pianos, we have to plan something better."

"No; not better, dear father, than those were in their time; only, as the editors would say, better suited to the 'spirit of the age,'" said Elsie, laughing.

"Yes, that will do. So then our young people have a 'society for improvement,' which meets every Saturday night, when the week's labor is done, at the house of its members, where we all join, old and young, in trying to do each other good, and to make each other happy."

"A grand idea," said Lincoln, trying to look pleased, while at heart he was secretly vexed at the thought of a 'society for improvement' on the banks of the Wahoo, instead of a pleasant evening with the interesting young ladies of the farm-house. . . . . . .

"Thank you, thank you, daughter," said the father,

as Elsie placed his favorite easy-chair in the centre of
the room, and seated him in it.

"There, father dear, is your place; you know you
are to be our monitor this evening."

"Ah! true; I had forgotten I held that post of
honor."

"We shall have a large party this evening, I fancy;
I hear merry voices now in the avenue.   Mr. Lincoln
and Mr. Walters will excuse us while we meet and welcome our guests;" and Elsie and Mary left the room,
while Alice held Walters listening to her merry jokes.

"I like to see the old and young mingling together
without restraint," said Richard, addressing Lincoln.
"I believe it the greatest safeguard against vice.   The
old people do a twofold work by joining in the sports
of their children — they keep their own souls full of
freshness and charity, while they curb the exuberance
of animal life in the young, which, when left to itself,
is apt to carry them too far.   I think the cold, austere
religions of this country have done great evil, by
denying to their followers the right to enjoy a proper
degree of mirth, thus throwing most of the reasonable
amusements of life into the hands of those who have
no religion at all.   Or rather, I should say, a wrong
theology has done this; for theology and religion are
very different things.   Some of the best and wisest
people I ever knew, and who lived nearest to the
true and undefiled religion of the olden time, were
condemned by the Christian world as infidels, because
they acknowledged no theological creed.   And that
theology that cannot discern between the use and abuse
of healthful and enlivening amusement, does not

deserve the name of religion; it is but an offshoot of that old Pagan superstition which worshipped God through self-abnegation, suffering, and sorrow; failing to read aright the great book of nature, which everywhere lies open to their view, with its lessons of cheerfulness and love."

The room was now rapidly filling with guests; fifty or sixty were soon assembled, and friendly greetings, jokes and mirth filled up the first half hour, then a selected choir sang, with great expression, several English and Scotch ballads, accompanied by Mary and Alice on the piano, while a young man from the town played his violin in concert.

Our city beaux exchanged bewildered looks as they saw the white fingers of the country maidens fly over the keys, and listened to the thrilling sounds of song from Elsie and her sister.

A question for discussion was next introduced, and each in his own familiar way expressed an opinion upon it. Frequent bursts of applause, or quiet merriment, gave token of the wit and originality of the talkers; and the young ladies found it not difficult to puzzle those who had spent years in lyceums and debates. After an hour of this free and easy chatting, the old topic was dismissed, and a new proposed for the next meeting.

And then came a discussion over apples, pears, and grapes, from the garden and orchard of the farmer — no one refusing to take part in this — when the meeting again composed itself to listen to a tale, from the talented Miss L——, who had been appointed to prepare an original story, poem, or essay, for the evening.

CHAPTER XXI

M ISS L—— was the teacher of the Smithville Female Seminary—a lady of fine educational attainments, and though past the heyday of youth, was neither a garrulous nor disagreeable "old maid."

She was neither tall nor slim, precise nor prim, as some persons would have us believe that women of that condition always are. Her full form, round, rosy face, and sparkling black eye, were significant of a joyous spirit, which had found its happiness along the way-sides of life, as naturally as the sky-lark finds hers amid the clustering clover and in the common air.

On the present occasion she did not flush, nor fool-ishly excuse herself as having nothing worth while to read, but took her chair by a light stand, and with a clear, musical voice, read as follows.

THE FIRST STEAMBOAT ON THE WATERS OF THE MUSKINGUM.

It happened to be my good fortune, ladies and gentlemen, to be training "young ideas how to shoot," in the beautiful little town of Marietta, in the year 1820. Marietta, you all know, is located at the junction of the Muskingum River with the La Belle Riviére, of the old French settlers, or, in plain Eng-lish, the beautiful river Ohio, and is famous for two

(214)

things. First, as being a place of mounds, covert-ways, dykes, ditches, squares, and embankments, or, as familiarly called, "ancient works and fortifications," supposed to have been made by a people far more cultivated than the Indians who roamed the forest, when the oldest civilized inhabitant first pitched his tent in the beautiful valley.

Secondly, it was famed as being the first point upon which the Ohio Company landed, after leaving Pittsburg, or old Fort Du Quesne, at the head-waters of navigation; and consequently, the first settlement of Ohio was made at this same town.

To me it was famous in another regard; that the early inhabitants, unlike most Western town-makers, had been too sensible to crowd themselves uncomfortably; and had in laying out theirs, provided a good common, wide streets, preserved their 'ancient works,' and left each landholder a lot large enough for a garden and door-yard. This liberality of land is often a matter of wonder to travellers among us; but I suppose our grandsires had not then dreamed of a half-acre lot west of the Alleghanies ever being worth half a million; or that they should live to see cities and towns strewn in grandeur and wealth, to the very slopes of the Rocky Mountains.

Ah, it was a delightful winter, that! Every day brought to me new treasures of history from the early times of this interesting people. I lingered many a day in their beautiful cemetery, where slept the last earthly remains of their leader, old General Rufus Putnam, who brought his gallant band so bravely through the wilderness, and stood steadfastly by them through the varied and sore trials of border life.

There, too, at the foot of a great mound, reared by the hands of a lost race, slept old Commodore Abraham Whipple, who, as his epitaph tells us, fired the first gun of the Revolution ; and performed the still bolder feat of taking the first ship, or barge, down the waters of the Ohio and Mississippi into the Gulf of Mexico ; a daring deed in those days, when the Indian hunting-grounds lay nearly the entire distance on either side.

Many a winter evening sped away, almost unheeded, as I listened to the tales of old Judge Cutler, of the valiant deeds of those valiant men, of their nobleness and courage ; of the heroism of the women, their unshaken faith and hope through the seven years' war, and their garrison life; tales of the hunt, and chase, and victory ; of the savage treachery and bloody massacre; of their losses and crosses, their hunger and toil, and their triumph at last, when they arose more than conquerors, from the conflict of years.

There, too, I heard the tale of the Fairy Isle, where Blennerhasset and his beautiful wife made their Eden home, ere a wild ambition swept over it, and left it all blackness and ruin.

These stories became to me as household words. Would that I could tarry to-night to give a worthy tribute to each.   From the Alleghanies to the buffalo-beats of Nebraska, every native-born Western man and woman owes these old settlers a debt of gratitude and love, for teaching the world how strong and brave the human heart can be.

But the one great topic of interest at the time of my residence among the people, was the new steam-boat building at the river-side, which was the first experiment of the kind ever tried there. Its builder was Capt. John Greene, born on the banks of the Muskingum, who had long followed its waters as a keel-boatman. The name of the trim little craft was the *Rufus Putnam*, after the memorable founder of this new world.

Many were the prophecies of failure. The "old fogies" of that day were as genuine antiques, as the same class of fossils of the present day; and shook their heads as ominously over any innovations upon the old order. But for all their glowering looks and dark sayings, Capt. Greene kept on the even tenor of his way, and accomplished his work. As the crowning feat of his temerity, he advertised that the "Rufus Putnam" would make a trip to Zanesville, in the month of March, and take, free of charge, any of the old settlers on the banks of the river. People did not so easily leave home then as now; and when the time came there were no more to accept the kind invitation, than could be accommodated on a craft of less than one hundred and fifty tons.

A steamboat upon the winding waters of the Mus-kingum? It was impossible! The man was crazed! He would run his prow into the crooked banks, he would stave her on a snag, get aground on the bars, or blow up, as had the "Washington," a few years before!

19

But Capt. G—— was not to be turned from his purpose by all their croaking. He had walked the crooked stream for years, with his shoulder to the setting pole, and stood with his hand upon the helm through storm and dangers. He knew it thoroughly, and he had no fears. So when the spring winds came, softening the icy chains, and setting the brooks and rills free; bringing down the gentle showers, and swelling the buds of the buckeye and red-bud, and the Muskingum rose half-banks to welcome his enterprise,—he announced the day and hour of his departure.

The fires in the sugar camps were not yet extinguished, nor had the swallows and bluebirds been wooed back to their old haunts, by the green boughs of the willows; though here and there a blue violet was peeping to see if the icicles were all gone, and wild anemonies in sunny nooks whispered of the "good time coming."

On the day fixed, a loud-mouthed cannon, posted upon her prow, told the people for miles around that the "Putnam" was on her way, and would call at their doors and take a breathing-spell, while they tied on cloaks and bonnets, and got ready to join the jovial party. . . . . .

In a long bend of the river, six miles above Marietta, called "Rainbow," by the old pioneers, from its resemblance to an arch; on the inner side of the curve, and hidden in the beautiful vale which it hugged in its embrace, were located several families of old settlers, who had lived through the trials and dangers of the Indian war, and who, as soon as the peace was declared, and the garrison opened its doors, had gone forth with their families, and settled on their farms in this beautiful area, surrounded by high hills, and bordered by the stream.

"Shall we go?" asked "uncle W——," as the loud report of the cannon came booming through the hills; but the smoke rolled up from his sugar camp, and the plough stood in the furrow, and he turned to his husbandry and smiled,—he could not be tempted away.

"Shall we go?" asked Frank of his father, a brave old veteran of the Revolution, who had lost one limb in battle, but was "worth as much as a well man yet." It was he, old Capt. Jonathan Devol, who built the first floating-mill on the waters of Muskingum, that gave bread to the settlers. As the "Putnam" poured out its salute before his door, and the band played the "Star-Spangled Banner," he hobbled out upon his cane, and bowed low his venerable head to the gallant Captain of the proud craft. The wind stretched out to their full size and length the stars and stripes that floated from her prow, and waved their recognition to the salute of the old soldier.

"Let us go," said Israel Putnam, a lineal descendant of the venerable Pomfret hero, — "let us go, Helen;" and in a moment they were flying in the light canoe to the steamer's side, while the cannon again sent out its signal.

"Shall we go?" asked the young Russells; but

the careful father and prudent mother shook their heads; how could they decide which of the half-dozen beautiful girls, or industrious boys, should leave the farm and its labors. On went the boat. The loud salute was fired before a brick mansion. Hats were flung high, and handkerchiefs waved, and the boat passed on. Now they were at the semi-circle that enclosed the farm of Col. Joseph Barker, the beautiful spot which the English novelist, Murray, has called Mooshanna.

"Shall we go?" asked the daughters, with beating hearts, as they looked down, from their home on the bluff, at the flying steamer.

But the old Colonel shook his head, as if not stirred by the excitement which called others from their homes to line the banks and wave their cheers to the flying stranger.

"Pho, pho!" said he, "can't you see it from here? I have seen it at Marietta; it's nothing but a steam-boat!"

And he hummed his tune, and worked away with a drawing-knife at a hoop for the rain-barrel. But what troubled his eyes just then?

"Plague take the dust!" he exclaimed, as he drew out his bandana from the pocket of his home-made, brown, hunting-shirt. He wiped his eyes again and again; the dust would not away. Ah! it was the dust and cobwebs of time that troubled him; of old memories, of early hardships, of dangers, toils and death; of friends long gone, linked to the present by every success and every triumph.

His heart was full — full to the brim, of those old stirring times; and, welling up they ran over at his eyes. Memories of days when he was young, when the hair upon his brow was not silvered; when he roamed the dense forest, rifle in hand, and peered cautiously for the savage foe behind every tree and fallen log; when the panther lay crouched in the path, and the rattlesnake coiled itself by the wayside, and the wild wolf howled nightly upon the hills; of the days when friends and brothers went out at morn, and returned not at nightfall; when sickness and sorrow came with heavy steps, and there were none to help; when the fire swept away the toil of years, and the hopes of days to come.

But the danger had passed; the savage and the wild beast were subdued. Friends, neighbors, children, peace, prosperity and abundance had come as the reward of past perils. It was no wonder that his eyes filled with tears, and his heart beat a loud response to the spirit-stirring notes of " Hail Columbia," as they came floating over his wide meadows. He tried to keep cool under it all; but the glittering blade made tremulous motions in his hands.

Boom! went the cannon, as the steamer shot by the line that separated his field from his neighbor. On, on went the boat, circling round the bend, while he whittled away at his hoop, unwilling, like many other old men, to own, even to himself, that nature was struggling for utterance in his soul; unwilling to let her speak aloud in the language of joy and triumph.

The girls had sped away to the river-bank, and

10 *

the mother stood gazing from the window; there were memories tugging at her heart-strings, too, as Capt. Green, who was an old friend, passed the spot where the settler's cabin had stood at first; where the tall pear-tree pointed to the sky, and the great elm spread its mighty arms over an acre of soil,—where he had often moored his keel-boat, and built his camp-fire, in years long gone,—and ordered another salute in memory of those days.

The Colonel could stand no more; his horse was out in an instant; and though no Bucephalus, he knew his master's will and did it. The Colonel mounted, the enthusiasm of boyhood and the vigor of manhood seemed burning in his veins, hurling the cool gravity of age from its seat; and, grasping the reins, down the hill and across the valley he dashed, and met the gallant Captain at the upper end of the bend. The old man raised himself in his stirrups, lifted his hat on high, and gave one loud, long *huzza* that went echoing through the hills far above the din of wheels or roar of the spouting stream, and was followed almost instantly by a blast from the old cannon which made the very tree-tops tremble. The band struck up "Yankee Doodle," and gave the gray-haired pioneer a hearty cheer. On flew the boat, on flew "old grey,"—but it was in vain; the new power subdued the old,—and with a bow and another wave of his hat, the proud old farmer went back to his thoughts and his work. . . . . .

The first eight miles up the Muskingum is a fair sample of the entire journey. People rushed to the banks for miles away, to see the mighty wonder of the age. Many had never heard of a steamboat, for newspapers did not travel the world as now; and fear and terror took fast hold upon such, when they first heard the report of the great gun.

It was not the Fourth of July, nor the Twenty-Second of February, — why then should guns be fired? Timid ones were sure that the " British were coming again; " others, who heard the roar of steam, ran to their neighbors for prayers; the day of judgment might be at hand. One old lady, who had heard of the fabulous sea-serpent, fled to the hills with her grand-children, lest, like Jonah, they should be swallowed alive. An old salt suggested that a whale had lost his way, and was floundering and spouting up the fresh water of the Muskingum.

All this excitement may seem strange to those who see daily the magnificent boats of the present gliding quietly by their doors. They can have no conception of the noisy, puffing crafts of forty years ago, which often heralded themselves from a distance of four or five miles, with every revolution of the wheel; and the curiosity and wonder they created could not be equalled now, were we to see a long line of rail-cars flying by steam through the air. Less a wonder would such a phenomenon be to us, than was the " Rufus Putnam " to a majority of the settlers on the banks of the *beautiful Muskingum* in the year of our Lord 1820. . . . . .

Miss L——— closed her article amid the acclamation

of the party. Conversation followed; each of the elder members warmed up by the allusions to border life, had something of personal experience to relate; and so closed the literary entertainment which had been both new and interesting to the Eastern gentlemen.

Dancing was now called for, and the young and old joined in a cheerful country-dance, filling the hall, the parlor, and the long dining-room of the farm-house; while those who did not join in the dance chatted and walked about, and made themselves happy as best they could; and at ten o'clock the company dispersed.

"How do you like our primitive society?" asked Elsie, as Lincoln drew his chair to the fire, after the departure.

"It is admirable. I have enjoyed it exceedingly."

"I have long felt," continued Elsie, "that if we would lead the young away from folly and vice, we must give them something better in their stead. We should have little need of moral or temperance lectures, if every neighborhood would gather together, in pleasant social ways, its young men and maidens; and the old and the wise would aid in governing and guiding the appetites and passions, and regulating the amusements."

"Your idea is a novel one, Miss Magoon," said Lincoln, "and I fear you will find, after all, that the human mind is sometimes perverse, and will run its owner into ruin, despite the most earnest effort."

"True; but will not that be the case, whatever instrumentalities are used? If the young man is made happy in the society of those he loves, without any feelings of uncomfortable restraint; if he can eat and drink reasonably, laugh and sing cheerfully, chat freely and dance merrily; will he, think you, wish to visit the low grog-shop, the tavern bar-room, or the secret club-room, or the midnight ball, where vice and depravity are his companions, and sin and shame the dark shadows that follow his outgoings?"

Lincoln started. Had she read the secrets of his city life? Did she know that he was a wine-bibber, a frequenter of the club-room? He felt as if his soul were laid bare before her searching gaze.

But ere he had time to reply, Alice and Walters, with Mary and George, returned from a walk to the willows, with their friends, in the moonlight.

If the young men had dreams of fairy-girls that night, it is not strange; nor shall we own that they have therefore *fallen* in love.

CHAPTER XXII

WELL, my most amiable friend, son of a wholesale New York merchant, and grandson to one of the double F's of the little Island of Great Britain,—educated at Yale, finished on the Continent, and dwelling in a palatial residence on Fifth Avenue,—will you be so good as to tell me how your lordship stands affected towards the country maiden, who mounts her horse so adroitly, waits on table so sweetly, and talks morality so preachingly?"

"Out upon your nonsense," replied Lincoln to his friend; "have done with your review of my descent, condition, and position! I'd barter all my so-called advantages with the veriest clod-hopper in creation, just now."

"Then I must say you would be immensely foolish, young man; for by the reading of your horoscope, I fear that if you were to make a blunder so egregious, you would find the heroine of the romance turning coldly upon you, to lean on the confiding breast of the Fifth-Avenue gentleman."

"But to think of it, Walters! that splendid creature gone mad on temperance! I learned from one of the boys here to-night, that she and her mother are the head and front of that great movement hereabouts. Tell you what, Charley, I shall have to keep a sharp look-out, or I shall gain no favor here!"

"Gain no favor here? what are you talking about; are you gone stark mad? Why, we must be off at our work on Monday morning, and probably you, nor I, will ever meet those really charming girls again."

"That's true. But I must say in confidence to you, Charley, that I have never before really felt as if the blindfold little god, in his haphazard shootings, had hit my heart. But I own up I am wounded;—whether mortally remains to be seen."

"Seriously, Albert, I think we'd better leave before breakfast to-morrow, for I find even the cold, slow pump that keeps my life-current ebbing and flowing, is moving a little faster than usual. The fact is, I am sick and tired of our fashionable beauties. Our dressing,—calling,—promenading,—waltzing,—gallopading,—schottisching,—polkaing,—precise-belles; that do everything by the rule of popular conventionalism, and never think, feel nor act, without consulting the book! Now I am a free man; my father was a farmer's son, and my mother was the assistant of *his* mother in the kitchen-duties; and they made a love match of it, and as near as I can discover, have never repented; and though we now tread marble halls, and bury our footsteps in " tapestry," I can well remember when a log-cabin home held as happy hearts as now beat under the blaze of chandeliers, and far more brilliant and merry smiles than are reflected now from ten-feet mirrors."

"And what has all that to do with my leaving before breakfast; am not *I* free?"

"Bless my stars, no! your Patrician blood would boil over if you were to *attempt* to be free on *that* subject,—I mean that in the veins of your honored progenitors."

"There *would* be a mighty fluttering among the aristocratic fathers of the C——s and L——s, if the hopeful scion of their lordly house were to take it into his head to unite his destiny with that of a common Ohio farmer's daughter."

"To bed, to bed, and be off with you, ere the sun gilds the hill-tops yonder, or there is no knowing what will happen."

This conversation passed between the two cheerful friends after they had retired to their room for the night; this and much more, for neither felt the least desire to sleep. The incidents of the evening had roused a new train of thought in their minds; and when at last, at a late hour, they fell into the embrace of the drowsy god, it was to dream of wild rides with ladies on horseback, of swimming silvery streams and sinking amid swollen waves, and rising amid dancing, laughter, and innocent cheer and mirth.

But both were awakened betimes from their fitful, changing vision, by a soft, sweet voice accompanying the piano, singing a cheerful Sabbath melody.

They sprang from their beds to find the sun already high in the heavens, and everything betokening a splendid autumn day.

They found breakfast waiting, and were soon again in cheerful *tête-à-tête* with the household.

A minister from the city filled the desk that day,

in the little brick church in the grove. Thither all
the family repaired, to listen to a sermon of ordinary
merit, to join in the choir-singing, and to kneel in
the fervent prayer. The walk through the shady
lane, the beautiful maple-forest, and by the river-side
was delightful, and gave the party opportunity for
much conversation.

Just as the twilight shadows were deepening down
the long avenue of maples, the young friends saw the
aged form of Granny Alison wending her way up
the road toward the farm-house.

"What can be the matter!" exclaimed Elsie, with
a disturbed look. "Grandmother is a strict observer
of Sabbath sanctities; I never knew her leave her
home before, on this day, except for church."

"There is some trouble, you may be sure," replied Alice. "Jenny is sick, or Willy is astray again;"
and both girls went out to meet the silver-haired old
woman.

"Why, grandma," said Elsie, "what brings you
so far from home at nightfall; what *has* happened?"

"Och, thin, it's not me that can tell yees, my darlint; but my heart is sick with fear that the worst
has come that could befall poor old granny."

"Are you very sick, grandma dear?"

"Nay, niver a bit, but with waping my eyes out
all the long day after him."

"After whom?"

"Och thin, I thought I'd told ye's. Ye knows
that Willy—the very bone of my body he is, in my
old age, sure—went down town to work with Mister

20

Forbes, who keeps the 'White Horse,' just to mind the gintlemen's boots, and carry water, and hold the horses for thim, and such likes. I trembled whin he went. lest the Evil One should be lading him astray, as it has often done afore, and but for your blessed works he'd 'a' niver been got back. Heaven bless and keep ye for the same! But thin he promised me, he did, over and over, that he would niver touch a dhrop.

" 'Do you think I'd be touching Miss Elsie's heart again,' he said, 'and be bringing the tears intil her eyes with my badness? niver, granny, niver.' And so I let him go, and two weeks he came back to me when the Saturday night came, and it was the beautiful quarter of tea, and a pound of sugar, and a new border for my cap, he fetched; and Jenny a pretty ribbon, too; and we were as happy as angels—asking your pardon for saying it—and och! but the Sunday was like heaven, down at the garden. But last night he came no more, and all the long night we sit up and waked for him, and sorry tears we dropt there, alone by the cabin-fire; and when the sun come up, I sint Jenny all the weary way down to the 'White Horse,' to be asking Mr. Forbes about him, and niver a word did she find of the poor lost darlint; and só I be come to ye's to tell me what to do,—for sure ye're the only friends poor old granny has now. Och! ahone, it's trouble, trouble."

"Cheer up, grandmother; we shall soon find out about Willy. Maybe Mr. Forbes has sent him away on business, or needed him, and did not like to tell Jenny."

"And sure, need he tell a lie to trouble my poor ould heart, thin?"

"No, no; it was wrong, if he did. But you return now to the cottage; it is a beautiful moonlight night, and George and I will ride to town and see, and come home by the garden and tell you."

"Heaven bless and presarve you, and may niver a drop of trouble get into your cup," said the aged and sorrow-stricken woman. "But I'se fearing it's tho whiskey again,— the whiskey that kilt my husband, and his father, and now,— och, Willie! Willie, it's breaking my heart for ye's."

The old woman turned down the lane, and sobbing heavily, took the way to her lonely home.

"I am not obliged to you, sister, for so unceremoniously engaging my services in this romantic business, this evening; for I am already pledged in another direction."

"Ah, indeed! then I shall, like the ladies of olden time, call upon this noble knight to be my escort."

"Most gracious lady, it will give me exquisite pleasure to do your bidding in this momentous affair," answered Albert Lincoln.

Elsie saw the half-concealed sneer couched in the last words. But it did not disturb her, and she turned instantly to order the horses.

"Oh! I would not bother myself, Elsie," said George; "you have already saved that fellow from destruction three times. and if he is determined to go, let him go."

"Three times three, George, and three times three

added to that, if needful. This last time he has kept
sober for a year, and how light and joy has come
through my poor efforts to the humble home of his
old grandmother and his sweet sister!"

"Yes, I know, but then it only raises hope to
make the coming disappointment more fearful. He's
not worth saving"—

"George, do not speak so," answered the heroic
girl. "Not worth saving! a human soul not worth
saving from that most dreadful of all fates — the life
of a drunkard! Is it not worth a moonlight ride,
and an easy effort, to still the anguish of that old
mother, who has walked her threescore and ten in
such sorrow and tribulation? Not worth an effort
to keep the sunshine of peace hovering over that little
garden, and the song of cheerfulness warbling from
the lip of that sister? Not worth an effort to lift
the generous, light-hearted, loving-natured Willy
again out of the slough of destruction, and place his
feet on the solid ground of self-reliance and self-
control?"

"Well I know," said George, subdued by her
earnestness, "it is a great thing to redeem a man from
the habits of intemperance, but I have not your faith,
that Willy can ever be redeemed. There is not much
help for an Irishman."

"There you are wrong again, my brother. They
are an impulsive, generous race; and if the oppres-
sions in their native land have driven them to ours
for protection, shall we let them die in their weakness
and ignorance? Let us save all who can be saved:

none shall reach out their hand to me for help in vain."

Elsie went for her bonnet and riding-habit, and the two were soon on their way.

As they rode towards the village, the eye of Lincoln rested upon the Old Still-House, gilded, as it rose in the vale below, by the full moon, which shone down upon its stillness and desolation.

"What is that old ruin?" asked Lincoln.

"It is, or rather was, a distillery, once owned by my father. But it is many years since he gave up the business, and it is now used only as a granary, and its outbuildings as a shelter for the cattle and sheep."

"Did he not find it *profitable?*" asked the city gentleman.

"*Profitable?*" responded Elsie, with emphasis, and turned her full blue eyes upon him, which flashed in the moonlight like blazing stars. "No, Mr. Lincoln, it was *not* profitable, nor can it be profitable to any human being in the best sense, to distil the waters of death for his fellow-men."

"You are a strong advocate of temperance, I see.

"And who would not be, knowing the vice and crime that it spreads over the world?"

"Intemperance is a sad vice, 't is true, but a *moderate use* of exhilarating beverages cannot be condemned, I think."

"But who is contented with a moderate use? Is the enjoyment obtained by this 'moderate use' of the poison by a few, an equivalent for the suffering and

20 *

sorrow brought upon the community by the immoderate use of the many?"

"Perhaps not. But I do not know that denying myself an occasional social glass would have the effect to reform the world: and I really feel that there is too much excitement upon the subject."

"Too much excitement!" she repeated; "can there be too much, when thousands, tens of thousands, and hundreds of thousands, of our fellow-beings, led on by a burning and unsatisfied desire, are sinking hourly into the drunkard's grave? When our ears are perpetually pained with the suffering cry of the victims of intemperance; when desecrated homes, widowed, or worse than widowed wives, and deserted, beggared orphans, meet us in all our daily walks? When this is so, shall we be told that we can feel too much?"

"But, Miss Magoon, I cannot see how any *individual* effort is to stay this evil, or clip the wings of unnatural and uncontrolled desire."

"Individual effort cannot *entirely* stay the evil. But individual effort can often avert individual wrong. And believing as I do, that there are more sober, self-denying men in any community than there are drunkards; and that each one of these may redeem at least one victim; I believe that we may, by this action, and by our outspoken testimony in favor of total abstinence, create a public opinion at length, which shall eradicate the dread scourge from among us."

"Ah! I fear it will be many a year, my fair friend, ere your Utopian scheme will reach any practical result. Surely I can most heartily wish its entire success."

" Of course we shall move slowly, while many of the best men of our country stand in firm phalanx disputing every step of the ground, and even erecting barriers in our path, which compel us to waste our energies in combating professed friends instead of leaving us a clear track and bidding us God speed in our missions."

" Surely no good man who has the true interest of the Race at heart, will be guilty of such treason to his country's good."

There was the least bit of sneer in the voice of Lincoln throughout this conversation, as if from a consciousness that he should confound the country maiden, and make her feel his superiority. Elsie perceived his feeling and answered promptly.

" Do you not see, Mr. Lincoln, that you stand exactly in that category? If you are a good and true man — a lover of your kind — and feel convinced that ardent spirits as a beverage, when taken to excess, are productive of untold evils, and the direct cause of a large proportion of the crimes committed in our country, — why do you compel me to waste my time and energies in arguing the question? Why not at once admit the wrong, and suggest a remedy ?"

" I think you state the case rather strongly. I am certainly an advocate of temperance: I only suggest that one can be temperate, while not pledged to total abstinence."

" May I ask you a question ?"

"As many as you please, Miss Magoon."

"How many men do you know who are moderate drinkers, who have grown old or even middle-aged, and do not at *some time* drink to excess — drink so as to make those who love them blush for their weakness, if not their depravity?"

Lincoln ran over his list of friends. He remembered his aged father, whose wine and brandy were every-day necessaries; and who, though not sixty years of age, was already yielding under his "moderate" system, to petulance, forgetfulness, and occasional inebriety. He remembered too, the tearful eyes of his beloved and venerated mother, when the excited father, after his wine, raised his voice angrily among his guests, or descended to silliness and disgusting suavity. He could not remember *one*, among them all, who was not, at times, less a man for his indulgence.

He answered the question promptly and honestly, as was his nature:

"Really, Miss Magoon, *I cannot think of one.*"

"One more question: If you had a brother who loved his intoxicating draught, and when one was taken was incapable of resistance; and, thus deprived of the power of self-control, would upon every possible occasion drink himself into the basest condition of inebriety; would you not be willing to forego the pleasure you take in moderate drinking, rather than —in the language of Shakspeare—'Put an enemy into *his* mouth, to steal away his brains'?"

" When the dark shadow enters our own circle, we all quail," was the prompt reply.

He was thinking of *just such* a brother, and of his mother's repeated request, that intoxicating drinks should not be placed before the children of the household. He was thinking of himself too ; of his college days; of his club-room sprees, and the times without number when he, the " moderate drinker," had risen from his bed after a night's social revelry, with blood-shot eyes and aching head, and a deep consciousness of self-abasement.

But they were now at the door of the " White Horse," and the conversation ended.

The "Still-House" fires no longer burned at the grove, it is true, nor did its shrieks re-echo through the valley. But while in its immediate neighborhood not a drunkard was found, the town of Smithville was accursed with more than one of those " breathing-holes of hell,"—as they have been not improperly named,—town groggeries. Indeed, as society advanced, and the foreign population poured in, there seemed to be an increased demand for alcoholic drinks. And while it was entirely excluded from the tables and sideboards of many, and total abstinence held rule in households, where twenty years before the idea was considered preposterous, the enemy still lurked in many a corner, and his victims were numerous.

Political strife ran high, hard-cider songs echoed from one party—while something stronger was not unfrequently found cheering the hearts of the other.

"Washingtonians," "Sons," "Cadets," and various orders, were meanwhile increasing in influence, and battling with the foe. But, with a few exceptions, the women—the wives and mothers, sisters and daughters—had taken no part in the great struggle except to attend the lectures, and to help at an occasional festival.

But the time seemed now approaching when woman's positive action was needed no less than her indirect influence;—and Mrs. Magoon and her noble daughter no longer stood alone.

CHAPTER XXIII

GOOD evening, Miss Magoon,—good evening, stranger," said the obsequious landlord of the White Horse, bowing and rubbing his hands, as the two entered his porch. "Does sore eyes good to get a sight of you, Miss Magoon. How's your father, and all the folks,—all well?"

This direct question seemed to require an answer.

"As well as usual, Mr. Forbes," replied Elsie, taking her way toward the bar-room door.

"Walk up-stairs, Miss Elsie,—Miss Magoon, I mean,—this way—this way, if you please; you will find all right up-stairs, and I will send in Mrs. Forbes and Cynthia, in an instant;" and the perturbed dram-seller almost drew her back with his trembling hands.

Lincoln stepped in between. His hand was ready to send the officious Mr. Forbes off the porch, for daring to lay his finger on one every moment becoming more and more sacred to him.

"Miss Magoon, sir, knows which way she wishes to go," said Lincoln, in a tone of authority.

"Of course, of course, stranger. But young ladies is n't apt, Sir, to want to go into bar-rooms, Sir—that's all, Sir—ask your pardon, Sir."

In the confusion of the moment, Elsie stepped

before the landlord, walked deliberately into the bar-room, and, nothing daunted, up to the bar.

There, sitting around in a small room of some twelve feet square, were one dozen or more men of the town, puffing cigars or pipes—some with feet over the backs of chairs—others half-lounging—others flat upon their backs; while the floor was literally dyed with the nauseous flood of tobacco-spittle, sent forth in every direction from wagging jaws. Three or four young boys were loitering round the room, inhaling the poisonous atmosphere, and taking lessons in profanity and obscenity from men, aged men—fathers and husbands—who were there on that Sabbath evening, leading, not their own children, but the children of others, down the dark avenues of vice and wrong.

Had an angel from heaven walked in among them, they could not have been more astonished and dismayed. They would have met a minister with jest and sneer; an officer of the law with oaths and resistance; but a woman,—and one whose character, by her undeviating rectitude, unflinching integrity and kindness, had enforced respect,—they knew not how to meet in a place like that, where all were ashamed of being seen.

There was the Justice of the Peace, Squire Murdock, —who had sworn before God and man to enforce the law,—listening to language that would have been actionable, had he done his duty. In one corner, just behind the bar, and screened by a frame on which was posted the show-bill of a menagerie, sat four young men engaged in a game of cards, with dollars and half-dollars upon the corners of the table. One of these was the constable; another, the youngest and best-beloved son of the judge of the county, whose fine residence on the hill-side near by looked down on the humble pretensions of the brick tavern. There was Dr. M'Guire, too, who was considered a very worthy and exemplary man — but who dropped in at the tavern bar-room to talk politics with Mr. Jackson, the grocer; and Mr. Edwards, who was running for Congress, who was restless to hear the news and to gain the votes of those who loiter on Sabbath-days and on week-days around the grog-shop doors, and who were sure to be influenced by his suavity and condescension in coming in to see them, in shaking hands all round, and giving them all a treat.

And there she stood in their midst, the pure, true woman, unabashed and unawed. "Unabashed and unawed!" you exclaim. "Could a pure-minded, true-hearted woman stand unabashed and unawed in a tavern bar-room, among the low and depraved, the sensual and vile?"

And why not? Is woman's purity of so frail a texture — like the lace of the satin in which she arrays herself — that she must stand watching and fearing, all through life, lest it become soiled, and tattered, and henceforth useless forever?

Away with such flimsy notions of woman's purity and truth. That which will not, like the diamond, bear, unsullied, contact with wrong, when that con-

21

tact becomes necessary to a great and wise purpose, is *not* the true, the pure, or the good.

And why should not Miss Elsie visit that bar-room on a Sabbath evening? The pew of Judge Heath was next their own, at church; and no one would have been shocked to have seen her in conversation with the finest-looking young man in Smithville — Walter Heath, who was the very "beau Brummell" of the town. Squire Murdock was the stanch friend of morality and virtue in the debating society, and at the new Lyceum. His family all went regularly to the Presbyterian church, and his children were regular Sabbath-school scholars. He only "dropped into the tavern to chat a little." Dr. M'Guire, too, was of the upper ten; and Mr. Edwards, the popular man on the Whig ticket just then; and Mr. Forbes, the landlord, was a man of influence among those who visited his bar, — he must be held firmer in his Whig principles; and, perhaps, that part of the democracy so easily bought over with a glass of brandy, might desert the standard of Polk, and come over to the help of Clay, and thus give an additional vote to Chauncy Edwards, and help him to "roast-beef and eight dollars a day."

Not a place for a young lady! Who says so? The very men who go there *daily*—who *know* how shockingly demoralizing it is; who have felt their own souls sinking into lower depths of infamy at each succeeding visit;—they,—the judge, the squire, the constable, the lawyer, the merchant, the doctor, the mechanic, — they know well that it is no place for any human being who would preserve himself in the image of God. *They* have said it,—lest in some hour of frantic solicitude, or dark despair, their own mothers, and wives, and daughters should, unannounced and unexpected, intrude upon their revelries, as did our heroine, and bring to light the dark, foul deeds enacted behind those dreadful screens.

No place for woman! Then is it no place for man to gather impurity till his whole soul reeks with filthiness, and carry it burning, steaming, bubbling, home to the bosom of his family, to be pressed upon the lips of his child, or poured in coarse curses into the ear of his victim-wife. . . . . .

Our Elsie paused not to ask what a cavilling world would say, nor even to consult the refined cavalier by her side. There she stood, in the midst of that den of beasts, who a moment before were sending up roars of ribald laughter over the drunken efforts of one Dennis Flinn, who could neither stand, nor talk coherently. Flinn was once a young lawyer of great promise, a fluent speaker, with all the rich imagination and impulsive genius necessary to have given him honor, wealth, and influence; now only a blear-eyed, bloated, wretched victim of licensed bar-room depravity.

Flinn was instantly pulled down upon a bench by Squire Murdock; Dr. M'Guire left in great haste; while Mr. Edwards, bowing to Mr. Forbes, caught his hat, saying—as if he had been in upon some business of consequence—"You will attend to that matter, Mr. Forbes?"

"Certainly, sir," was the ready reply.

Every man in the room was on his feet in an instant; cards were dropped; half-dollars slid into pockets; while the blood of yet uncorrupted innocence rushed to the very temples of the young men caught at what they knew was wrong—in a place in which they would not *for worlds* have had mothers and sisters, and young maidens of their acquaintance, know that they spent their leisure hours.

"Mr. Heath," said our heroine, as the young man stood blushing and stammering before her, "I want your help. I am after Willy Alison,—is he here?"

The young man stammered, looked at the landlord, then at Elsie, and then his eye turned toward an open door that led into a back room. "He is there," was the laconic reply, in husky tones.

"Come with me!" was her peremptory command, as she walked directly through the bar-room, where, among whiskey-barrels and other articles necessary to the trade, was the bed of Willy Alison; or, rather, an old frame or shelf against the wall, covered with a dingy straw bed, and an old quilt or two.

Here, lying on his face, his hair matted and tangled about his fair young brow, the dirt and stain of inebriation upon his clothes and face, lay Willy Alison —the darling boy of the old, doating, doubly-widowed grandmother; the brother, the only brother of that sweet, confiding child who had walked that long, weary road, in the morning, to ask for him there, and been told he was not with them.

The landlord naturally enough followed them.

"Did you not tell Jenny, Mr. Forbes, when she came down this morning, that Willie was not here?" asked Elsie, with an earnestness that admitted of no equivocation.

"Well, you see, Miss Elsie—Miss Magoon; that young man *can't* be kept straight. I've talked to him a great deal about drinking, but somehow he will get it, and then there is no stopping him."

"And do you advise him not to drink, while you are constantly, before his eyes, tempting others to do the thing you desire him not to do?"

"Well, you see, madam—Miss Elsie—Miss Magoon, ahem!—you see, Willy is a great favorite with my customers,—ahem,—and so ready and willing to wait on 'em, and the old woman has taught him to be so good-mannered, that they are always treating him and tempting him; I do believe, ma'am that the boy would have done well, if he'd 'a' been let alone, ma'am. But gentlemen like to be generous."

"*Gentlemen! like to be generous!*" repeated she, with a voice of withering scorn; "do you call *this* generosity? He has waited on them kindly, and they have repaid him by breaking down his good resolutions—by destroying his faith in himself—by robbing him of reason, and making him, there on that filthy bed, a lower thing than the brute that wallows in the mire!"

"Well, but you see, Miss—ahem."

"Do not attempt a justification, sir. No gentleman, or rather, I should say, no man true to himself, lifts the damning glass at your counter. They are

21 *

fiends in human form, who have done this terrible
thing."

"You are hitting some near by," said a day-laborer,
who had come there to smoke and talk, and who had
once been saved by Mrs. Magoon from a drunkard's
fate.

"Walter Heath, is it *you* who have done it?" she
exclaimed, turning her piercing eyes upon him, as if
she would read into his very soul.

"Go at once for a horse and vehicle; this boy
must be taken to his grandmother to-night. How
long is it since he went to bed?"

"Well then, Miss Magoon," again began the landlord, apologetically, "you know there was a club-
meeting, last night, out here on the square,—and the
speakers wanted a little to warm 'em up, and Bill
was right busy, and after they broke up, they stayed
warming themselves and treating round,—and—I
reckon Mr. Heath and Mr. Edwards can tell you
how it happened;" and the tavern-keeper cast a
malicious glance at the remaining respectables—who
shrank from him as from a demon,—"anyhow, about
midnight I found him a leetle the worse for liquor,
and told him to turn in."

" *Oh, Walter Heath!*"

"Indeed, Miss Elsie, I only offered him one glass
—I know it was wrong, very wrong."

"And did *one* glass lay him there?"

"You see, Miss—Miss Magoon, when the young-
ster woke up this morning, he felt pretty bad; he'd
the headache powerfully, and then he began to talk

about his old granny, and he couldn't stand it," said the landlord.

"And so he drank again?"

"Yes; but I reckon he's about sober now."

The landlord's wagon was now at the door.

"Willy, Willy," said Elsie, as she shook the stupid sleeper, who turned over, muttering. "Willy, wake up, I want you to go with me."

The young man stammered out an oath, with a thick and lumbering tongue.

"I'd 'a' thought that voice was Miss Magoon's," said the boy, "if I had n't heard it in this d—d rumhole. Oh," added he, stretching himself, "I wish to God I'd never come."

"Willy," again spoke his friend, "Willy look up, it *is* I—and in this fearful *rum-hole*—I have come to take you away, and to carry you to your poor old grandmother."

The boy started as if a serpent had stung him—opened his eyes, glanced wildly around him, and then at her. In a moment the whole truth seemed to flash upon him, and dropping his face into his open palm, he wept aloud, till the tears fell through his soiled fingers and washed away a part of the dismal stains.

"Come, Willy," she added, after giving his burdened heart time to vent itself. "I must leave this place; it is not a fit place for you or me."

"Oh, Miss Elsie, you have been *so good* to me, and how I have broken all my promises,—will grandmother let me come home again,—will you forgive me,—and let me have a chance to try once more?"

Elsie made no other answer than to take his tear-washed hand in her own, and say, " Come, Willy, come!"

And the boy, magnetized by her influence, arose and followed her to the door, and stumbled into the wagon without a word.

" Walter Heath, will you do me the favor to drive him to his grandmother's.

" Certainly," replied Walter, anxious to do any-thing to wipe out the fearful stain his character had that night received; and stepping into the wagon, he seated himself beside the half-drunken boy and drove away.

When they returned from the dark hole, in which Willy had slept away his inebriation, to the bar-room, there was not one loiterer there. What a change had been wrought in that room, in so short a space, by her presence there! She had repelled the degradation and shame, and cast it from her; no oaths, no vulgarity, no shuffling of cards, no smoking, no drinking were done after her foot passed the thresh-old. The guests had slunk away, one by one, and Mr. Forbes was busy with the broom, trying to sweep out the evidences of their recent carousal.

" Mr. Forbes," said Elsie, drawing herself up proudly before the man of grog, " William will not return to his place. I shall try and find a home for him elsewhere."

" Well, madam — Miss Elsie — that is to say, Miss Magoon, I reckon, maybe he would n't do the like agen — he 's a first-rate feller — does more 'n any two boys I git for common, and it's a mighty busy time. Really, Miss Elsie — Miss — I don't exactly know how to git along without him. He's a great favorite with my customers."

"No doubt of it. But he is also a favorite of mine, and I shall not show my love by making him a loathed, despised, and helpless thing. Is that your son?" she asked, as a fair boy of some eight years old stepped into the bar-room.

"Why, yes; that's our Ben. Ben, this is Miss Elsie — Miss Magoon I mean."

"Oh, yes," said Ben, "I guess I ha'n't forgotten my school-marm;" and the boy sprang into her arms, and ventured to kiss her cheek. She held his hand in hers, and looked from his bright eyes to his father's, where the great sweat-drops of agitation and shame were gathering.

"Do you love this child — this link that binds you to his dead mother, now in heaven?".

The tavern-keeper quailed before her searching look, and stammered out that, of course, he loved his only boy.

"Then, as you value your peace in life, — as you value your hopes of future happiness, cease the ungodly traffic, — or this boy, whom your soul loves, shall lay at your feet, the drunken worthless vagabond — the wretched drivelling sot that you have made of him whom you have sent home to-night, to bring sorrow and tears to the sleepless pillows of age and childhood! For as sure as there is an avenging God, the curse will fall. You may sow the wind, but you

shall reap the whirlwind;" and with one more kiss
upon the brow of the boy, she passed out, mounted
her horse, and followed the wagon to the widow's
garden in the wood.

"Father, what did Miss Elsie mean?" asked the
boy.

"Well, I don't know, 'zactly. Benny—you'd
better go in now,— I don't like to see you in the bar-
room Sunday night."

"Did n't she mean I'd get drunk some time, just
like Willy Alison, when I get bigger?"

"Well, I expect that was it;— but you won't, will
you?"

"Why, father, if you want all the rest of the men
to git drunk, why don't you want me to git drunk,
when I git a man?"

"Because, Benny — well — men are fools when
they git drunk, and act bad."

"What do they do, father?"

"Oh, they spend their money, and whip their little
boys."

"Then don't you sell them any more whiskey.
You would n't like to have a man sell you whiskey,
and make you come home and whip me, would you,
father?"

"Go into the house, Benny, go into the house,"
said he, as he pushed his boy out of door.

The doubly-rebuked landlord walked up and down
the deserted room. He had leisure now for thought,
for the customers, so strangely surprised, came not
back that night.

Sadly, silently, proudly, rode Elsie Magoon by Lincoln's side, on their return to the cottage. She knew he did not approve her course, that he had shrunk from entering with her, and had stood without, while she accomplished her work. But, promenading around the porch, he had heard through an open window all that passed in the back room. He had stood by the door when she met Benny; and she felt now in no mood to argue with him. Whatever he might have felt when she entered, he had now no disposition to call her to account for a work so nobly done.

Riding thus, side by side, in silence, they overtook the wagon, and the party arrived together at the gate, and were met by the aged grandmother and her little granddaughter, who were out walking to and fro in the moonlight, watching for the prodigal's return.

"We have brought him back to you, grandma," said the maiden; "but he is sore sick, in body and soul. Be kind to him; I will come and see you both, to-morrow."

"Oh, Willy, ye're welcome, darlint! come as ye will," said the aged woman, wiping her tears upon her apron, and following him up the path.

Jenny saw his condition, and shrunk among the vines to weep away her sorrow and mortification.

Walter Heath was about turning back, when Elsie rode up beside the wagon.

"Walter," said she, in a low, impressive voice, "shall I tell Mary what I have seen to-night."

"I dare not tell you, no," he replied.

"Last Sabbath evening, Walter, you sat by her side. I cannot believe that you truly love Mary, and yet can mingle in such a crowd as that. Come no more to us until I see you again. I will not tell her, but with your consent. Good night. God save you! Good night." Had vice and sin clung with their contamination to the white garments of this Angel of Mercy?

CHAPTER XXIV

AFTER leaving Grandma Alison's cottage, the two rode on in silence for some distance. The autumn winds rustled the foliage of the beech-trees, and the night-birds sung their doleful melodies. There is no more fearful sound in the dark, dim woods, than the hoot of the night-owl, and the cry of the whippoorwill seems ever like a note of despair.

The horses jogged along sociably together; they knew the road, and needed no guidance.

The riders were busy with their own thoughts. Elsie was sad. Willy Alison was so good, when he could be kept sober, and withal carried so much happiness or misery with him, according to his condition, that she could not be indifferent to his fall.

Lincoln was pondering his strange condition,— riding alone, with one of the loveliest and noblest-looking girls he ever saw, in the wild woods of Ohio, —one he had only known a day, to rescue from a village doggery a low Irish boy whom he would have found dead-drunk on the pavement of New York without a thought.

And what was all this coming to? How was he to get away from this enchantment? What could he say for himself, if she should ask him, in direct terms,

22   (253)

of his temperance principles? He began half to resolve that he would not drink any more, that he would go home and start a temperance reform in his own club; and actually ran over in his own mind the form of a preamble and resolutions; when a sound fell upon his ear that made the blood start from his heart with a livelier bound, and tingle with a pleasant excitement to his finger-ends. It was not owl or whippoorwill, the neighing of his steed, nor the bark of Cleo; but the voice of his companion.

"Well, my friend, what do you think of our adventure?"

"Really, Miss Magoon, I hardly know how to express my thought; it was to me a very singular experience."

"It will do for an item, if you journalize."

"But I fear I should fall short of doing the subject justice, were I to attempt it, or I *might* feel inclined to give such earnestness and self-sacrifice a publicity beyond my own scrap-book."

"Self-sacrifice! Do you call this pleasant ride in the sweet moonlight 'self-sacrifice?' I fear, Mr. Lincoln, you have not been well entertained."

"Oh! Miss Magoon, you mistake me; I certainly did not mean to imply any sacrifice on my part."

" And I, certainly, have felt none on mine. There is a pleasure in doing good to others, which overrides all the annoyance or inconvenience usually attached to its performance."

"That is true; but is it not very unpleasant for you, a ——"

"A young lady, to go into a tavern bar-room, just to save a human soul?" said Elsie, throwing into her tone the full force of her feeling.

"That is the question I was going to ask," was his reply; "but you have asked it and answered it at one breath, and leave me nothing further to say upon the subject, except that I admire your heroism. Would you do as much for every one?"

"Yes, I think I should, were I as sure that I could accomplish my object."

"And do you suppose that the young man will be permanently reformed?"

"Possibly not; but if I can succeed in keeping him sober and good even for a half-year, it will be worth far more than the effort has cost."

"That is true; but will he not be more difficult to save the next time?"

"Undoubtedly, if he fall; but do you think that he will be as incorrigible as if I had left him to drink until every feeling was deadened, and his loves and sympathies destroyed? Would it be easier then than now, think you?"

"Of course not," answered Lincoln, musingly.

"Besides, I feel sure that Willy is not the only rebuked one of the evening. I believe that young Heath will long remember that *he* met a *friend* in that den of wild beasts. I, at least, have now a knowledge of his predilections which I had not dreamed of before. I may not save him; but there is *another.*"

She paused suddenly, as if unwilling to speak family

secrets to a stranger. The conversation seemed as suddenly ended, for they found themselves emerging from the wood into a flood of moonlight, so beautiful and clear, that it hushed their tongues into silence, and their hearts into reverence and admiration.

"Miss Magoon," said Albert Lincoln, after a few moments' pause in the conversation, "the beauty of this night, the deeply impressive and interesting experience I have just passed through, together with the conversation we have had, will long be remembered by me. We shall leave your father's hospitable mansion to-morrow—whether we ever meet again, will depend upon *you*. May I ask of you a memento of this day, which will be to me, hereafter, as an oasis in the dreary desert of business details and uninteresting adventures? I know you write. I know, too, you write rhymes. Let me carry away with me something that will be a talisman against future temptations; for here, in this sacred moonlight, I pledge you my word and honor as a man, that I will strive to resist the habits which have grown upon me, and which have been enforced even by the training of my life. I have been an habitual wine-bibber, but I am resolved to turn reformer."

Elsie turned her face to his; the beams of the moon shone clearly upon her radiant brow, and, in her earnestness, she laid her hand upon his.

"God help you to keep in that mind," was her hearty response.

They were now at the gate, and were met by the

family and welcomed home, with many anxious inquiries after the success of the mission.

While Elsie and Albert Lincoln had ridden leisurely through the shaded forest, Charles Walters and Alice had been sitting beneath the same old beach by the river-side where Ellen and Dugan sat years before and talked their loves, ere the shadows fell upon their lives.

To make a long story short,—though Walters had **not** *fallen* in love, he had jumped, with a brave bound, out of the stagnant pool of indifference, and was as fairly and determinately wooing the country maiden as need be done. They will leave to-morrow—the two merchants' sons,—so, reader, let us bid them good night.

In the morning, Lincoln found a note awaiting him, which he crowded hurriedly into his pocket-book. An early farewell was spoken to the family, and the guests departed. Already had his intercourse with Elsie become too sacred for the observation of a third party.

GO FORWARD.

Art 'most resolved? Ah! pause not now,
　But on! with courage strong;
Go forward! with a stern good will,
　And help to right this wrong.

The people in their bondage groan,
　And for deliverance cry—
"Oh! save us from the drunkard's curse!
　Oh! save us, ere we die!"

22*

"Go forward!" was the Lord's command,
    When Israel's heart grew chill;
Go forward! He will part the waves,
    And bid the winds 'be still!'"

"Oh, touch not, taste not, handle not;"
    Be firm where'er thou art;
And thou mayest cast the demon from
    A thousand suffering hearts.

"Go forward"—every effort made
    Will be a blessing given
To woman's heart; and woman's prayer
    Shall waft thy soul to heaven.

At the first quiet opportunity Lincoln read eagerly
the lines which Elsie had given him; their refrain,
"Go forward," rang in his ears like the cry of fate.
Again and again he asked himself—Shall I turn reformer? Oh! there is need, there is need. Shall
woman suffer, and man boast of being her protector,
and yet withhold his hand, while this demon-scourge,
a thousand times knotted, is lacerating her heart, and
making life a curse instead of a blessing? And the
answer to all these inquiries came sounding on the
autumn blast, as he rode along, like the voice of inspiration—"Go Forward. Is there not one dead
in every house? Will you wait longer?"

As they journeyed on, Walters often rallied his
friend on his abstraction, but he could not bring him
back to his original conviviality. There was evidently something on his mind of which he did not
wish to speak. They arrived safely in the great city
of the West; and soon a party of old friends gathered about them—schoolmates and college chums,

whom they had not seen since they had parted at the door of their *alma mater*.

An evening at the Broadway Hotel was agreed upon; and the jolly company met in one of its finely arrayed rooms, intending "to make a night of it."

Wine was ordered by the Cincinnati boys in generous profusion, and a supper at midnight. And when the duties of the day were done, they came dropping in, one by one, until seven old friends were found chatting under the light of the brilliant chandeliers, of the old times, old loves and joys

Lincoln and Walters had not yet made their appearance. They were spending the evening at the house of a lady-acquaintance, and would not join the company before ten o'clock. The young men were growing impatient; for each longed to lift the wine-cup to his lips.

The expected gentlemen at last made their appearance.

"Why, Lincoln my boy, where the devil have you been keeping yourself so long?" asked John Melville, a young man of splendid physical proportions, and broad, open brow, which proclaimed him the very soul of generosity and good-humor.

"With my old flame—Ellen Morrow," replied Lincoln; "how she has faded and grown old, in three years.—What is the matter, Melville?"

"Matter! why, matter enough: Charley has taken to drink, and made a beast of himself.—But, come, the wine will burst the bottles, if we don't uncork it."

"*Not a drop to-night,*" answered Lincoln, who was the soul of the party.

There was coaxing, scolding, swearing, and jeering; but it was of no avail, Lincoln was unmoved.

"How long, in the name of all that is wonderful," exclaimed young Melville, whose eyes already showed the dim glare of inebriety, "how long since you have resolved to become a saint?"

"Ever since we have met to-day," answered Lincoln, with emphasis; "ever since we have met to-day, John Melville; and I saw in your eye and cheek, what that accursed wine-bottle was doing for you."

"Oh, the devil! Lincoln, don't come out West here with any of your canting;—we are not so green;—joined the church, eh? since we left the old mountains? Hurrah there, Walters! is Al going to take orders?"

"Blow me, if I know; he has been sober as a Methodist circuit-rider, these three days."

Melville by this time had drawn the cork from a bottle of champagne, and filled a goblet to the brim with the sparkling liquid; and in the tumultuous joy of the moment, he roared out one of their old songs:

"When Bibo went down to the regions below,
  Where Lethe and Styx round eternity flow,
  He awoke, and he swore that he would be rowed back;
  That his soul it was thirsty, and thirsty for sack.
     'You're drunk,' said old Charon,
     'You were drunk when you died,
  And know not the pains that to death stand allied.'
     'Row me back,' cried old Bibo;
     'I'll mind not the pain,
  Row me back, row me back, let me *die drunk again*.'"

Glasses were now filled all round; and Melville was just placing his to his lips, when Lincoln caught his hand, with the imperative word "stop."

"What's the matter, sir?" demanded the young man, indignantly.

' Remember your *Mother*," said Lincoln, in low, solemn tones; "have you forgotten, John, what every son should feel for the mother who gave him life?"

The song was checked. The impressive manner of Albert, the tone of his voice as he pronounced that holy word "mother," caused a pause in their mirth.

Melville set his glass upon the table.

"Your mother's last words to me, Melville, as I parted from her, in the old family parlor, were:

"'Oh! Albert, do try and find out what John is doing: he is so gay and wild, that I fear he may run into excesses; tell him *not to drink wine;* tell him, oh! tell him it was wine that brought his father to ruin, and sent him — my dear boy — away from his mother's arms, out into the world, alone. ' *Oh! tell him not to break my heart.'*

·" Now, Melville, do you wish to drink that glass of wine?" asked Lincoln, laying his hand on his friend's shoulder.

John walked to the window, but spoke not a word.

"Boys," said Lincoln, noticing that he had stayed proceedings, "now let us reason this matter a little. Here are we met, nine of us, who spent some of the

happiest years of life together; I ask you each, in
all seriousness, is it a reasonable way to enjoy our
reunion :

> ' To be, now sensible men, by-and-by fools;
> And, presently, beasts.'

"I have been learning some strange lessons of
late — lessons I wish we had all heard long ago;
and now let me implore you all to allow me to set
aside these bottles of wine, and let us compare notes
of the past, talk over the present, and lay plans for
the future. It will be a higher enjoyment than to
go to bed with muddled brains, to get up to-morrow
with aching heads, even if we escape committing
some disgraceful act, of which we shall all be ashamed;
and compelled perchance to burden our consciences
with deceptions and evasions,— to screen us from the
censure of friends. Oh, how could I dare portray
the scenes that *might* be enacted in this room ere
midnight, to John's mother?"

Melville turned suddenly upon the speaker. "Lincoln, give me your hand; you are right, let us be
happy without wine." Pressing the young man's
hand in his own, he rang the bell, and ordered away
what had hardly been placed before them.

Two of the party followed the wine, and sought
enjoyment in another room. A long evening of social
chat followed, and the happy frame of mind each
found himself in at the hour of parting, drew from
all a friendly pledge that they would, for the year to
come, drink no wine or intoxicating liquors; and

that they would use their influence to save others from their use.

Elsie Magoon, distant though she was, had been the inspiration of Lincoln's evening effort, and fervent were the thanks his heart gave her, over its successful termination.

CHAPTER XXV

WELL, I do say!" exclaimed Mrs. Deacon Hill, as she came from the porch and seated herself before the evening fire, rolled down her sleeves and buttoned the bands around her wrist, before she took up her gray-mixed knitting for the evening: "I do say *that's* the queerest thing yet."

"What?" said the Deacon, who had just put on his "specs," and opened the *Smithville Luminary*, preparatory to a long set-to at the news.

"Why, Pete Jones says that Elsie Magoon is going to give a lecture on Temperance, next Tuesday night, in the Methodist Church; I would n't believe a word, only that it's in the papers, and great bills is stuck up all round town."

"Pho," said the old man, "what's the world a-coming to?" and he fumbled over the paper and found the simple notice to the citizens of Smithville, that Miss Elsie Magoon would address them on the subject of Temperance, on Tuesday, December 24th, in the M. E. Church. "There it is, in black and white!" said the Deacon.

"And all that's in the paper must be true," responded Helen, who had already found her place at the fire-side. "But you don't catch me going to hear a woman make a speech."

(264)

"Well," said Mrs. Deacon, as she held up her knitting between her and the fire, to pick up a stitch. "I am right sorry, I am, to see Elsie gitting so crazy; it 'pears as if she could n't be content to do like other women. There was lots of things said about her going there to the White Horse, that time, and saving Billy Alison; and now I guess they 'll say harder things than ever."

"Pho, pho!" said the Deacon, looking over his spectacles; "wonder if it's not as right for young women to talk and preach if they want to, as it is to be for ever telling their 'speriences in meeting."

"No, Deacon, I don't think it is; for I reckon when St. Paul said, 'Let women keep silent in the churches,' he knew what he was about."

"Yes," said the Deacon, slyly, "I guess he did; and when he said, 'If a man be ignorant, *let* him be ignorant,' he knew jest as well. And particularly, he was wise when he tell'd the women about wearin' gold and jewels, and sich like;" and the Deacon gave a knowing, mischievous look at Helen's great ear-rings and breast-pin, which were glittering in the bright fire-light.

Helen's blushes, had they been interpreted by a psychologist, would have revealed the fact, that Calvin Douglas, the young Methodist Circuit-rider, whose father was rich enough to allow him to give presents of such value, was the very servant of the Lord who had disobeyed the injunction of Paul, and hung the gold and jewels through the pierced ears

23

of Miss Helen Theresa Hill, who had returned only
a few weeks before from boarding-school.

"Well, Deacon," said Mrs. Hill, in the motherly
wish to soften her husband's wit upon their daughter,
"I reckon things ar'n't as they used to be in them
days; *everybody* wears jewelry now, that can get it."

"I know," responded the Deacon; "and when *all*
the women get to talking in meeting, and going down
into the old rum-holes and saving the poor boys from
destruction, you'll be saying 'It's right enough,' and
that times ain't as they used to be when Paul said,
'I suffer not women to teach;' and, 'Let your women
keep silence;'"—and the Deacon chuckled heartily.

"Why, Deacon Hill, I am surprised at you for
speaking so! Do you raly think now, that it is
right and becoming in Elsie Magoon to git up there,
before everybody, and go to talking about Temperance?"

"Sartain I do,—for whatever Elsie Magoon does,
she does well, and good comes of it. Where do you
think we'd all a-been on Temperance now, if them
wimmen folks of Magoon's hadn't a-tuck hold of
him, and that 'Old Still-House'?"

"Well, I know, I know; but then this lecturing is
a little too much."

"Pho, pho, wife! can't see any harm in it—mean
to go and take Helen, here; and if the Parson (and
the Deacon called up Helen's blushes again with
another wink at the ear-rings) says anything about
it, I'll just tell him that whosoever is guilty of
breaking one commandment, is guilty of all."

Helen bent over her embroidery, and made no reply.

"By the way, mammy," asked the Deacon, "how did that scrape about the 'White Horse' come out? Did Billy stick?"

"Ha'n't drunk a drop, they say, since that blessed Sunday night. He's worked for Magoon all the fall; earned flour and meat for granny, and got up a pile of wood, nuff to last her all winter."

"Well, that was pretty well done! Guess the neighbors did n't make anything by talking 'bout her that time."

"No, of course," said Helen, a little mollified; "all the stories they told about her were false."

"Guess they 'll get over this, just so," answered the Deacon, as he settled himself to his newspaper, and was soon so absorbed in the political drama of the day, that he heard no word of gossip that still went on between the mother and daughter in an undertone, as each pursued her evening work.

In the opposite corner from the one occupied by the Deacon, beside a small stand, with a solitary tallow candle upon it,—the mother and daughter sat for some time in silence; until a deep sigh from the elder caused the younger to look up from her needle; when, to her surprise, she discovered great tears rolling down her mother's cheeks.

"Why, mother, mother," she whispered gently, "what is the matter?"

Mrs. Hill lifted her apron and wiped away the pearly drops; then answered in the same low, murmuring whisper:

"It is seven years to-night, Helen, since your father drove poor Fred from home, and bid him never let him hear from him, or see him again."

"So it is," mused Helen. "Mother, I was only thirteen then,—and I know *I* thought father was more to blame than Fred,—and you know father has never been willing that we should talk about him since. But, mother, do you think his offence was so very terrible?"

"It was very wrong for Fred to speak to his father as he did. Yes, Helen, it is terrible for a son to call his father a liar, before a room full of company. But the poor boy had been drinking, and really did n't know what he said."

"Oh, why did n't he ask father to forgive him, and not go off so suddenly?"

"Well, you see, after his father struck him down so, and ordered him to leave the house, and never to come near him again, Fred thought he could not. He said they would never feel right, and he had best go away and take care of himself. Oh, he was such a good boy, and smart boy; he'd been twenty-seven this very night, if he 'd 'a' lived."

"Why, mother, he 's not dead! you don't think brother Fred is dead?" asked Helen, in alarm.

"Dead to me, child,—dead to me, when I can't see him, nor hear him, nor tell him how much I love him;" and the true-hearted mother bent her head and wept without restraint.

Helen's tears flowed in sympathy. For though impetuous and positive in her bearing, she was kind and gentle when her heart was touched. She had often seen her mother's sad tears over the absence of her boy — whom the temptations of that old " Still-house " had led to speak unseemly words to his passionate father, who was laboring under the same excitement. It was at an evening husking that the dispute had arisen. The unruly tongue had angered the father, who in return hastily struck him a blow more heavy than he had intended, and ordered him never to appear again in the house. Gathering up his scanty wardrobe, he prepared to depart. The mother, with tears and sobs, bade him adieu, thinking that a few weeks would bring him back penitent; and with her last embrace prayed as a mother only can, that her child might spurn the tempter, and save his noble heart from utter wreck.

Fred Hill was a boy of great spirit, and of much personal beauty, and a favorite throughout the town. He was the finest scholar in school, the best talker at the debating club; and he would not allow that he could not drink as much egg-nog, or toddy, at a husking frolic as any one. He drank and became mad, and went forth a wanderer from the home of his childhood, — and so the mother's tears had fallen in her quiet lonely hours, through the seven long years, over the fate of her lost child. He had never written. They had heard of him at Cincinnati, at New Orleans, but only that somebody had seen some other body, who had seen Fred Hill.

"Mother," asked Helen, speaking still lower, and bringing her head nearer to her mother's ear, "don't

23 *

you think Elsie Magoon and Fred used to love each other very much?"

"Yes, I think they did; but how can you remember it, you were only a little child then?"

"Little children have eyes and ears, and I have always remembered one circumstance. Fred had been down to Cincinnati with a load of corn, you know, along with Mr. Thompson; (it was just before he went away;) and when he came home he was standing here by the window, and I saw him take something out of his pocket, and take up the corner of his coat and rub it; and I stepped up and asked him what it was. He said, 'Oh, nothing much,' and put it into his vest-pocket; but when father asked him to bring in a back-log for the night, he pulled off his coat and vest and hung them over a chair, and I slipped my finger into the vest-pocket, and found that it was a beautiful ring. That night he went to singing-school, and the very next day I saw Elsie Magoon have that ring on her finger,—and she has worn it ever since."

"Well, that makes me think of a good many other things.—And Elsie has never married," said Mrs. Hill, musingly.

"Some people think she's going to marry the New Yorker who rode with her to the 'White Horse,' the night she saved poor Willy Alison."

"Don't believe it," said Mrs. Hill, with spirit, speaking louder than she thought.

"Don't believe what?" asked the Deacon, and started up from his paper.

"Don't believe that James K. Polk will make as good a President as Henry Clay, do you?" answered his wife, looking roguishly in the fire.

The Deacon was a strong Democrat, and of course started off in a tirade of invective against the other party, relapsing again to his paper, and at last fell into a nap, when he found that he could not engross the undivided attention of his small audience.

Elsie delivered her lecture, on the appointed evening, to a crowded audience; for, although the majority of the towns-people opposed the idea of a woman speaking in public, few had the self-control to deny themselves the gratification of being present.

There was a breathless silence, when she rose before them. Her face was colorless as marble, her voice trembled perceptibly, and her lip quivered with uncontrollable emotion. But her eye was calm and clear, her heart strong in purpose, and soon self was utterly forgotten, and she only felt conscious of the sacredness of her opportunity to plead the cause of temperance to a people who, though partially redeemed from old-time excesses, were loitering far from the goal.

Oh! with what stirring eloquence she besought the fathers and mothers to come forth and take their stand on the side of right; that through their influence and power the young might be saved from the gulf which now yawned beneath their unwary feet.

She plead for the suffering wives, the helpless children. Pointed them to the past, and ran over in

quick succession a list of the loved and lost, whom
most of them had known and mourned. At the con-
clusion, she offered a simple pledge, and asked, "Who
will put their names here, and thus say to the world
and to each other, they are ready to stand over against
the enemy of man and God?"

When she had closed, the audience, stilled to perfect silence by her power, sat as if unwilling to break
the spell that bound them. At length, Deacon Hill
arose, and asked, in subdued voice, if there were any
clergyman present who would make a prayer. Not
one responded, although the faces of three or four
were seen in the back of the room. But this prop-
osition dissolved the spell which had held them, and
the people began to realize where they were. The
pledge was placed before them, and they rushed forward to place their names upon it, by scores,—and
foremost among them all, the landlord of the "White
Horse."

"Gentlemen," he exclaimed, "when a man knows
he's done wrong, the best way to atone for it is, not
to do so any more. So here goes my name. Come
on, boys; and New-Year's morning we'll make a
clean sweep of it,—and if you'll help me tumble it
out, we can make a bonfire of the cursed stuff on the
square."

"Hurrah! hurrah! hurrah!" shouted the boys, with
wild enthusiasm, as they pressed forward, with a new
impulse, to sign their names; and before they left the
house, three hundred of the men and women, boys
and girls of Smithville, had pledged themselves to
total abstinence.

All this while, Elsie had her head upon her breast and wept in silence. Do you ask why she wept? She wept that she had waited so long, distrusting the powers that God had given her, while souls were perishing about her. Wept over that weakness of the human will, that sees the right, yet allows the wrong to triumph. Wept that she could not reach loftier heights of truth and wisdom, and attain that calm self-poise, that purity and strength, which she felt conscious she should need in this great conflict with evil which she had now so resolutely begun.

The true, earnest spirit is always humbled by its triumphs. While the world sends up its impulsive huzzas, and offers its tumultuous, or more dignified approval, the struggling soul feels the more keenly its own weakness, in the warmth of its newly-awakened zeal,—longs the more intensely to be worthy of the praise it wins, by nobler deeds and loftier living. So felt Elsie, as she rode home by the side of her father; and as they sat round the farm-house fire after their return, Elsie shading her eyes with her hands, her mother broke the silence.

"Elsie, my child," she said, with unusual fondness in her tone, "you have reason to feel very proud of your work to-night."

"Proud! mother; how can you say so?"

"Certainly you have produced a deep impression."

"Yes; I have stirred the surface; but, mother, I would stir the waters to their very depths; stir them till their impurities shall roll to the surface with a fearful vividness of pressure that will admit of no loud 'huzza,' no noisy applause. I am thankful for having troubled even the surface. But my work is deeper, and self-denial and sacrifice must meet me at every turn."

She rose and clasped the hands of her parents in her own. "Let me have *your* love and blessing, and I shall be strong to meet them all;"—and her day's labor was crowned by the hearty, tearful blessing of both.

CHAPTER XXVI

A DIVISION of the "Sons of Temperance" had just gone into operation in the town of Smithville, and was doing a noble work. But they refused to recognize the right of woman to labor publicly in the cause, although Elsie Magoon had brought members into their organization, and done, apparently, more by her influence, than all others. Ministers stood in their desks, and spoke strangely severe and censuring words of the gentle girl who was winning, with persuasive eloquence, the young and the thoughtless from the errors and temptations that were leading them to ruin.

Petty persecutions, wicked misrepresentations, willful perversions of truth, followed her day and night, and made her sometimes weep bitter tears in silence and solitude. But not for an hour did she quail before her persecutors, or regret the steps she had taken. The voice of Christ seemed ever near, "As ye would that others should do unto you, do ye even so unto them." She *knew* that she was striving for the highest good of her fellows, and her conscience upbraided her not for using methods not hitherto employed by her sex, but entirely proper in themselves, and successful in her hands.

"Shall I," she cried, "who can win one soul as precious as Willy Allison's from the haunts of vice,

(275)

faint or fail because of the sneers of the sinful or the heartless?"

She heard, sometimes, of unkind words and bitter jests at her expense, dropped from lips which once never spoke of her but in her praise. Parson Simpson, who had succeeded young Manford, was bitter in his opposition; and to the plea that she was eloquent, and was doing good, his answer uniformly was:

"'Though she speak with the tongue of an angel,' I will anathematize her work, for it is unchristian. St. Paul has said, 'Let your women keep silence in the churches;' (he quite forgot to tell them *to whom* St. Paul was writing.) Her apparent good works are of the devil."

Orders called "Daughters of Temperance" were multiplying, but they also refused to recognize the efforts of Elsie as in harmony with their own.

Despite all this active opposition, the fame of the new lecturer spread far and near, and she was frequently invited to address the people of neighboring towns.

One hot August day, as she was travelling through the hills to meet an appointment in an obscure country town, where the people had become liberal through the influence of the numerous Quakers among them, she stopped at the roadside to get a draught of cool water from a well which stood, with its unpretending curb and bucket, before the door of a log farm-house. An old man, with his broad-brimmed hat drawn over his eyes, sat upon the step.

"Can we get some cool water here?" asked her companion.

"Sartain, sure," answered the old man; "and you can't git nothing else,—ain't a better well in —— county."

"Well, that is good news, for we are very thirsty."

"Then water is the thing to cure you. But don't get out; I'll fetch it."

"That's too much trouble for one so old."

"I ain't too old to give a cup of cold water to a weary feller-critter travelling in this hot sun," responded the old man, as he whirled the old oaken bucket to the bottom of the well. "It's mighty little I can do now for the folks; but I've seen the day when I could do as much as anybody."

The windlass soon wound the bucket, dripping with its sparkling contents, to the top of the ground, and, filling a large white bowl, the old man approached the carriage. As he came near, and lifted up his face to the travellers, Elsie recognized an old laborer of her father's, who had left the "Still-house" ten years before, a beastly, wretched drunkard, whose wife had fled from him long before that, and gone, no one knew where, to get out of his reach.

As long as he could do anything, he had loitered about that den of pollution and shame; but when his hand had become so palsied that he could no longer work,—when he lay in the fence-corners, imbecile as a log, and the swine rooted him about and tore his flesh,—then the overseers of the poor took him away

24

to the county poor-house, and she had heard of him no more.

"Why, Mr. Bell," exclaimed Elsie, "is this you?"

"Yes, this is me. But who are you? It seems like I'd heerd that voice afore to-day."

"Yes, indeed, you have. Look up and see if you don't know me."

The old man raised his head, and, shading his dim, bleared eyes with his old withered palm, looked her steadily in the face.

"Know you? Why, Lord bless me! yes, I do; yes, I do; it's Elsie Magoon, the distiller's daughter, who always spoke a kind word to the old drunkard. God bless ye! How's your ma?" and the old man seized both her hands in his, and shook them, and laughed and wept.

"Come, come; you must get out and rest; *you must*—I can't take no. The old woman lives here with me, and Tom and little Kate. She ain't little now, but as pretty a great gal as ever ye see. You must stop; it's nigh noon, and the old woman has a chicken for her pot, and a pot for the fire, and a fire for it all; for I don't drink any more, Miss Elsie. But come out with ye now. Rachel, here!" he called, and forth came the old wife, with her neat white cap and checked apron.

"There, old gal; do you know *her?*"

"Why, la! yes; it's Elsie Magoon; who'd 'a' thought it? Where did ye come from, and where be ye going?" was asked in a breath, as the travellers were ushered into the neat room of the farmer's home.

"I am from Smithville, Mrs. Bell, and am going to ———— to lecture on temperance."

"That's right! that's right!" almost shouted the old man; "that's what *the women ought to do.* Look at my old gal there; *hain't she suffered?* Didn't I curse her,—and beat her—and starve her,—and frighten her,—and beat the children,—and pour whiskey down their throats, to make her suffer,—and get up nights to drink, and then throw the dregs of the cup into her face and eyes, while she lay asleep with her baby in the bed?—and did n't I drag her round the floor by the hair, till I made her give birth to a noble, great boy, that died by my hand? and yet men let me go on, till she ran off, like Hagar, into the wilderness with her children—fled here—alone —out of the world; and the few settlers and neighbors rolled her up that old log cabin you see yonder; and there she set up her loom, and spun, and wove, and worked,—till she paid for this bit of land, and took care of Tom and Kate; while I—like a beast —was sucking at that old plug down at the hollow, till the hogs rooted me about like a dead dog; and if I had n't been steeped in whiskey—which even the hogs can't bear—they'd have eat me up, every shred of me, body and bones, for all my will; but they ran away in disgust. Ah! Miss Elsie, it was your sainted mother that had me took up that cold day, and drove me home on the fodder-cart, and lodged me in the old corn-house, bound up my wounds, and then sent me to the poor-house to get me out of reach of the "old Still;" and then she wrote to Tom here, who was twenty years old then,—his mother had been away ten years,—and he came and told me if I'd behave he would bring me home and take care of me; and so I came, ten years ago, Miss Elsie,—and I've not had a drop since, nor I don't want it, neither; and you may ask Rachel there if I haven't tried to atone for my sins." The old man paused for breath, and wiped the sweat from his brow.

"Yes, indeed, he has," said the wife, in gentle tones, looking kindly upon him as he sat before her.

"The old gal never loved me drunk,—and never did anything else, when I was sober," responded the farmer, while tears of joy and penitence mingled together and stole their way from his red-rimmed eyes. "You see my eyes; they are almost blind, most burned out with whiskey. There, Rachel, let me lift that pot; I am stronger, I guess, than you;" and he sprang to her side and lifted the heavy dinner-pot from the crane, and then set out the table; and while he helped spread the ample repast, talked garrulously of his efforts, and trials, and victories.

"And now," said he, exultingly, "I am a free man, Miss Elsie, and nobody's debtor, and no longer a slave to Rum! I have earned five hundred dollars this last year with my tools; and I have put it in bank, in *her* name, (pointing to his wife,) for fear I might be tempted agin. Kate is keeping school, and I'm going to send her to college,—and *she* shall be a temperance lecturer; yes, she shall; I never thought of that before. But *she shall*,—she can talk like a book, and she shall tell all the world how her old father cursed his whole household and brought ruin and sorrow on them all."

The old man, generous and tender-hearted by nature, covered his face and wept at the thoughts his last words recalled.

"There, there, Jacob," said his wife tenderly, "let by-gones be by-gones. You're good now, and would *never* have been a bad man, if whiskey had n't tempted ye."

How the thoughts of the wrong done by that old "Still-house" smote upon Elsie's heart!

"I must struggle for the right," was her inward cry. "If children are visited with the iniquities of the fathers, then, too, it is the children's duty to strive to undo the wrongs that their misguided parents have done."

This incident made a deep impression upon her. She compared the now gathered family, living in peace and plenty, in harmony and love, with the shattered, miserable household of ten years ago; the wife and mother then bearing her burdens alone, the father of her children a *drunkard;* steeping her pillow at night with bitter tears, and rising to find the day darkened with forebodings, lest his wandering steps might lead him to the door of her humble home, to seize, under the law of the land, all her hard-earned savings as his own.

"Oh! to redeem one such misguided soul is opening the door of heaven for *many*, is it not?" she asked, as she left the door with their blessings upon her head; "those children, and their children, and

24 *

their neighbors! Who shall tell where the influence of such a work will end?"

"Only in eternity, Miss Elsie; only in eternity!" answered the woman, with a look that told how much she had suffered and how much she had gained.

And Elsie went her way, strengthened anew for her work.

CHAPTER XXVII

THERE was a great bustle in the farm-house on the first of May, 1845. Ducks, turkeys, and geese, had looked their last on the bright skies and fresh green clover-fields, and lay side by side on the kitchen-table, trussed up in their comfortable fatness, and ready for the oven and the spit. Girls were busy — busy as bees — beating the whites of eggs to foam, or putting butter and sugar into good-natured relations with each other, till they grew so close a union, that, as old Nora Sweeney said, "Sure it was nobody could be telling which from tither."

Old Nora! she whom we knew long ago,— though her head is white as snow, her face wrinkled, and her hands trembling and weak, can still scour knives, and dust, and sweep; and put a gloss on the carpet strips, and door-sills, "with any on 'em." So she says.

Her husband has been gone this many a year. The "Old Still-House" was the death of him. One cold January night he had been to get his jug filled; it was Saturday, and how could he, poor droughty soul, get on over Sunday without a wee drop, to warm his spirits, and keep him cheerful? It was dark when he reached the dram-shop, and he was numb and cold. A dram gave him comfort, and the good fire under the grate thawed him out; so he sat and chatted with old Scruggs until ordered off home.

The gallon jug was already much lightened, but before he ascended the great hill, he stopped and took another "swig." Half way up he seemed to have paused again, probably for the same purpose, as his staggering foot-marks on the snow the next day, indicated. There had been a fall of snow in the morning, and a light rain at noon, which had filled all the pools and ruts, and left the snow still upon them. The wind blew up cold, and now it was freezing fast; at the top of the hill he staggered back and forth again, showing that he had halted for the third dram. Now he was thoroughly drunk. The footprints ran from side to side, sometimes long, sometimes short, till he reached a turn in the road, where the swine had rooted out a wallowing place in the summer, which was now full of water. He could probably keep his footing no longer, and fell head-long, his face breaking through the fast-forming ice, and sinking in mud and water over his ears, leaving only the back of his head above the surface.

Here he had died, and was found in the morning, his face buried in the ice.

Old Nora rose early and went to find him,—whether she really felt troubled for his safety, or only lest she should not get her share of the contents of the jug, no one knew.

She says she was "warned in the night by a quare drame that something mighty awful had happened him." Terrified and screaming, she had hastened to

Mrs. Magoon, who was her refuge in all time of trouble.

Old Pat was taken up and decently buried, and old Nora ever after lived at the Magoons, and did such work as she was able. Pat's death left a fearful impression on her mind; or not so much his death, as that he died drunk, and in the manner he did.

"Indade, it was no honor till him, either here or hereafter!" was her constant remark, when the subject came up. . . . . .

So, on this first-of-May morning, old Nora was the busiest of them all; scouring the candlesticks, the knives and forks, the door-knob, the hand-irons, the fenders, and any thing that would glow and brighten under her hands.

Mrs. Magoon walked about, overlooking the various workers, in her usual quiet way; but it could be easily seen that a sad feeling was tugging at her heart-strings.

It was the first marriage under the roof-tree of the old homestead. Alice, her good kind-hearted Alice, was to leave her,—to be no more by her side. And though her heart yielded cordially to the claim of young Walters, she could not altogether quiet her motherly regrets and anxieties, nor repress her womanly tears.

Mary was bright as a sky-lark in a June morning, and warbled her song of love, up-stairs and down, as with fairy fingers she touched everything with fresher beauty, and imbued the household with her own cheerful spirit. Frank was at home with his bonny young wife, and his sweet young babe. George had plenty to do; and Elsie was supreme manager in the kitchen, and maid of honor in the dressing-room. Many were the jokes played off upon her as "the incorrigible old maid," but she laughed as cheerily as the rest, and told them "her time would come some day."

It had been quite generally believed that Albert Lincoln and Charley Walters were going to bear away both the sisters on the same evening,—as the postmaster did not fail to circulate through the neighborhood an exact report of the letters received monthly from the city by both young ladies.

Mr. Magoon sat feeble and pale in his arm-chair by the parlor-fire; he was sad. He had held a long talk with his wife, the purport of which may be drawn from the following conversation between Elsie the elder and Elsie the younger, as they stood together in the bridal chamber after the last touches had been given,—Elsie, at the foot of the bed, her left arm around the post, as with downcast eyes she listened to the words of her mother.

"I do not even say I wish it, Elsie; but you are now twenty-six years of age, Mr. Lincoln is devoted to you, and he seems devoted to the cause of truth, too; every temperance paper is giving new assurances of his goodness and popularity. You would risk nothing, I think, if you could only feel justified in giving him your hand; and your father desires it so much."

"Why should he, mother?"

"Because he likes Mr. Lincoln, and would be made happy by seeing you united to one who seems to be so unalterably attached to you. He feels as though you were almost perverse."

"Mother, *you* would not ask me to marry where I do not love? And, also, though there are few men in this world whom I hold in higher esteem than Albert, yet I cannot love him as I must love, if I ever marry.

"Elsie, you know I do not urge you, but your father is so feeble and nervous, and your coldness in this matter puzzles and irritates him."

"Mother, do you remember Fred Hill?" asked Elsie.

"Oh! yes."

"You know we were always friends; I have always loved and trusted him. I don't think from the time we were fourteen until his unfortunate departure, we ever had a secret from each other. I love him still, and wear on my finger the ring he gave me as a pledge of love and faith. I cannot, cannot marry, until I know his fate.

"He is probably not living, my child."

Elsie shuddered. "He may not be, but if he is, and should return after these long years of wandering—return as faithful as I *know* he is—to find me wedded to another,—mother, would not my life be accursed?"

"But what makes you think he is faithful?"

"I *know it*, and I feel that he is not dead. I beg you, therefore, mother, do not ask me again to marry

Lincoln; if he is not strong-hearted enough to live without me, in a life of usefulness, he is not strong-hearted enough for me."

"I will not urge you, my child. You are right, I feel, but your father will be offended."

"Do not speak to him of Fred. Let that secret rest between you and me;" and Elsie arose, and went on steadily with the wedding arrangements.

Mrs. Magoon went to communicate the result of her mission to Richard, who had quite set his heart upon the union of Elsie with Lincoln.

"And what did she say?" he asked nervously.

"That she cannot possibly consent to marry Lincoln."

"What does possess the girl!" he exclaimed, pettishly. "Here is a young man, educated, travelled, rich, and talented; and she refuses to marry him."

"It cannot be helped, husband; she *does not love him.*"

"Fudge!" said Richard, impatiently; that's the effect, mother, of a woman's getting out of her sphere— one of her Utopian notions. She is getting so much praise, that her brain is turned. She is absorbed in her own fame."

The mother longed to tell him the truth, but she dared not; so she only answered, "Richard, do not misjudge our faithful, noble daughter; if she chooses to live singly, and do the work that seems to be waiting her hands, shall we call it ambition and love of fame? May not a woman live single after the ordinary time that women usually marry, as well as a man?"

" If she is a mind to make herself such a simpleton, I suppose she can," answered Richard, pettishly.

Mrs. Magoon saw how much he was disappointed, and thought that a silent hour would best calm him: so she slipped away quietly, to attend to duties that required her care. . . . . . .

Richard sat looking into the fire. What should he say to Lincoln, who was expected that night? Lincoln had written to him, and to the mother, begging them both to intercede for him with their daughter.

Mr. Magoon had been delighted with his proposal, and greatly pained that Elsie would not accede to it; and had this morning asked for a final decision.

But it was time to drive over to Smithville, for the two young men who were to arrive that evening; and in a few moments he was on his way, guiding his spirited team with his usual calm hand.

I am not going to describe the meeting of Alice and Charley; I was not there; and you who have met your " Charley " under similar circumstances, will know all about it; those who have not, should not have their curiosity gratified until their own time comes.

Lincoln and Elsie were to wait upon the bride and groom. A beautiful pair they were, as, hand in hand, they entered the parlor. He was pale, oh, how pale! but the vigorous soul within still beamed from his lustrous eyes.

Elsie had met him the evening before, and told him frankly that her heart was not his; that as a brother

25

and friend she should always love him, but in no other light.

"Is there no hope?"

"None!" she answered, in a voice tremulous with her womanly sympathy.

"God help me!" he gasped, "to learn to bear this disappointment manfully."

"Let us be friends," said Elsie.

"Aye, more than that, brother and sister," he answered, involuntarily. Their lips met to seal the compact; and they parted, to meet hereafter, only as friends, faithful in the great work of life, that engrossed them both—the cause of human redemption from the thraldom of intemperance.

CHAPTER XXVIII

OH! these weary days and nights, these long-drawn hours of pain, that no medicine can alleviate, no care or nursing make lighter. How long, oh! how long are they to last?" exclaimed Richard, as he turned with a deep groan on his bed, and fixed his eyes on his pale wife, who sat writing by a window.

"Can I do anything for you, Richard," asked Mrs. Magoon, laying down her pen and springing to his side.

"Yes," was his prompt reply, as she stood holding his hand between hers; "yes,—there is one thing, Elsie."

"What? Richard; what can I do?"

He looked up at her, and fixed his eyes, those deep, firm, intent gray eyes, upon the face he had loved so long. His spirit seemed struggling within him; struggling for the mastery over pride, which almost refused to speak what he felt should be spoken.

Again Elsie asked, "What is it, Richard? do not hesitate to tell me,—for I will do *anything in my power;*" she passed her arm around his neck, and drew his head to her throbbing heart.

"*Will you promise* to do what I ask?"

(291)

"Most surely I will,—if it is in my power, Richard. Why, what have I done that should make you distrust me?"

"You have done everything, wife, that a human being could do, for my comfort; but this that I am about to ask will be laying too heavy a burden upon you, I fear."

"Well! let me hear what it is. I have promised, you know, and I seldom break my word."

She spoke gayly, but her heart was full of sadness, as she looked down on his wan, dying face.

"*I want you to write my life.*"

"I? Oh, no, Richard; you don't wish me to do that! How could I?"

"Yes,—I want you to write my life. To tell the world, as you only can, of the danger of attempting to do evil that good may come. To tell how miserable, even from my first step, the building of that 'Old Still-House' has made me; how I groaned and tossed to and fro upon my bed, that first awful night after the poor mutilated body of Scott was laid in his coffin; how the very iron pierced my soul, when his poor wife plunged into his grave in frantic madness and grief; how I scorned your prayer to stop then, when I might have stopped; how I smothered conscience, spurned the right, and went on my way. Tell them how, like demons, the staggering forms of my neighbors and friends came in nightly dreams to taunt and reproach me for the withering curse I had made for them."

"Oh, no! Richard!"

"Yes,—yes,—write it down, write it as you can write; for *you know* how I have suffered."

"I? how could I know, Richard? you did not tell me."

"By the throes of agony in your own heart! Do you think you had a real pang that I did not suffer?"

"I did not know!"

"Aye, I knew well that you did not,—but let me go on now, while I have strength; now, while we are both alone. Write out the story of Henry, of Mike, of that anguished widowed mother, and the crushing of her hopes, of the Fourth of July, of the death of the beautiful, innocent Emma,—oh! my God, spare me now, let me not think of that;" and the poor sufferer covered his face with his hands in an agony of emotion. "And you, Elsie,—oh! Elsie, —I must leave alone, *alone* in the world! No, not alone; for our beautiful children, whom your precept and example have led into all that is good and noble, are with you. But *I* must go, Elsie,—*I* who promised to be, and who should have been, your protector and helper to the end. I must die, slain by my own hand!"

"Be calm, Richard," said his wife; "you are not strong enough to talk of these things."

"I shall never be stronger, my wife, than now. Let me speak on. Tell them *all*,—every wrong that you have ever known, that had its origin in that 'Old Still-House;' and when you have finished the black catalogue of crimes, and the world, the cold,

25 *

severe world, is ready to cry out, of its utter hatred
to the human race, because I was one of them; then,
begin a new chapter, and tell them what has been
done for temperance since that fearful hour, when I,
a prisoner to my own household, learned to be a sober
man. How East and West, and North and South,
on the wings of the morning have floated the songs
of rejoicing, over a land awaking from its long sleep
of crime and wrong. Tell them how you and others
have struggled; and how, while others rested from
their labors, you, with your ever ready pen, have
plead and prayed, and striven to rescue the tempted,
the suffering and lost. Write it all, all, all,—all
your labors and your prayers, all the self-sacrifice of
our noble child; of the martyrdom — *that is the
word* — which she has suffered day by day, that she
might undo some portion of the wrongs that I had
done."

"Don't speak of that, my husband, let me —"

"Yes, I will speak now — lest I never have time
or chance to speak again. Tell all; and then add a
third chapter, longer even than the other two, of the
three years of patient endurance, of nursing and
watching, of love and duty, which you, too, have
shown here at my bedside. Tell all that I have
suffered,— leave out not one pang or groan, for every
wail of agony shall prove a sermon from your pen
against intemperance; for each and every one had its
origin, in the violation of my own conscience and
the laws of nature and of God; in doing what, in
my soul, I knew was wrong, while I was laying the

plaster of worldly wisdom and philosophy upon the smarting wound, in saying to myself, '*I am not my brother's keeper — if he will give his money for that which destroys him, what is it to me?*' Tell the young, the old, the middle-aged, how intemperance planted the disease in my manly frame, which has been eating out my life for fifteen years; until now, at sixty, I must die,—die the victim of my own wrong. Tell them of my repentance too, of the struggle I have made for a higher life. Tell them that my angel wife and daughter have saved me; and that God, through my repentance and reform, has spoken peace to my soul. But fail not to show above all things the fearful truth, that *the body must die of its own sins.* Will you write all this for me?"

"Richard, I have said I would grant your request, if I could; but you are too sick now, too much racked with pain, to talk of it; wait until you are more easy, and your mind more calm."

"Elsie, I am as easy now and as calm as I shall ever be; and I again repeat it, every pain and suffering through these long, long three years, had its origin in that 'Old Still-House' now rotting to the ground; and—"

A fearful pain racked the poor dying man, who had for three years been stretched upon his bed, from a disease, said by his physicians to have had its origin in the use of alcoholic drinks.

"A weaker constitution," said Dr. Lee, his attendant, "would have failed, ere half his career was run, but he will die by inches. Had his life been at all times temperate, fourscore years would have found him, no doubt, still at the post of duty, doing good work for future generations."

Elsie laid him back gently upon his bed; his eyes closed and a shudder passed over his frame. The lips quivered, and all was still. In affright, Elsie called for her daughter, who had lain down to rest in the next room.

"Oh! mother, is he gone, our beloved father?"— exclaimed the child; "let us bless God, that his pains are ended."

As she spoke, his eyes opened once more. With a sudden effort, he raised himself almost from the bed.

"Yes! bless God, my child, that my pains are ended. Oh Father! receive my spirit. Elsie—wife —daughter—all of you, farewell,—the body has lived out its penalty, and the soul is free; farewell."

He sank back again upon his pillow, his lips moved, and in indistinct murmurs were heard the words, "write—write—write it all;" and with a pleasant smile playing over his wan features, as if he rejoiced in his release, and saw some beautiful vision of his future, his soul passed away.

The scene just described transpired in the spring of 1851, six years after the marriage of Alice and Walters, as described in the last chapter.

We left Richard, then a nervous invalid. Day by day had his pains increased, and his weakness kept pace with them, until years after, while on a visit to his daughter, in Philadelphia, a surgical operation revealed the fact, that a fearful cancer, the effect of the irritation of his stomach and vital organs by alcohol, must end his life.

He talked much with his patient nurses, his wife, and daughter Elsie, who, through the long three years, had never been both absent from his sick-room.

It seemed an ever present thought with him, to do something or say something to warn the thoughtless and unwary against destroying the beautiful temple in which God had seen fit to shrine the spirit. "Let them both be kept pure," he would say, "to the end." "Oh! if men could learn to appreciate *the body* as well as the soul, how soon would the world be redeemed from its glaring sins. The temple must be kept holy and pure; for it also, as the spirit, is of God.

Elsie, the mother, was yet active and strong; and though lonely in her widowhood, folded no idle hands in grief; but still took charge of the home, and with her domestic duties and public efforts filled the hours to the brim.

Frank was among the foremost men of his time, and as a member of the constitutional convention of Ohio, in 1850, stood forth boldly as the champion of temperance.

George, in a far city of the West, was leading a gallant band in warfare against the hydra-headed monster which in all new countries is so destructive to public morality and peace. Young Heath was active in the same cause in California. Henry, the youngest, was pursuing his college studies in an Eastern city.

Mary had become the wife of young Heath, and gone with him to the land of gold. The care of the loved old farm fell upon Elsie, who, equal to every emergency, proved herself invaluable as a manager of it.

Old Nora had been gathered to her kindred, and she and Granny Alison lay side by side in a quiet nook in the corner of the churchyard, at Maple Grove, where Elsie had planted the wild spring flowers and the willow. Jenny, the pure-hearted little granddaughter, had, like other girls, been wooed and won, and now held undisputed control of the little garden and home; and still made the old loom do its work, in weaving carpets for the neighbors.

Helen Hill was still single, and the principal of a flourishing seminary in W——. The Deacon and his wife jogged on in life, every day growing into truer harmony, now that the mischievous habit had been utterly abandoned.

Mrs. Hill had her odd ways; but she was, nevertheless, a good woman, and in the infancy of her boys and girls had taught them faithfully the way of right. Blunt and plain were they, but honest and true; and her heart rested in her labors, except when she thought of Fred, for whom she still yearned.

The Falconers had followed their now beloved son-in-law, who, by a lifetime of self-sacrifice and devotion to the good of his fellow-men, was trying to wash out that dark stain of his early youth that never failed to send a shadow over his face when it was called to mind. He was rich and fortunate, and gave with liberal hand. The temperance reform had no truer friend.

The Trumans were scattered, doing as well as they could be expected to do, with their early training and hereditary tendencies. Smithville was without a grog-shop; and it was often said there was no more moral town in the State. The Seminary that Elsie started was still a thriving institution; and an institute for boys stood on the site of the old warehouse, where the Fourth-of-July sufferers had found a temporary refuge.

Elsie was now over thirty years of age; but so harmonious and true had been her life, that one would not have supposed her over twenty-five. The prettiness of eighteen had given place to a more attractive beauty. She had chiselled her face with high and holy thought. Day by day the truthful-ness and beauty of her life had been impressed upon her features, and so radiant were they with goodness, purity, and truth, that the stranger who passed her upon the street paused to ask her name and to learn something of her character.

Elsie had been in correspondence with many ear-nest workers in the temperance cause, and among them were men and women who felt that its best interests required the establishment of an organization which should follow the type of the family, and rec-ognize equally both sexes, in its privileges and duties. And thus came into existence the "Order of Good Templars — *Christian* knights — who reverence the saying of the Master, that "In Christ Jesus there is neither male nor female."

WALTER HEATH was young, ardent, and ambitious. The slow process of making wealth in the older States found no favor in his enthusiastic mind ;· and in 1848 he had left, with his bride—then in her twentieth year—for the distant Eldorado—California. Mary was delicate and spiritual ; sensitive to an extreme, that had made her life almost a sorrow ; shrinking and fearful, without strength or nerve ; beautiful as the white lily that droops over the stream, and as fragrant and frail as that far-famed flower.

For the first year or two the pair seemed to prosper well. A beautiful little daughter brought sunshine to the mother's heart, and helped to reconcile her to separation from the loved ones at the old home. Every mail brought letters from them, and every mail carried out others to them. In 1853 came news of the entire destruction of all Heath's property by fire. The letter of Mary was a sad moan. The mother of three children—with shattered health—now in poverty ; and worst of all, Walter, whom she looked to as her ideal of all that was good and beautiful, had, in this hour of fearful trial, proved too weak to bear the burden of misfortune laid upon him, and was striving to subdue his melancholy in the exhilarating bowl. The letter, so full of sadness and trouble, ended thus :

"Oh! Elsie, my sister, can you not come to us? I know it is a long way, and full of dangers and trials; but your spirit is brave and strong; you saved him once for years. Oh! how often has he said, in our happy and prosperous days, 'I owe all that I am to sister Elsie. I was going to destruction as fast as a thoughtless self-indulgence could carry me, and but for her timely care should have finished my wild career long ago. How she watched me; plead with me; found me out, till I was forced to yield.' Think of it, my sister. Come to us now in our days of tribulation. Come, oh! come; 'save the father to the mother and children.'

"What shall I do, mother?" asked Elsie, as, with tears coursing down her cheeks, she finished the letter.

"Another victim of that 'Old Still-House,'" said Mrs. Magoon, sadly, as she slowly paced back and forth before the fire, on the chilly March morning. "No man more perseveringly encouraged your father in continuing his work, than Judge Heath; and I have often, when Walter was a boy, seen his father put the glass to his lips and allow him to drain the dregs of sugar from the bottom. Your father always sent him a barrel of his best whiskey."

"Yet, Judge Heath never was a drunkard?" said Elsie, inquiringly.

"No, never. But many a poor fellow has gone to the penitentiary by his decisions, that was less a dram-

26

drinker than he; and could perhaps trace his first steps in wrong to the indirect influence of that influential man. But, Elsie, you *must* go to our dear Mary. She is unfit to grapple with so many enemies, alone."

"What will *you* do, mother, while I am away? It will take a long time."

"Oh! never mind me,—I am hale and strong,— and if you were not so much better able to do the work that needs to be done, I should go myself."

"You, mother?"

"Certainly; a woman at sixty is in the prime of life, if she has lived with proper care; and if it were not for the fallacy that women of my age must begin to lay themselves upon the shelf, there is many a woman who would be worth twice herself at twenty, because of her gathered experience and judgment. It is a great pity, Elsie, that the world wears itself out so soon."

So it was resolved at once that Elsie should go to California.

Helen Hill was at home on a visit, and it chanced that she, her mother, and Elsie, sat chatting by the parlor fire of the old homestead, one bright evening, a short time before Elsie's departure. They had been talking of the past, and Mrs. Hill had given utterance to the yearning of her mother's love for her long-lost boy.

"Five years it is, Miss Elsie, since I have heard of him." Elsie started.

"I did not know that you had heard so lately as that."

"Yes, five years ago, last autumn, he wrote to his father, asking if he would receive him, if he should return."

"And what did the Deacon say?" asked Elsie, anxiously.

"Oh! it was so cruel. He enclosed his letter, and wrote him back: Never to let him hear from him again. That he never could or would forgive him."

"And what did he say of himself?" asked Elsie.

"We don't know. Father would never let us see the letter, for fear we should answer him. Oh! my poor forlorn boy," sobbed Mrs. Hill; "I think he is dead now."

"He is not dead!" spoke the old voice to Elsie; yet she dared not give comfort to the mother. How could she, when she could only say, "it is a thought, a feeling"?

"But why," she asked again, "is the Deacon so determined?"

"Because," answered Helen, "it is a matter of conscience that his word must never be broken; and he has so often said that he would never forgive poor Fred, that now he thinks it would be wrong to yield. But, mother, do not weep. If Fred lives, we shall see him again. If he is dead, let us try to feel it well."

We will not tarry to trace Elsie's pleasant land-journey,—her visit to Alice in her city home, where she met Lincoln, still unmarried,—a cheerful philanthropist and earnest reformer. Had Elsie been a woman of the ordinary stamp, he would have renewed his supplications and begged on bended knees for permission to endeavor to win the love which he would have laid down his life to possess.

But like a true woman, she gave to every look, and tone, and gesture, that calm dignity, yet kindly friendship, that precluded the slightest thought of a renewal of the subject. Aye, even more than that,—it subdued the passion, while it purified and harmonized the love, till she became to him a sacred thing; an altar for no profane worship, but upon which to lay his highest and holiest thoughts.

When he bade her farewell, on the deck of the steamer at New York, he could not forbear saying, "I cannot endure, dear Elsie, to see you going out to sea alone; were it as easy to make perfect the tie of brother and sister, as that of husband and wife, I would beg to go with you as a protector and brother."

"A woman who cannot protect herself, Mr. Lincoln, in these days, when men treat women with so much kindness, is scarcely worth protecting, if she be not ignorant and weak. You have a larger and nobler work to do, than to waste your time on one poor body like me."

Lincoln looked pained, and turned to go.

"Bless you, however, for your kind intentions," she added quickly, looking cheerfully into his face, "and write me at San Francisco,—will you not?"

"I will, most certainly."

The ship weighed anchor, the great wheels commenced their motion, and ere Lincoln reached the shore, the gallant bark was standing out to sea; while

Elsie turned away into a corner of the saloon, to give vent to a few womanly tears.

Perhaps no passenger ever had a more pleasant or more prosperous voyage, than our heroine. The weather was propitious, and the passengers, though numerous, were either naturally of the most amiable class, or made so by their surroundings. Elsie was like a sunbeam to that great crowd, who were, for the most part, floating away from country, home, and friends.

Some in search of 'fortunes,' not knowing, poor fools! that to-day's fortunes shall be a life of hopes lost to them.

Some in search of friends; or, like Elsie, going forth to lift the burden from a loved heart.

Wives in search of husbands, who had left home, children, all that was dear to them, for gold.

But among them all—no husband searching for a wife—no father his daughter—no son his mother. The truants and wanderers were all on the male side.

The days flew rapidly by, and brought them at last safely into port.

Elsie had no difficulty in finding the home of her sister in San Francisco. Mr. Heath, as a merchant, had been well known, and in his prosperous days well beloved. Creditors, who would have driven a bad man from their door, bore with him, for the goodness that was in him, and the hope, that some who loved him still cherished, that he would reform. His wife, too, so gentle and amiable, so earnest to help herself, claimed the sympathy of old friends; and they still

26*

kept the house which they enjoyed before the misfortune, although stripped of its luxuries and adornments, which went out day by day to procure food for the family, or drink for him,—the largest proportion for the latter.

An Irish servant-girl answered the door-bell, and led Elsie through the cheerless, uncarpeted hall, to an inner room.

"Just be taking a seat, Miss; it's a bad way Mistress Heath is in, to be sure, the day."

"What is the matter?" asked Elsie, her heart beating almost audibly.

"Och! thin, it's nothing uncommon at all for the likes of him. You see, mem, he'd been drinking hard, and last night he gets hisself into a scrape, and they takes him off to the calaboose—"

"Oh! my poor sister," exclaimed Elsie, clasping her hands in sadness. "Go, tell her a friend from the States wants to see her."

"And axing your pardon—hain't ye the sister she's been praying for?"

"I am her sister."

The girl bounded away, three steps at a leap, and Elsie followed as fast as her faltering limbs would carry her, and left her time only to cry out,—"And sure it's your sister, darlint, that's come to spake pace to you."

Oh! what a meeting was that! The poor frail mother, wailing like a sick child, lay on her sister's breast, sobbing out her sad tale of suffering and wrong.

Elsie did not stop to think of herself, nor of the long fatigue of her journey. She kissed the pale cheek again and again; and with comforting words tried to still the clamor of the little ones.

"Oh! my sister, they are starved; all the day we have had no food. He left us without a cent, and how could I go out to ask help with this great trouble upon me. Every hour I have looked for him. Hush, hush, my poor children."

Elsie drew out her purse, and dispatched the faithful Bettie for food; then, with the old impulse to fondle the once petted one of the home, she drew out her comb and smoothed back the long masses of beautiful hair that hung around the white neck and shoulders,— chatting the while of home and kindred, neighbors, and other pleasant things, to still the aching heart.

Bettie soon returned with all the necessaries of a frugal meal; and when it was ready, rang the tea-bell, with all the energy of other and better days.

The little ones were in ecstasies,— but alas! poor Mary, though half-famishing, had no desire to eat or drink. The fate of her husband was still a mystery; and although his conduct had been so unworthy of late, she still cherished a hope that he would return to the paths of rectitude. She could not think that he had done anything very criminal, so strong was her faith in him.

She suggested it as probable that he had been taken to the calaboose for breaking windows, or some like rowdy conduct; "for," she said, "his exhilaration, when he has been indulging, is wonderful,—he is like a mad boy. I sometimes fear he will kill the children with his pranks."

While they were talking, Bettie was called to the door by a man who came to inform them that Heath's crime was of a more serious nature. He had been arrested for murder. "There had been a man killed by the discharge of a revolver,— some by-standers said that Heath fired it,— others that it went off of itself He came by the request of a gentleman, to let Mrs. Heath know how matters stood. Maybe if his wife were there, it would help him, he said."

The man, whom Bettie knew to have been a dray-man in Mr. Heath's employ, departed; and Bettie, uncouth as she was, had wit enough to know that her mistress must not be unceremoniously told his errand.

"Who was it, Bettie?" languidly asked Mary.

"Only a man asking after one Kitty O'Phelan, ma'am, that used to live along this block somewhere; and it was nothing I knew, to be telling him; but niver a bit would he be off till I sprung the door into his face, the spalpeen. Shure he might know that I had something to do as well as hisself."

Bettie fluttered about the dishes, waited on "the childer," talked and scolded, and finally broke out:

"Indeed, Mistress, it's no use in the born world for you to be sitting here; shure, now, you'll be swooning away like as ye did the ither day; just git back to the parlor now, and lave me to care for the childer."

Mary, who was extremely weak, followed the rude advice, so kindly given, and suffered Bettie to lead her back into the parlor; where she left her safely in bed, for the parlor and bed-room had become one.

"What is it, Bettie?" exclaimed Elsie, as soon as she returned.

"Och! thin it's wourse than I thought. Mr. Heath is charged with murther."

"With murder? How,— when,— where?" Elsie sprang to her feet in alarm.

"Sure I didn't learn exactly whin, nor where. Jimmy Regan it was that called out of good-will, to say: 'Tell Mistress that there was a scuffle like, in the strate, and a gun went off and shot a man stone dead, and there was some as said it was Mr. Heath that did it.'"

"Oh! thou invisible spirit of Rum! if thou hast no other name to be known by, let us call thee *Devil!*" exclaimed Elsie, springing from the table with energy.

"And troth, ye may well say *that*, for it's a devil he is in liquor. Sure isn't it from a bating he gave her the other night, that the poor creature is so sick now?"

"Beating? *Did Walter Heath beat his wife?*"

"Faith, thin, he did, and the children too, and driv me out of the house. It's a devil he is in drink, shure."

"Mary must know nothing of this, Bettie. Where is the justice's office, and the jail?"

"Will, thin, Jimmy Regan said it would be down

to the Racorder's; and troth, he did n't name the strates."

Elsie made all haste, and sent Bettie for a cabman, who would know where to drive her; and went directly to the place where her poor wretched brother-in-law was reported to be undergoing his trial. She made inquiry of a policeman at the door, and found that it was as the drayman had said, and the investigation was now going on. Elsie drew her veil closely over her face, and entered the room. The crowd gave way before her, supposing her his wife; and one of the attorneys placed her a chair near the prisoner.

Walter was so changed that, had she not known she was to find him there, she would not have recognized him. His beautiful complexion, once so clear a red and white, was now crimson and purple; and his fine blue eyes, lurid and blood-shot. His hands hung listlessly between his knees—his fine form drooping from weariness and exhaustion.

Elsie's emotion almost overcame her, but by a strong effort of her will she subdued every outward sign, and sat calmly as the examination proceeded.

The witnesses for the prosecution testified to the death of Mr. Hunt, a famous gambler and roué, by a pistol-shot. There were three or four engaged in the affray. The pistol belonged to Mr. Hunt, but Heath had threatened to kill him. The witnesses for the defendant testified to a row,—that Hunt drew his revolver, gave it to Heath, and told Heath to 'shoot if he wanted to,' at the same time abusing him as a coward and a drunkard. That Heath made some aggravating reply. Hunt then seized hold of him, and in the scuffle the pistol was discharged, lodging the contents in the neck of Hunt, cutting off the jugular vein, and causing almost immediate death.

Elsie had taken little notice of any one but the prisoner at the bar, and the witnesses as they came forward. But now a figure arose before her that even more than Walter Heath stirred her deepest emotions. As he came to the side of the besotted man, and stood there in his manly strength and health, he looked in the contrast like an angel of light.

A man of most winning face, with the mildest eye, and hair of glossy brown; a high broad forehead, and upon every feature the stamp of humane feeling and undaunted will.

When he arose to speak, there was a general murmur and rush forward, as if the crowd outside was pushing upon the crowd within, to hear him, and the people closed round the chair in which Elsie was sitting,—shutting out her view of the judge, the prisoner, and his counsel,—and also preventing the tremor which shook her frame like a genuine ague, from being noticed by the by-standers.

"Can it be possible?" she thought; "have I seen those eyes, that brow, that face?" Her heart stood still. The house whirled, the light grew dim, and her head drooped against the back of a man who did not heed the weight. When her senses returned, a rich voice was pouring forth a stream of eloquence, that hushed the house into entire silence. She had never heard that voice,—its full, round, rich tones

were new to her, and her heart sank again,—but her
ears grew dull no more.

Oh! what a speech was that to the gaping crowd.
A speech full of truth, of beauty, and temperance.
After summing up the evidence of the witnesses, and
showing from the reports of the coroner and physicians, that the wound must have been made while
Mr. Hunt was stooping forward, and might have
been the result of the scuffle while he held the weapon
in his own hand, he proceeded to detail the character
of the prisoner before he took to the practice of drinking ardent spirits. He called to mind, in the most
severe yet polished manner, the late conflict upon the
liquor question; alluded in the most studied and
gentlemanly terms to the position held in that conflict by the judges, and incumbents of office through
the city; appealed to the people whether it were just
to place a snare for the feet of the unwary, and then
to punish the poor wretch who fell unawares into the
snare set by their own hands. He charged home
upon every man holding office, or entitled to a vote,
the responsibility, in a greater or less degree, of every
murder and outrage committed on society by the
agency of ardent spirits; and concluded his short
but magnificent argument, by an appeal to the social
feelings of the justice and spectators; describing the
condition of the good but helpless wife, of the small
children; of the young man, full of energy, talent,
and health,—his future of respectability and usefulness all hanging upon their decision; then turned to
the crowd, and for a few minutes poured a scathing

fire of condemnation on their sins and follies, and sat down amid shouts of applause, which the justice could hardly subdue into silence.

The decision was '*not guilty*,' and the prisoner was released. Twenty minutes before, every one had felt that he would be sent back to jail to await a trial, so strong did the testimony seem against him. Such power had the magic words of eloquence.

The court adjourned, and the crowd slowly dispersed, leaving only a few gathered about the speaker and his client.

For the first time, the gentleman noticed Elsie, who had not yet risen from her seat, but sat quietly waiting the time to speak to her brother-in-law. He stepped forward and reached out his hand. She placed hers in his; whoever he might be, she thanked him in her heart.

"Mrs. Heath, I presume," said he, in gentle tones.

"No!" was the answer of Elsie, as she lifted her veil and revealed her face.

There was a closer pressure of the hand. The blood left the cheek — the lip quivered — the frame tottered, and the manly figure staggered into the nearest chair, murmuring, "Elsie." The tongue could say no more.

"Oh, Fred, is it you?" and she sprang up and bent over him.

"It is I," was the answer; "would to God we had never met."

All this passed so quickly among the crowd, in its

27

bustling to and fro, as hardly to be noticed; and Elsie soon turned away to speak to Walter, who seemed bewildered, and scarce knew what to do. He recognized her at once, and allowed her to lead him away without resistance to a carriage at the door.

CHAPTER XXIX.

ELSIE hurried home with her astonished and bewildered brother-in-law. Leaving him with
Mary, she withdrew to the unoccupied front parlor.
The night winds whistled through the closed blinds,
and the echoes of her footfall, as she walked to and
fro through the empty room, sounded hollow and
mocking. "Would to God we had never met?"
rang fearfully in her ears. Why that wish? Why
that terrible emotion? Was he married,—had he
forgotten his first love, taken another to dwell where
she once ruled supreme? Why wish they had never
met?

How grand he was; how forcible his thoughts;
how just his conclusions; how withering his de-
nunciation of wrong. Where had he been, through
all these long years? It must be that he had forgotten her, or he would have returned for her sake,
long ago.

To and fro, like the caged lioness, walked the
usually calm and self-possessed woman. ▆▆ deep,
unstirred fountains of years were troubled; the faith
and trust which never for a day or hour had faltered,
were driven back by those ominous words: "Would
to God we had never met!"

What shall I do?" she asked, in trembling accents, as if to some invisible spirit who could answer her. So we all ask in our hours of sorrow and anguish! And is there not an invisible spirit to answer our inquiries; the spirit of God, the all-pervading, all-satisfying! to which the yearning heart, after all, conscious of its own dependence, turns involuntarily. And aid comes alway, if we are careful to live true to what our own souls, holding this conference with the highest, tell us to be right.

At the same hour and moment, another was pacing to and fro, in a solitary office in another part of the city. "What shall I do?" came also from the lips of the high-souled man, whose frame trembled with its inward emotion, and whose great heart was beating wildly, with its new and strange experience. "What shall I do?" and a voice seemed to answer in tones of authority,—"Go seek the woman you have loved so long,—go hear from her own lips the story of her broken faith,—ask of your mother, of your father,—old, and no doubt stricken with his own violence of passion,—go as thou would'st have her come to thee, Fred Hill,—act like a man; as thou art above all meanness, so be above all fear."

"It's going down the strate I am, for a little, Miss Magoon," said the faithful Bettie, thrusting her head inside the parlor-door, "and shall be laving the key with yese; and ye'll plase let me in whin I get back." So saying, she handed Elsie the key, and the hall-door closed with a bang.

Elsie continued pacing the floor of her solitary apartment, absorbed in thought, and unconscious of time, until she was startled from her reverie by a vigorous ring of the doorbell. Supposing it to be Bettie, she stepped out and unlocked the door. As it opened, the lamp upon the opposite corner flashed into her face, and revealed her to a stranger, who immediately entered and extended his hand.

She placed hers in his, and he asked, in tones almost inaudible.

"By what name shall I address my once valued friend, Elsie Magoon?"

"The one you knew her by, long years ago," was the unwavering reply.

"Have I then been misinformed,—are you not married?" he asked.

"Let me reply by asking you the same question, Mr. Hill." Her voice, her tone, the electric thrill that shot instantly through his whole being, told all that he wished to know. There was no need of labored explanations. Each felt that the other had been true, and without further word, he folded her to his heart.

"My own! my long-lost! mine forever!" burst from his lips. And she answered, "*forever!*"

Shall we follow them farther,—shall we tell the earnest love that each pledged the other in that lone, desolate room? Shall we repeat the ▲ of his wandering,—how in the depths of his despair, when driven from home and friends, he had enlisted in the Mexican army? Then his adventures in foreign lands; his endeavor to return home, when he met a person who told him that Elsie was wedded to Liu-

27 *

coln, which made him resolve to remain a stranger
from his people.   That, striving earnestly for wisdom,
it had met him at every turn; wealth, too, seemed to
have come to him as a natural heritage.   His fine
open brow, and frank manliness, gained him stanch
friends.   He learned the language and lore of
many lands, and used them in the best service of
his race; and, endeavoring to atone for that early
fault which had driven him forth a wanderer, he was
temperate in all things.   He had been shipwrecked,
imprisoned, wounded, and robbed, yet his faith had
never deserted him, nor his hope grown dim.   For
years, Elsie had been his guiding star.   But when
the crushing news fell upon his ear that she had wedded
another, he only blamed himself that he had been so
long a wanderer.   He had written and re-written,
but as no letter had reached her, she, of course, could
never answer; his letters to his mother and sisters
had met no response; and he had learned to feel that
he was alone in the world.   Though he believed Elsie
married, he had not blamed her.   But her purity of
thought and feeling, her strength of character, were
to him so far above those of other women, that he
never sought to fan into a fresh flame the smothered
embers of a first love.

Such the brief history of those long years of
wandering and absence.   Now they had met, and
though standing almost upon the summit of life, they
found no diminution of that deep and earnest affection which had first bound them together.

"Oh! shall I never hear of him again?" moaned Mrs. Deacon Hill, and she laid her head on the shoulder of Helen, one cold September evening. After a few moments of silence she added. "Mrs. Magoon told me to-day that she looked for Elsie by every train, and there is the whistle now. Somehow, when I think of her, I always think of him."

"Hope on, dear mother," replied Helen; "I am not willing to give him up yet."

A low sob made answer.

"Do you think we should know him, mother?" asked Helen, wishing to turn her mother's thoughts in a more cheerful channel.

"Know him, Helen? Does *a mother* ever forget?" answered Mrs. Hill, reproachfully.

"But he was not fully grown, mother; and you know William Eldon told us, seven years ago, how much he had changed."

"Yes, yes, I know; but I could never forget those eyes,—so deep and full of meaning, even when Fred was a baby. I used to tell his father I did not know how we came to have so beautiful a child. I often wished, Helen, it had been you, instead of Fred."

"Why, mother?" answered Helen, with a silvery laugh, more sad than merry.

"Because, Helen, it does better for girls to be pretty than boys. Handsome girls almost always find good husbands."

"And I am on your hands yet, and over thirty!" continued Helen, glad to make her mother forget the object of her sorrow.

"Well, as to that," said Mrs. Hill, "I am sure I ought to be thankful to the good Father for giving you a homely face, or maybe I might have been left alone."

"Oh! now, mother, that is too bad, to credit all my love to a homely face; and now I am going to tell you a secret, just to pay you for thinking it was my want of beauty, and not my heart, that has kept me without a home full of cares, so that I can fly to you every time you are down with the *rheumatics*."

"Well, well! there child,—I know;" and the mother's eyes filled with tears as she thought of ten years of careful kindness and unwearying affection from her noble girl.

"You don't want to hear my secret, then?"

"Oh, yes! to be sure I do; only I thought you were taking me in earnest."

"Not at all, mother dear. Well, I have not had time to talk with you since I came home. While I was with Alice Walters, they received a visit from Mr. Lincoln, Elsie's old beau; and we had a nice trip to Nahant, and up to the White Mountains, and all around, as I told you; only I did *not* tell you that Mr. Lincoln was one of the party. We were together six weeks; and I don't know whether it was my great hands, so used to hard work, or my plain dress, or my homely face, that attracted him; but he has offered to give me a place as housekeeper in his beautiful mansion in Fifth Avenue, New York."

"You did n't agree to go, did you?" inquired Mrs. Hill, in alarm.

"Well—yes, mother; if you and father are willing."

"Why, child, I never can consent to your going out to be a servant for anybody."

"What! not in a marble palace, mother?" asked Helen, while her eyes danced with a mischievous light that her mother's spectacles were too dull to catch.

"*I* don't count a housekeeper in a marble palace any higher up, Helen, than a cook in a good old brick house like this; and I'm sure there is enough for us all here."

"Well, mother, suppose I say he offered to make me the lady of the house—his wife."

"Helen, child, what makes you talk so?"

"Because, mother, Mr. Lincoln has offered me his hand, heart, and princely fortune. I only await your consent."

"God bless the child! what a trick she's been playing on her old mother!"

The Deacon, who was ill, had been dozing on the lounge; but now, as it approached nine o'clock, he arose and came to the fire, laid his old, time-worn Bible upon the stand, and read his chapter and page with fervent heart, closing his evening supplication with the Lord's Prayer. When he came to the clause, "Forgive us our debts as we forgive our debtors," his voice trembled, and a tear rolled from the eyelids, and slid down the furrowed cheek. The mother sobbed, and Helen's heart was touched. As he concluded the last words, and they rose from their knees, a heavy rap at the door startled them.

"Who can that be, at this time of night?" asked the Deacon.

"May be it's Fred," gasped his wife; "something has been telling me all day he'd come."

Helen had gone to the door and opened it. A tall stranger passed by her, directly in, before the blazing fire of the sitting-room.

"Oh! Fred, my child, my darling!" shrieked the mother; and before he had passed half around the room, the aged hand was resting on his bosom, and the trembling form pressed to his heart. "I knew it was he! I knew the rap!" exclaimed the mother, disengaging herself. "Oh! father, forgive him."

Her words were cut short. Fred advanced a step towards his father, and stretched out his arms. With a cry of anguish, the old man fell prostrate at his feet. Frederick raised him. He seemed dead; but on feeling his pulse, he was still alive. It was half an hour ere the old man showed any signs of conscious life. Slowly he opened his eyes, and gazing around him as if in search of something, uttered the words, "Forgive him!"

"Father," said Helen, passing her hands over his cold temples, "dear father, do you know me?"

"Where is he?" feebly ejaculated the old man. "Did I not see him—Fred—was he not here? I dreamed he came, and I forgave him."

"Father, I am here," burst from the swelling heart of the returned wanderer. The old man lifted up his arm, as if to embrace him. Fred bent down, and the quivering arm clasped his neck, while the low, hollow voice uttered,—

"My son, my son, forgive your cruel father."

"My father, say not so; let me be forgiven."

"Oh, God! forgive us both," answered the old man with fervor, and swooned away again upon the breast of his boy.

It was some hours before the Deacon fully came to himself, and became conscious of the presence of Fred. Never was a heavier load lifted from any man's heart. Alas! what agony, what torture pride compels the stubborn soul to bear, ere it will allow itself to yield to the power of conscience and acknowledge a wrong!

Slowly the old man recovered. Never was man prouder of a son. Once, and once only, he told them all how he had suffered, and begged them to forgive him, and allude no more to the past. . . . . .

It is five years, the 10th of October, 1858, since Frederick Hill and Elsie Magoon were married, and the sunlight of wedded love beams as brightly to-day in their home, as on that eventful eve when, his wanderings passed and her waitings ended, they joined hands to live and love till death should part them.

Two beautiful children claim the noble mother's care, and find a nestling-place in the grandmother's lap. But they fill not all the measure of human love in the hearts of either.

Elsie, the elder, still pursues the even tenor of her way,—still bears her testimony against intemperance and wrong, and implores the mothers of the land to be up and doing in this great work that is to redeem so many millions of the living, and of those yet unborn, from fearful ruin.

Elsie, the younger, finds it quite as easy to work for the world, with her home, and husband, and babes, as it would be to make fashionable calls, or go to parties and operas, and quite as compatible with duty to give her leisure to the wants of others, as to the amusement of herself. She still perversely insists that it takes her no longer to make a lecture than to listen while Gen. Cary, or John B. Gough, or Neal Dow gives one; and that, indeed, it costs no effort to prepare a temperance speech : "Just open your mouth," she says, "and if you love temperance and abhor intemperance, thoughts will not be wanting; for 'out of the abundance of the heart the mouth will speak.'"

THE END.

PUBLICATIONS OF J. B. LIPPINCOTT & CO.

Will be sent by Mail on receipt of price.

NOVELS BY "OUIDA."

Chandos.

A Novel, by "OUIDA," author of "Strathmore," "Granville de Vigne," etc. 1 vol. 8vo. Cloth, $2.00.

CONTENTS.

BOOK FIRST.—Chapter I. Pythias; or. Mephistopheles. II. "La Comete et sa Queue." III. A Prime Minister at Home. IV. The Queen of Lilies. V. Poesie du Beau Sexe. VI. "The Many Years of Pain that Taught me Art." VII. Latet Anguis in Herba. VIII. A Jester who hated both Prince and Palace.

BOOK SECOND.—Chap. I. Under the Waters of Nile. II. The Dark Diadem. III. Butterflies on the Pin. IV. "Straight was a Path of Gold for Him." V. Clarencieux. VI. The Poem among the Violets. VII. The Poem as Women read it. VIII. In the Rose Gardens. IX. The Watchers for the Fall of Ilion.

BOOK THIRD.—Chap. I. "Spes et Fortuna Valete." II. "Tout est perdu fors l'Honneur." III. The Love of Woman. IV. The Last Night among the Purples. V. The Death of the Titan. VI. "And the Spoilers came down." VII. The Few who were Faithful. VIII. The Crowd in the Cour des Princes.

BOOK FOURTH.—Chap. I. "Facilis Descensus Averni." II. "Where all Life Dies Death Lives." III. In the Net of the Retiarius. IV. "Sin shall not have Dominion over You."

BOOK FIFTH.—Chap. I. In Exile. II. In Triumph.

BOOK SIXTH.—Chap. I. "Primavera! Gioventu dell' Anno!" II. Castalia. III. "Gioventu! Primavera della Vita!" IV. "Seigneur! ayez Pitie!"

BOOK SEVENTH.—Chap. I. "Do well unto Thyself and Men will speak good of Thee." II. The Throne of the Exile. III. "He who Endures Conquers." IV. "Qui a Offense ne Pardonne Jamais." V. "No chercher qu'un Regard, qu'une Fleur, qu'un Soleil." VI. "Nihil Humani a me alienum puto." VII. "Pale, commo un beau Soir d'Automne." VIII. "Record One Lost Soul More."

BOOK EIGHTH.—Chap. I. The Claimant of the Porphyry Chamber. II. "Magister de Vivis Lapidibus." III. "To Tell of Spring Tide Past." IV. "To Thine Own Self be True." V. The Codes of Arthur. VI. "Et tu, Brute." VII. Liberta. VIII. Lex Talionis. IX. "King over Himself."

Strathmore, or Wrought by his own Hand.

By "OUIDA," author of "Chandos," "Granville de Vigne, or Held in Bondage," etc. 1 vol. 8vo. Cloth, $2.00.

Granville de Vigne, or Held in Bondage.

By "OUIDA," author of "Strathmore, or Wrought by his own Hand," "Chandos," etc. 1 vol. 8vo. Cloth, $2.00.

PUBLICATIONS OF J. B. LIPPINCOTT & CO.

Will be sent by Mail on receipt of price.

LIPPINCOTT'S PRONOUNCING GAZET-TEER OF THE WORLD,

OR GEOGRAPHICAL DICTIONARY.

Revised Edition, with an Appendix containing nearly ten thousand new notices, and the most recent Statistical Information, according to the latest Census Returns, of the United States and Foreign Countries.

Lippincott's Pronouncing Gazetteer gives—

I.—A Descriptive notice of the Countries, Islands, Rivers, Mountains, Cities, Towns, etc., in every part of the Globe, with the most Recent and Authentic Information.

II.—The Names of all Important places, etc., both in their Native and Foreign Languages, with the PRONUNCIATION of the same—a Feature never attempted in any other Work.

III.—The Classical Names of all Ancient Places, so far as they can be accurately ascertained from the best Authorities.

IV.—A Complete Etymological Vocabulary of Geographical Names.

V.—An elaborate Introduction, explanatory of the Principles of Pronunciation of Names in the Danish, Dutch, French, German, Greek, Hungarian, Italian, Norwegian, Polish, Portuguese, Russian, Spanish, Swedish, and Welsh Languages.

Comprised in a volume of over two thousand three hundred imperial octavo pages. Price, $10.00.

FROM THE HON. HORACE MANN, LL.D.,

Late President of Antioch College.

I have had your Pronouncing Gazetteer of the World before me for some weeks. Having long felt the necessity of a work of this kind, I have spent no small amount of time in examining yours. It seems to me so important to have a comprehensive and authentic gazetteer in all our colleges, academies, and schools, that I am induced in this instance to depart from my general rule in regard to giving recommendations. Your work has evidently been prepared with immense labor; and it exhibits proofs from beginning to end that knowledge has presided over its execution. The rising generation will be greatly benefited, both in the accuracy and extent of their information, should your work be kept as a book of reference on the table of every professor and teacher in the country.

PUBLICATIONS OF J. B. LIPPINCOTT & CO.

Will be sent by Mail on receipt of price.

Bulwer's Novels.

A New Library Edition of the Works of Sir Edward Lytton Bulwer 12mo., in 42 vols., viz.:

The Caxton Family,	2 vols.	Zanoni,	2 vols.
My Novel,	4 "	Pelham,	2 "
What will he do with It?	3 "	The Disowned,	2 "
Devereux,	2 "	Paul Clifford,	2 "
The Last Days of Pompeii,	2 "	Godolphin,	1 "
Rienzi,	2 "	Ernest Maltravers—First Part,	2 "
Leila Calderon,	1 "	Ernest Maltravers—Second Part	
The Last of the Barons,	2 "	(i.e. Alice),	2 "
Harold,	2 "	Night and Morning,	2 "
Pilgrims of the Rhine,	1 "	Lucretia,	2 "
Eugene Aram,	2 "	A Strange Story,	2 "

Each work furnished separately if desired. Neat cloth, per vol., $1.25; library style, $1.60; half calf, $2.50; half calf, gilt, extra, marble edges, $2.75.

Hospital Life;

From November, 1861, to August, 1863. With an Introduction by
. BISHOP POTTER. 12mo. $1.25.

May and December.

A Tale of Wedded Life. By Mrs. HUBBACK. 12mo. Cloth, $1.75.

A Rebel War Clerk's Diary at the Confederate States Capital,

During the entire Four Years of the existence of the Confederate Government. By J. B. JONES, Clerk in the War Department of the Government of the Confederate States. In two vols., crown 8vo. $5.50.

The Ladies' Guide to Perfect Beauty.

By ALEXANDER WALKER, M.D., LL.D. 12mo. Cloth, $1.25.

Mayhew's Illustrated Horse Management.

Embellished with more than 400 Engravings from Original Designs made expressly for this work. By EDWARD MAYHEW, M.R C.V.S. One vol. 8vo. Cloth, $3.00.

Mayhew's Illustrated Horse Doctor.

With more than 400 Pictorial representations of the various diseases to which the equine race is subjected; together with the latest Mode of Treatment and all the requisite Prescriptions written in plain English. By EDWARD MAYHEW, M.R.C.V.S. 1 vol. 8vo. Cloth, $3.00.

Goldsmith's Complete Works.

Edited by JAMES PRIOR. With four Vignettes engraved on steel. 4 vols. 12mo. Cloth, $6.00; sheep, library style, $7.00; half calf, neat, $11.00; half calf, gilt, extra, $12.00.

Adventures of Gil Blas of Santillano.

Translated from the French of Le Sage. By T. SMOLLET, M.D. With an account of the Author's Life. 12mo. Cloth, $1.50.

PUBLICATIONS OF J. B. LIPPINCOTT & CO.

Will be sent by Mail on receipt of price.

Arabian Night's Entertainments.
8vo. 100 engravings. $3.50. 12mo. $1.75.

The American Gentleman's Guide to Politeness and Fashion.
By HENRY LUNETTES. 12mo. Cloth, $1.50.

At Odds.
A Novel. By the BARONESS TAUTPHŒUS. 12mo. Cloth, $1.75.

The Sparrow Grass Papers, or Living in the Country.
New Edition. By FREDERIC S. COZZENS. 12mo. $1.75.

Libby Life.
Experiences of a Prisoner of War in Richmond, Va., 1863-64. By LIEUT.-COL. F. F. CAVADA, U. S. V. 12mo. Cloth, $1.50.

Don Quixote De La Mancha.
Complete in one vol. 12mo. Cloth, $1.50.

Dickens's Works.
The Illustrated Library Edition. Beautifully printed in post octavo, and carefully revised by the author. With the original illustrations.

Pickwick Papers. 43 illustrations. 2 vols.	$6.00
Nicholas Nickleby. 39 illustrations. 2 vols.	6.00
Martin Chuzzlewit. 40 illustrations. 2 vols.	6.00
Old Curiosity Shop. 36 illustrations. 2 vols.	6.00
Barnaby Rudge. 36 illustrations. 2 vols.	6.00
Sketches by Boz. 39 illustrations. 1 vol.	3.00
Oliver Twist. 24 illustrations. 1 vol.	3.00
Dombey and Son. 39 illustrations. 2 vols.	6.00
David Copperfield. 40 illustrations. 2 vols.	6.00
Pictures from Italy, and American Notes. 8 illustrations. 1 vol.	3.00
Bleak House. 40 illustrations. 2 vols.	6.00
Little Dorrit. 40 illustrations. 2 vols.	6.00
Christmas Books. 17 illustrations. 1 vol.	3.00
A Tale of Two Cities. 16 illustrations. 1 vol.	3.00
Great Expectations. 8 illustrations. 1 vol.	3.00

Dickens's Works.
Cheap and Uniform Edition. Handsomely printed in crown octavo, cloth, with frontispiece.

Pickwick Papers,	1 vol.	$2.00	Hard Times, and Pictures from Italy,	1 vol.	$1.75
Nicholas Nickleby,	"	2.00			
Martin Chuzzlewit,	"	2.00	Oliver Twist,	"	1.75
Dombey and Son,	"	2.00	Sketches by Boz,	"	1.75
David Copperfield,	"	2.00	Christmas Books,	"	1.75
Bleak House,	"	2.00	Great Expectations,	"	1.75
Little Dorrit,	"	2.00	A Tale of Two Cities,	"	1.50
Barnaby Rudge,	"	2.00	American Notes,	"	1.25
Old Curiosity Shop,	"	1.75	Uncommercial Traveller,	"	1.50

Gulliver's Travels into several Remote Nations of the World.
By DEAN SWIFT. With a Life of the Author. 12mo. Cloth, $1.25.

PUBLICATIONS OF J. B. LIPPINCOTT & CO.

Will be sent by Mail on receipt of price.

GOLDEN TREASURY SERIES.

London edition. Uniformly printed in 18mo., with Vignette Titles by T. WOOLNER, W. HOLMAN HUNT, T. NOEL PATON, R.S.A., etc. In 15 vols. Price, $28.25, viz.:

A Book of Golden Deeds of All Lands and All Times.
Gathered and narrated anew by the author of "The Heir of Redclyffe." $1.75.

The Sunday Book of Poetry for the Young.
Selected and arranged by C. F. ALEXANDER, author of "Hymns for Little Children." $1.75.

The Book of Praise, from the Best English Hymn-Writers.
Selected and arranged by ROUNDELL PALMER. $1.75.

The Golden Treasury of the Best Songs and Lyrical Poems in the English Language.
Selected and arranged by F. T. PALGRAVE. $1.75.

The Children's Garland, from the Best Poets.
Selected and arranged by COVENTRY PATMORE. $1.75.

The Ballad Book. A Collection of the Choicest British Ballads.
Selected and arranged by WILLIAM ALLINGHAM. $1.75.

The Fairy Book. The Best Popular Fairy Stories.
Selected and rendered anew by the author of "John Halifax." $1.75.

The Jest Book. The Choicest Anecdotes and Sayings.
Selected and arranged by MARK LEMON. $1.75.

The Poems of Robert Burns.
Edited, with Prefatory Memoir, by ALEXANDER SMITH. 2 vols. $4.50.

Bacon's Essays and Colors of Good and Evil.
With Notes and Glossarial Index, by W. A. WRIGHT. $1.75.

The Song Book.
Words and Tunes selected and arranged by J. HULLAH. $2.25.

Pilgrim's Progress, from this World to that which is to come.
By JOHN BUNYAN. $1.75.

The Republic of Plato.
Translated into English, with an Analysis and Notes, by DAVID J VAUGHAN, M.A., and J. L. DAVIES, M.A. $2.25.

Robinson Crusoe.
Edited after the original edition by J. W. CLARKE, M.A., Fellow of Trinity College, Cambridge. $1.75.

PUBLICATIONS OF J. B. LIPPINCOTT & CO.

Will be sent by Mail on receipt of price.

INNER ROME:

POLITICAL, RELIGIOUS, AND SOCIAL.

BY THE

REV. C. M. BUTLER, D.D.,

Professor of Ecclesiastical History in the Divinity School, Philadelphia; author of "The Book of Common Prayer interpreted by its History;" "Lectures on the Apocalypse;" "St. Paul in Rome," etc. etc. etc. 1 vol. 12mo. $1.75.

From the Philadelphia Inquirer.

. . . . No modern volume within our knowledge has so thoroughly entered into an exposition of the government and the social condition of Rome.

From the Cincinnati Gazette.

The book is the result of personal observation as well as the careful study of documents only made public since the surrender of the Venitian capital to Victor Emmanuel. Hence we find disclosures of long permitted wrong, oppression, and cruelty, that startle us even in this day when rebellion has given so bloody a record of crime. It is the duty of every man to read a volume so opportune, and which so clearly indicates that the Old World is about to pass through an ordeal more severe, if possible, than that in which our own land and people have been tried, and, we trust, purified. We commend the volume to the student, the politician, and the practical man.

From the Rev. Dr. S. I. Prime.

. . . . No book on Rome or Popery has met my eye so well fitted to show the world what Romanism is at Rome, as this book of yours.

From Judge Advocate General Holt.

My dear sir: I write to thank you sincerely for the volume "Inner Rome." . . . . I have read it carefully and with much interest and instruction, and think you have done your friends and the country a good service in thus presenting to them the results of your diligent study of the principles and policy and habits of those who have now the guardianship of this "lone mother of dead empires." Be assured that I shall prize the offering alike for its own worth and as a token of that friendship with which you have so constantly honored me, and which I gladly and gratefully reciprocate.

From the Rev. Horatius Bonar, D.D.

My dear Dr. Butler: . . . . I am busy with your work, and find it exceedingly interesting and instructive. One likes to get a view of the interior from one who knows it so well as you do; as for a traveler, like myself, he is not qualified for the task at all, and his pen can only sketch exteriors. You have seen a great deal both of Rome Inner and Rome Outer, and it is pleasant to be introduced by you into one chamber, and another, and another.

PUBLICATIONS OF J. B. LIPPINCOTT & CO.

Will be sent by Mail on receipt of price.

"The Grand Addition to the Geography of Inner Africa made by Mr. Baker."

SIR RODERICK I. MURCHISON, BART.

JUST READY.

In 1 vol. 8vo. Cloth. Price, $6.00.

With Maps, numerous Illustrations, engraved on wood, by J. Cooper, from Sketches by Mr. Baker; and a Chromo-lithograph Frontispiece of the Great Lake from which the Nile flows, and Portraits of Mr. and Mrs. Baker, beautifully engraved on steel, by Jeens, after photographs:

THE ALBERT NYANZA,

GREAT BASIN OF THE NILE,

AND

EXPLORATIONS OF THE NILE SOURCES.

BY

SAMUEL WHITE BAKER, M.A.F.R.G.S.,
And Gold Medallist of the Royal Geographical Society.

In the history of the Nile there was a void: its sources were a mystery. The Ancients devoted much attention to this problem, but in vain. The Emperor Nero sent an expedition under the command of two centurions, as described by Seneca. Even Roman energy failed to break the spell that guarded these secret fountains. The expedition sent by Mehemet Ali Pasha, the celebrated Viceroy of Egypt, closed a long term of unsuccessful search.

The work has now been accomplished. Three English parties, and only three, have, at various periods, started upon this obscure mission; each has gained its end.

BRUCE won the source of the Blue Nile; SPEKE and GRANT won the Victoria source of the great White Nile; and I have been permitted to succeed in completing the Nile sources by the discovery of the great reservoir of the equatorial waters, the Albert Nyanza, from which the river issues as the entire White Nile.

The journey is long, the countries savage; there are no ancient histories to charm the present with memories of the past; all is wild and brutal, hard and unfeeling, devoid of that holy instinct instilled by nature into the heart of man—the belief in a Supreme Being. In that remote wilderness in Central Equatorial Africa are the Sources of the Nile.—*Preface.*

PUBLICATIONS OF J. B. LIPPINCOTT & CO.
Will be sent by Mail on receipt of price.

GOETHE'S WORKS.

Goethe's Autobiography.
Truth and Poetry from my own Life. Including also Letters from Switzerland and Travels in Italy. Translated by JOHN OXENFORD, ESQ., and the REV. A. J. W. MORRISON, M.A. 2 vols. crown 8vo. $3.50.

Wilhelm Meister's Apprenticeship.
A novel from the German of Goethe. Translated by R. DILLON BOYLAN, ESQ. Complete in 1 vol. crown 8vo. $1.75.

Dramatic Works of Goethe.—Comprising
Faust, Iphigenia in Tauris, Torquato Tasso, Egmont: translated by ANNA SWANWICK: and
Goetz Von Berlichingen: translated by SIR WALTER SCOTT, and carefully revised by HENRY G. BOHN. 1 vol. crown 8vo. $1.75.

Novels and Tales by Goethe.
Elective Affinities; The Sorrows of Werther; German Emigrants; The Good Women: and a Nouvelette. Translated chiefly by R. D. BOYLAN, ESQ. 1 vol. crown 8vo. $1.75.

Goethe's Works: uniform in Sets. In 5 vols. Cloth, $8.75. Half calf, gilt backs, $15.00.

Wilson's Pre-Historic Man.
Researches into the Origin of Civilization in the Old and the New World. By DANIEL WILSON, LL.D., Professor of History and English Literature in University College, Toronto; author of the "Pre-Historic Annals of Scotland," etc. 2d edition. 8vo. Cloth, $10.00.

Comparative Anatomy and Physiology of the Vertebrate Animals.
By RICHARD OWEN, F.R.S., D.C.L. In 3 vols. This work will be illustrated by upwards of 1200 engravings on wood. Vol. I. published. Vol. II. nearly ready.

Mrs. Browning's Poems.
Selections from the Poetry of Elizabeth Barrett Browning, with new Portrait, and engraving of Casa Guida. 1 vol. crown 8vo. $5.25.

Globe Edition of Shakspeare's Works.
Complete in 1 cap 8vo. vol., including the Plays, Poems, Sonnets, and a Complete Glossary. Edited by WILLIAM GEORGE CLARKE and WILLIAM ADDIS WRIGHT, of Trinity College, Cambridge. $2.50.

The History of Usury, from the Earliest Period to the Present Time.

Together with a brief Statement of General Principles concerning the subject in different States and Countries; and an examination into the policy of Laws on Usury, and their effect on commerce. By J. B. C. MURRAY. 1 vol. 8vo. $2.00.

Mr. Murray, in the very interesting volume before us, contends, wo think justly, that these usury laws embarrass business, check enterprise, and offer a premium for unfair dealing, and strongly commends the example of England in this respect as deserving of imitation. His volume is very comprehensive, and presents, in a comparatively brief compass, a mass of information on this subject nowhere else to be met with. As a manual for the guide of reformers in the United States it is of value, but as an historical monograph it cannot be too highly estimated—it should take its place by the side of our standard histories, and hereafter, when the laws against usury are forgotten, it will be treasured alike by the antiquarian and the historian for its curious facts, and its indirect references to curious social problems.—*Trubner's Literary Record.*

Cerise: A Tale of the Last Century.

By G. J. WHYTE MELVILLE, author of "The Gladiators," "Digby Grand," "The Brookes of Bridlemere," etc. 1 vol. 12mo. $1.75.

Here is a capital tale of the last century. Melville is well known as the writer of "The Gladiators," "Digby Grand," "The Brookes of Bridlemere," etc. The book is written with the pen of a skilled and ready genius at narrative, the incidents running rapidly upon the heels of each other. The French and English characters of the last century do good duty in illustrating the sense of the Saxon and the elegant frivolity of the modern Gaul.—*Boston Post.*

* * * It is rarely that a volume contains so much compressed and varied interest. England, France, and the Indies; sea and shore; life in the palace and in negro huts; insurrection among slaves and rebellion among freemen; love and war; wealth and poverty—almost all the paraphernalia of fiction is enlisted to give spice to the tale.—*North American.*

The Story of Gisli the Outlaw.

From the Icelandic. By GEORGE WEBBE DASENT, D.C.L. With illustrations by C. E. ST. JOHN MILDMAY. 1 vol. small 4to. With maps and beautiful full-page illustrations. Price, $3.50.

The "Story of Gisli the Outlaw" is one of the choicest gems of Icelandic Legendary Lore. The volume is executed in the highest style of the art of book-making.

Hidden Depths.

One vol. 12mo. $1.75.

This book is not a work of fiction in the ordinary acceptation of the term. If it were, it would be worse than useless, for the "hidden depths," of which it reveals a glimpse, are not fit subjects for a romance.—*Preface.*

Resources and Prospects of America.

Ascertained during a visit to the States in the autumn of 1865. By SIR S. MORTON PETO, BART., M.P. for Bristol. 1 vol. 12mo. $2.00.

* * * It will be observed that I have carefully confined myself to my subject—the "RESOURCES AND PROSPECTS OF AMERICA." As far as possible I have avoided all political allusions: and I have not attempted any descriptions of the country, or of the manners and habits of the people, which have been rendered familiar to us by far abler writers than myself. That which I have been anxious to afford my fellow-countrymen is an opportunity of forming a more correct judgment than that at which many have hitherto arrived, of the progress, means, and probable future of the great nation on the other side of the Atlantic, with which, by every tie of fraternity, we ought to be so closely allied.—*Preface.*

Chambers's Encyclopædia.

A Dictionary of Universal Knowledge for the People, on the basis of the German Conversations-Lexicon. Illustrated with Maps and numerous Wood Engravings. Published in parts. Price 25 cents each. The whole to be comprised in nine volumes royal octavo. Eight volumes now ready. This is the only authorized edition that will be published in America. Price, per volume, cloth, $4.50; sheep, $5.00; half Turkey, $5.50.

FROM R. SHELTON MACKENZIE, D.C.L.,

Editor of Noctes Ambrosianæ, etc.

Upon its literary merits—its completeness and accuracy, and the extent and variety of its information—there can be only one opinion. The work is worthy of the high aim and established reputation of its projectors. Art and science, theology and jurisprudence, natural history and metaphysics, topography and geography, medicine and antiquities, biography and belles-lettres, are all discussed here, not in long treatises, but to an extent sufficient to give requisite information, at a glance as it were. Sometimes, when the subject justifies it, more minute details are given. * * * Its fullness upon American subjects ought to recommend it especially in this country, and its low price makes it one of the cheapest and most accessible works ever published.

FROM EDWARD HITCHCOCK, D.D., LL.D.,

Late President of Amherst College.

I have looked the work over as attentively as my time would allow, and it appears to me well adapted to the objects in view. Judging from those articles on which I feel most qualified to give an opinion, the work seems to me to be prepared by men thoroughly acquainted with the subjects about which they write; and the whole work must prove a cheap and invaluable source of information to almost every class of the community.

www.ingramcontent.com/pod-product-compliance
Lightning Source LLC
Chambersburg PA
CBHW020934030726
47496CB00005B/1191